Good
Sex

Good Sex

REAL STORIES FROM REAL PEOPLE
JULIA HUTTON

with an introduction by Isadora Alman
2nd edition

Copyright © 1992, 1995 by Julia Hutton
Introduction copyright © 1995 by Isadora Alman

All rights reserved. Except for brief passages quoted in newspaper, magazine, radio or television reviews, no part of this book may be reproduced in any form or by any means, electronic or mechanical, including photocopying or recording, or by information storage or retrieval system, without permission in writing from the publisher.

Published in the United States by Cleis Press, Inc.
P.O. Box 8933, Pittsburgh, Pennsylvania 15221, and
P.O. Box 14684, San Francisco, California 94114
Printed in the United States

Cover design and production: Pete Ivey
Cover photos: David Pickell
Cover model: Colleen Lye
Text design: Ellen Toomey

Library of Congress Cataloging-in-Publication Data
Good sex : real stories from real people / [compiled by] Julia Hutton : with an
    introduction by Isadora Alman. — 2nd ed.
        p. cm.
    ISBN 1-57344-001-9 : 29.95. — ISBN 1-57344-000-0 (pbk.) : $14.95
    1. Sex customs—United States. 2. Sex. 3. Hygiene, Sexual—United
States. I. Hutton, Julia, 1958–
HQ18.U5G59 1995
306.7—dc20   94-44750
                                                                          CIP

CONTENTS

Introduction by Isadora Alman ... 7

I. DESIRE ... 13
Ricky • José Antonio • Bea • Anne • Harlan • Dave
Carol • Dennis • Christopher • Lissa • Cooter

II. SEX TALK ... 49
Ben • Guy • Jackie • Amanda • Msafiri • Lani • Terry
Halima • Jay • Paula • Anthony

III. FE/MALE TROUBLE ... 83
David • Mark • Tede • Vaughn • Cybelle • Andy
Diane • Shannon • Richard

IV. MIXED MEDIA ... 115
Kris • Mishell • Steven • Paris • Bill • Carolan
Pamela • Morgan • Sybil • Jack

V. SEXUAL HEALING ... 147
Barbara • Luke • Veronica • David • Judy • Cathie
Darrell • Maya • Jim • Rachel

VI. ECSTATIC OUTLAWS ... 179
Mike • Ginger • Peter • Patricia • Buzz • Angela
Phil • Toni • Marting • Don • Lena

Notes from the Author ... 215
Appendix: Safer Sex Guidelines ... 221

INTRODUCTION

Think back to the last time you were sexual. Once you have fixed the occasion in your mind, the *who*, the *how*, the *when* and the *where*, and, I hope, have spent a moment in smiling reminiscence, the question I pose to you is: *what?* Not what did you do, but what made your last sexual experience a memory to smile over? If, alas, that last time was not a particularly stellar event, compare that occasion with a shining moment in your personal history which was or which would have been truly outstanding, if only.... In other words, it is unlikely that you are unaware of the general outlines of what, for you, constitutes the difference between ho-hum activity and a truly unforgettable sexual happening. But the specifics? Could you write a recipe for good sex as exacting as one, let's say, for soufflé?

Have you ever pondered other people's recipes for sexual pleasure? Of course you have. Satisfying that curiosity is the raison d'être for the "entertainment news" industry. Who are the current commercial idols, what do they wear, where are they seen, with whom, and most importantly, what are they doing in bed, and is it any better for them than it is for you?

We are treated to facts and fantasies of the glitterati's social and sexual goings on (and comings off) not only in *People* and similar magazines. Turn on a TV talk show or MTV. Listen to the Top 40 songs of the moment. Open the pages of a best-selling novel, go to a movie, a play or a display of current photography. Sex might be dressed up in the ribbons of romance, the little lacies of love, but as often as not it's right out there, practically naked, enacted by bodies you have come to recognize. Love might be what makes the world go 'round but "sex sells."

Even if you eschew commercial television for the public broadcast stations, view only documentary films and confine yourself to news magazines, you get the message. Every day, in ways both blatant and subtle, we are told what a big deal sex is. It's used as a sales tool for everything from life-enhancing luxuries to life-destroying substances. Unique in the history of human-kind is our culture's endorsement of sex as a realistic basis of lifetime mate selection. Sex is promoted as life's all-purpose magic bullet, a wonder drug more powerful than aspirin and, being Americans, we must have the biggest, the newest, the best.

Given the continuous and omnipresent media ballyhoo about sex and given the enormous burden of expectation each of us brings to sex (if we are good, he/she is good and sex is good, Loved One and I will surely live happily ever after) it's a wonder that anyone ever comes away satisfied from any sexual interaction. What's absolutely amazing is not that sex often disappoints, but that it even occasionally surpasses our most fanciful hopes. Why? Because in spite of all this multimedia hoopla we are given precious little real information about what might constitute acceptable sex, let alone the good stuff. We don't get real information about real people's thoughts, feelings and acts. Oh, there are scientific reports that do reach the popular media—statistics on how many times how many people do how many specific acts. But that's not very helpful when what you're striving for is quality.

Magazine features promising secrets to improve your sex life instead detail relationship hints like leaving love notes under the pillow or offer commercial nonsense such as perfuming your private parts. Even instructional videos specifically devoted to such matters as finding her G-spot or women who ejaculate like Old Faithful don't really help us to define what good sex is or could be.

One important way most of us set standards and define goals for ourselves is by first sifting through information available to us, lifting out what is relevant to our particular situation. About the subject of sex we are provided many forms of "information"—what our parents told us, what we inferred from what our parents did not speak about, locker room hints, treatment in classics as well as popular media, hit or miss (usually painful) personal experiences and—*big* and—the experiences of others. If we don't get reports that we can trust or any reports at all on the sexual realities of others we lack an extremely important source of information upon which to base our own expectations.

I have been a provider of nonjudgmental sex information, the hows and whats of the human pursuit of pleasure, for more than fifteen years. I have done my part for sex education by volunteer-

Introduction

ing on a free information phone line, by hosting a call-in radio
show, by giving public lectures and workshops to university
classes, businesses, singles' organizations and church and syna-
gogue couples groups, by producing educational tapes and by
writing articles, books and, of course, my syndicated advice
column on sex and relationships, "Ask Isadora." I mention my
bona fides as proof of my experience with an enormous variety
of audiences, questions about sex and methods of asking them.

These activities have allowed me to formulate what I refer to
as Three Miserable Myths about sexual behavior, common
beliefs which seem to underlie most of the questions people ask
me: (1) that there is one right way to conduct a courtship (e.g.
she speaks first, he phones next), (2) that there is one right way to
have sex (e.g. Partner A must spend specified amount of attention
doing Activity Q to Body Part X of Partner B) and (3) that there
is one right standard of desirability you must achieve in order to
take part in all these exciting goings-on (young, thin, able-
bodied, glossy of tooth, shiny of mane and attractive in face and
form).

While some may firmly believe that every sexually active
person on the globe adheres to rules she somehow missed learning, most of us are smart enough to have a doubt or two. Because
we suspect there are many routes to pleasure and, let's face it,
because we still hope someone will have "the" answers, we're
curious about what people like us do during sex. We are also
extremely interested in The Other—men about women, heterosexuals about lesbians and gay men, monogamists about non-tra-
ditionalists and so forth. Herein lies the beauty of *Good Sex:
Real Stories from Real People.*

There is no doubt that the interviewees in this book are real
people speaking in their own voices. For one, no one could have
made up such an assembly! For another, a commercially con-
structed collection would have had far more commercially standard people speaking the standard party line—missionary intercourse within a socially sanctioned couple, with perhaps a
person of bisexual sensibilities or unconventional fantasies
thrown in for good measure. The dizzying array of thoughts and
feelings and activities and labels, of ages and desires and even
genders encompassed here speaks not only to the investigative

thoroughness of Julia Hutton but to the realities of her respondents. The explosion of those miserable myths requires acceptance of the revolutionary fact that, particularly when it comes to good sex, there is no one right way.

If even a small proportion of the seekers and askers I encounter could accept the idea that there is no gold standard of human sexual behavior, that each of us makes it up as we go along—what feels good to us, what might feel good to another person—and that all of us are in that same universal learning endeavor together, more similar than different, a great deal of pain and fear would vanish from the lives of good people everywhere. This book you now hold in your hands is one very important tool of this much to be hoped for enlightenment. May you enjoy *Good Sex*, learn from it, and pass along the good word.

Isadora Alman
October 1994

I. DESIRE

There are relatively few ways to tuck bodies together in sexual interaction, but those couplings hold countless meanings. This chapter matches action with appetite in eleven spunky interviews that trace the ever-shifting shape of desire. All different, the anecdotes itemize kinks, proclivities and breath-taking pleasures. What the stories share is an undertow of longing. "Desire is a bridge to fulfillment," said Lissa. "We are alone in this world, and we can't truly connect minds and hearts except through the tools we have—language, art, music, and sex. When I was younger, the need to connect was so powerful it felt almost uncontrollable."

"As a teenager," one man recollected, "I was like a heat-seeking missile." Many interviewees remembered a single touch or glance that brought on shock waves of lust. For Dennis, who has known his wife since grade school, an incident from their high school dating days became a powerful erotic icon. "We were sixteen . . . virgins . . . I remember vividly the sun shining on her breasts. Her breasts were just *gleaming*," he said. "It was the most beautiful, sensual moment. I have *always* carried that memory."

First impressions linger, but desire undergoes considerable transformations over time. Harlan remembered when girl-chasing matured to longing for companionship—a need no less compelling. The night he met his wife, "there was so much attraction, it was scary." An older woman described the development of her take-charge attitude towards sexuality, and a number of stories explored shifts in sexual orientation. In one, a late-blooming lesbian mused over the "intrigue of being with a woman"; in another, a gay man offered a humorous history of his painful coming-out process. Throughout the chapter, attractions change, along with the nature and quality of desire. Ricky, reflecting on heterosexual dating and mating, said, "It used to be that what turned me on was their desire, but now . . . the main thing is *me* . . . my desire."

This chapter serves up polymorphous perspectives on good sex, from casual sport to marital mixed doubles. Presented in the context of life stories, desire emerges as a deeply informed and evolving internal drive. Here, choices in partners and pleasures show a personal coherence; sex is no inexplicable outside force. Certainly not every red-hot throb fits a pattern, and not all patterns are healthy. Rather, sex is intricately intertwined with identity and reveals less about the workings of the glands than the psyche. In one man's words, "I've realized that my deepest sexual fantasies are a mirror of myself. I used to look at sex as a game, a macho act, but now I see it differently. Desire is a consuming flame. You experience the life force. You start touching your essence."

As a catalyst for self-revelation or a means of connection, sex has marvelous powers. It is profound that so few acts can convey so much of human experience. Still, in *Good Sex*, not every wanton clinch is described in reverential tones. "Sex is not like the movies, where people look like Patrick Swayze," noted one woman. "The kitchen table is about as wild as it gets. To me, desire is like rock and roll: raw, not pretty, passionate."

Ricky

Ricky caught the Southern gift for conversation when her family moved to the Bible Belt. She first attempted intercourse with her boyfriend during his forty-eight hour R-and-R from Vietnam. "When we turned the lights on, the carnage was horrifying," the blonde forty-two year old remembers. "He was so sweet. He picked me up, tore the sheets off the bed. Actually, it was the only time in our relationship or marriage that he changed the sheets." Divorced and working in television in San Francisco, Ricky reveled in being a bad girl who would hit the bars after getting off the late-shift—a lifestyle abruptly swept into domesticity when she got pregnant by the filmmaker with whom she has lived for seven years.

Attraction is almost completely subconscious. It does go back to childhood things: somebody who has eyes like your cousin. I tend to go with men who remind me of other men that I have or have not been with. My husband reminded me of Elvis Presley, and a lot of men since then have reminded me of my husband. And then there's a couple standard types, and anyone who talks like them or gestures like them or looks out of the side of his eye like them, turns his head in a certain way . . . That's a signal. That's recognition. Heat-seeking. It seems to be familiarity of some kind, and it seems to have been familiarity from the get. It's probably my father, the movie stars I've liked, my mother— I've gone with a couple of men who reminded me a lot of my mother.

I want to be in his car, laughing. Preferably him laughing at something I'm saying. I want him to call me up and say, "When are you coming? I thought you were coming now. Come on, come *on.*" He has to be enlivened by my presence because we have the same sense of humor, because we have the same real grievous irony, because we are proud of our bitterness. A match is just heaven—a match of even just *one* quality is the most seductive thing to me . . . I want him to tease me in a personal way that implies that he knows me. I want him to mimic me, say my words back to me. I don't want him to talk about me in the third person in front of me. I want somebody who will see me and suggest to me that I'm not invisible after all.

The second time you do it is real good, because it's not foreign territory. The second time you do it, it's like you've known each other a million years and you're old friends: "Oh, I've been here before. But look, it's not tarnished. I don't hate this person yet, I don't know any bad information about him. I don't know what he's going to do next. I'm pretty sure he's not going to hurt me. I like what he did the last time, and I am interested enough to move." The main thing is *me* for goodness sake, is my desire. It used to be that what turned me on was his desire, but now I'm just so happy to feel desire, to yearn.

Whatever the attraction, it doesn't last long, not long at all. It turns out to be a mistake. It turns out that what I thought we were connecting on, we were not. The politics that we were agreed on, when we get to a more subtle point, are acted out in completely different ways. Almost opposite. Somebody has on some clothes that look a certain way, and I think, "Hey, I wonder if he's brilliant." Much later, I realize that it was something his old girlfriend gave him, and he put it on by mistake, and never wore it again.

I have this ridiculous theory about why I like black men, and why they like me—certain black men. It's political. It's a lot of suffering on either side of a line. We don't have the same suffering, but we suffer from the same source. We haven't suffered together so we don't despise one another, like black men and women sometimes do, or black women and white women sometimes do. We can see the other's suffering, their cunning and their fury, their meanness and their hate—and *welcome* it. What I love about black men is that they're furious at white men, and so am I. That's sexual. We have this great thing in common, and we're so happy to see each other. All those other people are out there, and we're in here.

I think if you can't have other kinds of communication, you can't have sex. You've gotta be hittin' on it in some way: if you laugh at the same thing, if you hate the same thing, if you love the same music, if you can catch somebody's eye across the room and laugh at somebody else. That whole notion of being conspiratorial is what's sexual to me: "It's me and you against all these morons." That's fun, that's intimate.

If you can't answer me, if you can't talk to me, if you can't laugh at my goddamn jokes, don't touch me. Don't touch me. This assumption that you can disagree in your minds but overcome that in your bodies . . . I believe that's true for some people, but it's not true for me. You can't disagree. You can't offend me with something that you say or think and then touch me. I want to touch somebody when he says something *wonderful*. If he gives me a sense that he's trying to figure out something to say that will either catch my interest or make me laugh, it drives me mad with desire. And gratitude.

When I was married to David, good sex came out of tenderness in the marriage, and it was rare that I felt that, because I was angry most of the time. We were just married, and I was horribly frigid and cracking up, and he was just acting horrible, and he got this ulcer—age twenty-one—and goes into the hospital and is horribly sick for two years. Every time he got really, really sick, I would get uncontrollably turned on. We'd be sitting up in bed reading or something, and the next thing I know, I'm just crawling all over the poor thing, who's barely sitting up. I don't know what that was about, but it was real strong.

Sex is the only thing we've got. It transforms us completely, one day to the next. It's still the main thing after all these years that I really care about. How do you get good sex? Pray. Give money to the homeless. Eat your carrots. You don't get good sex on purpose. You can keep away from bad sex. But you don't know who's going to make sweet sex happen or if there's ever going to be another chance for it. To find somebody who can slow-dance with you, match you and lead you just a little . . . . It's like, "My God, there is method in the universe." You circle around each other with centrifugal force and *resonate*. Humming. Sex has a voice of its own. It's like speaking in tongues, a phenomenon outside of yourself that you're driven by. Straight ahead.

José Antonio

Raised in Houston, José Antonio exhibited gay traits so early that his parents panicked. "They pushed me so hard towards girls," he jokes, "that I ended up identifying with them." At nineteen, he had his first gay date, a Christmas present set up by a friend. Bright and quick-witted, José Antonio has worked for many years as a professional in the mental health field. At forty, he is now entering law school.

I always picked very sensitive, seemingly-heterosexual men. In college, it seemed that the men I loved and wanted to have relationships with were unavailable to me. There was one guy I was attracted to. He was attracted to me, but he couldn't give himself permission to act on it. We'd go out drinking, and he'd say, "Do you want to dance?" And this would be in a heterosexual bar! Or he would make sure nobody'd be looking, and he'd throw kisses at me. We'd get drunk, and it would be snowing, and I'd pretend to be slipping towards him. He loved it, he loved being pursued. This went on for a year. Approach, avoidance. We never had sex.

I learned that if I ever wanted to have an emotional relationship, I was going to have to have a relationship with a woman and just trick on the side with men. So I got a job at a university in this little hick town back East and fell in love with this one woman, a student of mine in the residence hall. She was dating another staff member who was gay. As a matter of fact, he came on to me in the bathroom one day. She and I fell in love. Her mother had taught her to date gay men, because they were safe—she could have a good time but no sex. Well, this woman had *radar* for gay men.

We dated and eventually got married, and she accepted the fact that I would trick with men. I would take her to gay bars. She thought that she was special, because she was the only woman I was attracted to. She felt special, and our sex life was great. She was very free in her sexual activity. As a matter of fact, I

18

Desire

couldn't keep up with her on our honeymoon. At the university, I think she did the whole hockey team. But when we moved West so I could get my doctorate, I took her to a gay church. My present lover was sitting in the back pew, and I said, "That's him."

That was on Sunday. Friday we broke up, because we both knew that I had found what I needed. She left. And actually, I almost committed suicide. I was going through this identity crisis. I was afraid to own my gayness and lose my heterosexuality completely. I wrote a suicide note, and I was going to take some pills, and I cried myself to sleep. I called a crisis center that night. It wasn't a twenty-four hour crisis center. They had an answering service. And I'm crying my heart out to this woman, and she says, "Yeah, yeah, it seems like everything happens on a Friday night." I had worked in a crisis center, and I'm thinking, "This isn't how she's supposed to respond to me." Finally, a real counselor called me at seven-thirty the following morning. She was able to help me. For three months, all I did was watch Lawrence Welk with my mother on Saturday nights.

Mark was still going to the church. I liked him so much—I had already fallen in love with him, just from looking at him. He's a gorgeous man, tall and handsome, the all-American type. We started dating. After three or four months, he cleaned out a closet for me, and I moved in. We've been together thirteen years.

He had a sexual dysfunction, because he had always gotten negative messages about being gay, and his sexual activities had always been at adult theatres. He was a premature ejaculator. Cured him in three sessions. Just gave him permission: "Just let it happen," and so he learned he had control. He's shy. He's shy in bed, too, still. He doesn't enjoy sex, which makes it hard for me, because I love sex. But the unconditional love this man gives me is unbelievable.

He likes to do more than to be done. He wants to get his over with. So I usually do him first, then we can spend some more time on me. Mutual masturbation. Oral sex: we suck each other off before coming, but we never come in each other's mouths. I have very sensitive nipples. Most of the time, I just have my lover work on my nipples while I work on myself, because he does nipples better than anyone. We kiss a lot, we hug a lot. Our sex acts . . . we don't have marathons. By the time we get to bed, the emotional part has been going on for a long time. He never liked anal sex—to do it or be done. I've learned that his favorite fantasy is mine, too: that we're doing it with each other, but there are people watching. Discovering that is creating a little more aliveness in our sexual relationship.

I haven't been totally faithful to him, and he knows it. I'm allowed sex at conventions. Whenever I go away to a convention, I play around. It's usually with a married man from the Midwest. I tested HIV-negative, and I never do anything unsafe with other partners. I don't have a problem with condoms. For many Latinos, birth control is complicated. There's the issue of a guy's manhood, because generally the guy also wants the woman to have his baby, so putting on a condom prevents that. The other thing is that if a woman shows a man a condom, she is loose, she has bad morals, she's sleeping around: "If she's ready to have birth control, she can sleep with other men besides me." If you took away that part of it, and just talked about the logistics of the spread of AIDS, it would be a hell of a lot easier. You could teach people how to have more sensitivity with condoms: putting lubricant inside the condom, putting the condom on inside out, with the ridges on the inside.

On the continuum, I'm probably on the gay side leaning towards bisexual. I find myself attracted to certain women, but my identity's very gay. For Latino men, you're not allowed to own that you're gay, typically because of the Catholic Church. You have the same priests sleeping with men who condemn men sleeping with men. I have a priest that I see, and the *stories* he tells me! The people in the parish will just come and offer themselves for anything. Married men. I told my lover, "When you die, I'm going to be a priest."

Anne

One of four tow-headed immigrant kids on a dairy farm outside Los Angeles, Anne developed a gentle manner and a stubborn streak she calls typical of Norwegians. She became sexually active in college, while rooming with a friend bent on worldliness. "She came from a Seventh Day Adventist background where everything was forbidden, so she said things like, 'Anne, you really should smoke,'" laughs the silver-haired grandmother. "It was the same with drinking and sex." Now sixty-five and in her second marriage, this retired teacher makes her home in the Berkeley hills overlooking the Bay.

The message from both my father and my mother was that women were as good as men, and it was important to get a good education as women, because we needed to be able to take care of ourselves, be independent and not be under the thumb of a man. My father would take me out on the milk route with him and talk politics. I argued with him, and he liked it. When I was four and a half, my neighbor's teenage son came into our garage, and he wanted to look at my sexual organs. He was really pushing me. I started to remove my pants, and then it hit me that I didn't like him and didn't feel right about it. Suddenly I looked up at him and said, "No, I *won't!*" He tried to pressure me, and I said, "No, I *won't!* And you'd better go away and leave me alone." I think I was able to be so forceful because of my parents' message that as a woman, you're empowered.

I met my first husband in the medical library at college. He knew Los Angeles in a way I'd never seen it before—art places, concerts, parties with interesting people. I don't know when we ended up making love, but I enjoyed it tremendously. I was really surprised when he asked me to marry him—absolutely taken aback. The only thing I could think of was, "I don't want this to end." I was twenty, and I didn't have the nerve to say, "I don't want to get married, but I'd sure like to keep having sex with you and fun with you." In the first two years, he was so loving and kind to me. He was gentle and always tried to please me in love-making.

There were years of sex. He was *always* turned on by me: I'd kiss him, and he'd want to have sex. I'm naturally affectionate, and I had to be careful not to be too affectionate with him unless I wanted to have sex. But sex was going to happen every night anyway. Then my mother died, and her death made me aware of how lonely I was in the marriage. I realized he was gone so much of the time, and when he did come home late at night, he'd wake me up, and there was sex. I was never ready for it, but he'd keep stroking me and turning me on. I acquiesced. Then he'd be gone in the morning before breakfast. No time together. Life continued this way for seventeen years, and I raised four children. Eventually, I found out he'd always had a lot of other women. Within six months, I filed for divorce. He said, "The only thing that's wrong is that you found out."

The last time we had sex, I knew I was going to divorce him, and I hadn't told him. I reached over to him and said, "Let me show you how to make love." We made love. It was absolutely marvelous. I said, "There. Can you tell the difference?" It was the best love-making we'd ever had. It was really communicating, beyond passion. It was being totally sensitive. I was responding to him, directing the whole thing, completely communicating my needs. I wasn't holding back in any way. It was my way of saying good-bye.

After the divorce, I had the most wonderful sexual experience of my life. It was on a date set up by a friend. The man was a lieutenant commander from the Navy—the classic blond, blue-eyed, square-jawed, handsome devil. His whole goal was to sexually please the woman, and he knew more about it than any man I have *ever* come across. He knew how to touch me, feel me, please me, stroke me, and listen. As soon as he ejaculated, he was hard again, and he had a nice size penis. He was gentle and did everything to please me, until I was so exhausted from sex I couldn't move. Sensation of the first order. Totally responsive to the way my body moved. Totally.

I certainly didn't feel any intimacy with him. I enjoyed it as a pure sexual experience. But with my husband now, and we've been married twenty-one years, sex is totally emotional. I enjoy

Desire

the warm feeling, the friendship, the lovingness, the lying next to him, the complete ease that I feel with him. We're affectionate with one another, we laugh a lot, and we just have sex when we feel like it. It's friendly and part of the conversation. It's a give and take. I've evolved into certain decisions: I'm in charge of my body, and I'm not having sex with anybody unless I want it and on my terms. And I think that was pretty well established, the kernel of it, when I was four and a half, when I somehow or other knew to be so forceful with that older boy. I'm nobody's slave. I'm doing it because *I* want to. My husband gives it to me on my terms and says he's never enjoyed sex with anyone as much as with me, that he never really knew sex before.

I like a lot of foreplay, in terms of feeling my body all over and appreciating it, kissing one another and stroking and then intercourse. If he wants to have oral sex with me, that's okay, but I don't like having a penis in my mouth. I've tried all sorts of positions, and I don't like most of them. I'm very conservative in what I find pleasurable: I like the traditional missionary position best of all. To me, good sex is communication. We have our best sexual experiences when we've resolved a problem. When we come to agreement, we have this incredible respect for one another, love for one another, and we have sex. As we've aged, it's less passionate, but it's really lovely. We're so comfortable with one another. It's funny to say you're comfortable about sex, but I am.

Harlan

Harlan is a lanky, long-haired man in a baseball cap. Scottish, Irish and Cherokee, he grew up Southern Baptist on a North Carolina farm. As a terrified twelve-year-old, he was seduced by a sister's friend. "We went to a local bootlegger, got a pint of whiskey, went up on a ridge and got snockered. That's when the girl decided she and I should go for a walk. I owe her a lot." Married four times, at forty-one Harlan is happily settled in a monogamous relationship with Thea, his wife of fourteen years. He works in construction.

Being raised on farms, I can't remember not knowing about sex. But we're taught about the plumbing, not the sensitivity. I learned at an early age to keep my ears open and my mouth shut. So when my sister and her girlfriends would be talking, I would listen. When my mother got together with her sisters, I would listen. I learned that women didn't care about rough sex, that they wanted tenderness and for men to go slowly, that a kiss and caress was worth more than a large penis. By listening to them, I learned that the things my father had passed on to me about women were totally wrong. He told me once, "There are two kinds of women: whores and mothers." However, I found out there's a measure of good girl and bad girl in all women, just as there's a good boy and bad boy in all men.

I came back from my first tour of Vietnam, having lost a very dear friend from high school. He died in my arms, and I came within six inches of getting killed. Just six weeks later, back home, my brother introduced me to this young girl, still in high school. I was twenty, vulnerable, fell for her. My second wife. When she left me, I went nuts sexually. For fourteen months, the remainder of my second tour, I was like a rabbit, from one girl to the next to the next. I feel now that I was trying to get back at women for the hurt I experienced when I found out my wife was leaving me.

Desire

1975. That's when I met her. Thea. There was so much physical attraction there, it was scary. I knew prettier girls, girls with more money, but I'd never met anybody who attracted me so much. We got married May 14th in People's Park, and we've been lovers and best friends ever since. The best sex I ever had was with Thea. We'd been married a couple of years. We decided to take a three-day weekend off up in the mountains, and we took a couple of hits of good Owsley acid with us. The stuff had been stuck in the freezer in San Francisco for years. We took this by the light of a full moon on top of a mountain. No one around for miles and miles. We made love in every conceivable position, some I didn't even think were possible. We made love for six solid hours. The woman had me so turned on that I could sit across an open area from her, look into her eyes and orgasm. And she could do the same.

I like long, slow kisses. Petting, touching, staring into each other's eyes. And if foreplay don't last at least an hour, I'm not happy. One of our favorite positions is laying face to face on our sides, me on my right, her on her left. She grabs my penis in her left hand, moves me back and forth up against her clitoris. I enjoy oral sex a lot. Butterfly kisses are better than a hog in a trough.

Thea has multiple orgasms, and I enjoy them more than my own. She screams and hollers, and I was never so proud as the first time she told me, "No more." She's an adamant lover. She's not afraid to let me know when she wants to make love, to tell me when she wants something done differently. Ninety percent of the time, she comes before I do, and I like that.

I had a vasectomy because of my warped genes from Agent Orange. It caused a blood clot on my left side. Took 'em six weeks to schedule corrective surgery. It took me two years until my left nut could even be touched, and sex was hell. At one point, I would come blood. I didn't want to be touched. I went down on her more. We used toys, a vibrator and dildo. Not much finger-play, because my hands are rough from construction work—I always put on hand lotion before we make love because of the toughness of my skin. I recovered. Once I was sure I was sterile, sex became ever so much more enjoyable. No more worry about damaged chromosomes, about my wife getting pregnant.

A great weight was lifted from my mind, love-making became

more free. Orgasms seemed more intense. And multiple orgasms, while not commonplace, were more frequent.

They say multiple orgasms don't exist for men, but I'm here to tell you that they do. There's the initial build and climax, and then a building even higher, even stronger—not as extended in time, but more intense physically. I stay hard the whole time, come with each orgasm. There's never any pattern, never any clue that it's going to be that way. I've experienced multiple orgasms with Thea when we're having intercourse, oral sex, masturbating. It's always a surprise. First time it happened was a real mind-blower: what was *that*? I'd just come in Thea's mouth, she pulled her head back and I came again all over her throat. Surprised her as much as it did me, but I was too busy writhing in ecstasy to react. When I'm straight, twice is usually the limit. When I'm on LSD or mushrooms, it goes on for hours. We trip once a year just to experience it.

I don't understand a lot of folks: Thea and I have been married over fourteen years, and we *still* have good sex. Love-making eases tensions. We discuss more when we're sexually active than in periods where we're not: "This has been causing me some concern, I'm worried about that." When we don't make love on a regular basis, it seems like we lose communication. For the most part, we make love a lot, and it doesn't matter what time of day it is or whether the lights are on. We make love at least every other day—and we have the whole time we were together, except when I was physically unable to. It's a melding of souls.

Bea

At seven, Bea discovered masturbation, a pleasure she occasionally tried to give up for Lent. Her secret childhood games included peeping at a male boarder in the bathtub and playing "butt doctor" with young friends. Bea grew up on Chicago's South Side. As a teenager, she set her sights on college, avoided dreaded pregnancy, and had a series of crushes on boys and girls. A willowy forty-two-year-old who says she has always been tantalized by body parts, Bea teaches dance and lives with her girlfriend of nearly three years.

I didn't deal with a lot of boys as a kid. I'm dark, and being dark when I grew up was a no-no. It was long before Black Power and "Black is beautiful." I wasn't intimate till I was twenty-one. A late bloomer. Twenty-one years old before the big one, and then it was *so* big! His penis was huge, absolutely huge. He got to the doorway, and it was like, "Well, baby, you ain't coming in *here* with *that*!" I like to woke up the whole dorm screaming. He must have really been in love, because it was a long time before his dick ever saw the inside of me.

From there, I was off and running. Until age thirty-two, I dealt with twenty-some men. There were some I wanted to marry, and there were time periods I just wanted to be that single girl hanging out. I was the "other" woman twice. Intercourse was exciting, but it never took off. With most guys, I went through the motions, because that was my role as a woman. Two guys were clever enough to understand a woman's body and knew to move the clitoris. Two guys. One was oral. Back then that was really a big deal, because you couldn't always get black men to do oral. They'd want you to go down on them, but they didn't want to go down on you. I do not ever remember having an orgasm with a penis in me. But it didn't matter to me, because I knew I could have an orgasm: they'd fall out dead, I'd do my little thing and go to sleep. I would do it on the side, and that was fine.

At thirty-three, going to a dance class, I was very into the instructor. One day I came home and realized that it wasn't because she was such a great dancer. I liked her *body*. I was into *her*. I remember my first sexual encounter with a woman. I thought it was great: "Hey, this is very smooth." You set up a whole different rapport when you deal with men than when you deal with women. Men are *quick*: they want to get right to it. Very few men know how to build up a situation. Women aren't necessarily like that. There are things they want to do: caressing, taking time, drawing it out. You still have to talk, "I like this or that." Just because you're two women doesn't mean you have instant ESP or mental telepathy. Different women like different things.

I like the softness, the fullness of a woman. That womanly feel. The wetness. Men: they're dry or you get the gush of life. With women, there are degrees of warm wetness. I like to be touched gently, teasingly, breasts caressed. I like to be held, kissed, soft touches all over my body. I love being stroked with a brush, with a feather. Whispering past the vaginal area, just teasing. Kissing the thighs, kissing the vaginal lips and then getting into a whole oral thing. I like to have fingers inside me in the build-up phases, but I'm really into the clitoral thing. Anything to do with the clit. The first climax is the biggest. When I come, I close down, but then I can build back up again.

I love sucking my lover's breasts, being oral, kissing her all over. Sending her into levels of excitement through a build-up. Whispering in her ear, kissing her ears, sticking my tongue in her ears. Kissing the fullness of her mouth. Her tongue and my tongue together. I like using my hands, stroking her on each side of her clit and going inside, sliding in and out of her. Going down, just being right there, going oral with the clit and using the tongue in the vaginal area.

I like to play, to use my body in subtle ways. I like wearing skirts with no underwear and then letting my lover know that, sitting across from her in a risqué position, where not only she could see, but somebody else could, too. I love to pose for my girlfriend—in bed, out of bed, especially in places you wouldn't think of. I'll come out the tub and wrap my leg around the door frame, or I'll sit in a chair and spread my legs. Very *Vogue*. I like driving along, playing around in the car. Or on a crowded dance floor: bop, bop, reach for a breast, get brave and reach

Desire

down. That has a real erotic thrill for me. Or being out shopping, or in line at the movies, and brushing my breasts against her. I like to do things in situations where she cannot react. I like to push that to its limits.

There's this whole intrigue about being with a woman. I like that people wonder if I'm a lesbian. I like the sense of, "I know what it's like to be in bed with a woman, and you *don't!*" I'm not into dating; I'm into a relationship. Lots of girls jump into bed on the first date, but I have to drag the ordeal out. It seems to me if you're fucking while you're dating, then good sex is just hitting the right spot at the right time. But with a long-term partner, the sexual act is a bonding, a check-in. Sometimes it's a communication when words aren't there. Things can be happening that you can't talk about, and sex is a way of saying, "I'm still there."

Good sex is satisfying to you and your partner. You can communicate—in or out of bed—what you want to do, not what some book or standard says it's supposed to be. It's something you love to do.

Dave

In 1980, office gossip alerted Dave to swing parties, which he and a female co-worker promptly investigated. He did not know what to expect. "I went into this group room. People said to take my clothes off, sit down and talk. I did, and some woman grabbed ahold of me, and next thing you know, we were having sex together," he recalls. "It totally blew my mind. I thought it was the way to live, and I was sorry I'd never done it before." Today, swinging remains central to Dave's sex life. A forty-two-year-old Asian American, he works in civil service and lives with his parents.

I have such a good time with sex that it's one of my main forms of fun. It's something that's really exciting. It's a very physical experience for me, and one of the most fun things anyone could ever do, anywhere, any time. Swinging, to me, is like when people are into running and they have a running club. Well, some people feel this way about sex.

About five years ago, I met the woman I go to parties with now, and that's when I started going regularly. For two or three years, we went every other weekend. We like each other, we're close friends, and we see each other outside the parties, too. She lives in a rooming house, and I can't go up into her room, so we go to swing parties or hot tubs. When we go to a swing house, we have sex together, and then we split up and don't see each other for hours. If I conserve my energy, get to the party early, and haven't masturbated for a week, I can usually have sex three times. I do it with my partner, take a good shower and get cleaned up properly—hygiene is really important. Then I try and meet someone else, do it with her, come a second time. Then I have to wait a long time, like an hour and a half, before I'm ready for sex, so I clean up again, get something to eat, rest. I spend a lot of my time trying to get in as much activity as I can.

It's a dimly-lit environment. A lot of people are there to have anonymous sex, so they really don't want to know your name or

30

Desire

who you are. Every swing house has its unwritten social rules: it's okay for women to have sex with women, but men never have sex with men. That's probably an old-fashioned, macho-type thing. Some of the rules are pretty good: respect for other people, meaning you don't go over and grab them, "Come *here*!"

For the most part, there isn't too much discussion. You might be in a private bunk with someone, and you'll see a couple get into the bunk below, and pretty soon you'll hear all these oohs and ahs. When people are in a group situation, there isn't really a lot said. A woman may position her body in a certain way: she'll be on her knees giving a guy head and she'll have her rear end sticking up in the air. Usually, but not always, that's an invitation to do it to her from behind, so I go over and check that out, maybe first putting my hand on her back and asking, "Am I bothering you?" If she indicates no, then I keep going.

My big thing is intercourse. I don't do a lot of kissing with strangers, because I don't know where someone's mouth has been. The softer, gentler, romantic things that I'd do with a girlfriend, I usually wouldn't do at a swing house. In the context of a swing party, I like to start by touching a woman's breasts, putting my arms around her, holding her close and then reaching down between her legs. My woman friend is always complaining that there are a lot of thirty-second jockeys out there, and I try to be more considerate. If the woman's not getting wet, I'll ask, "Is there a certain way you'd like me to do it?" If I don't ask, I don't think she'll necessarily tell me what she wants. If I want to make absolutely sure that she's going to come, then early on I say, "I'm going to get on top, and I want you to play with your clitoris while I fuck you. I want to feel you come, and I want you to tell me when you do."

I like a partner to play with my penis, feel myself get hard and start doing it. Going inside a woman's body is a really neat experience. A hard-on is like an extension of your whole body. Entering a woman, you're hard and stiff, and you feel good, and that's making *her* feel good. You feel a rush throughout your whole body. If I have sex often enough, I can control how long I can have that feeling last. Sometimes I can build myself up to just before orgasm and keep that sexual excitement for a long time.

I use condoms all the time. The little pleasure that they interrupt is greatly outweighed by the safety that they provide. At the swing house I go to most often, right at the door, there's a big dish of condoms. I'm always filling the thing up, so hopefully people are using them. You see a lot of people grab them, but it's hard to tell whether other guys are using them, because the condoms are translucent and the rooms are dim. I don't ask women to do me orally—although if they really want to, I won't say no.

Two or three months ago at a swing house, a woman told me, "This is exactly what we're going to do. You're going to eat my pussy, then I'm going to suck you, and then we're going to fuck." I said no. It was a group situation, and people gave me kind of a hard time. But people there don't use latex barriers *except* for condoms, and I don't like to put my mouth where maybe she's just had unprotected sex with some guy who didn't wear a condom. I've seen guys who think that's the greatest thing in the world, and that's *why* their mouths are there. But to me, that's really dangerous. I got tested for HIV a couple of years ago, but not recently. I'm really careful: after intercourse, I grab hold of that condom and pull out carefully to avoid exposure. This might be false, but I feel that because I use condoms and lubricants with nonoxynol-9, my chances of getting AIDS are pretty slim.

What's good sex? To me, that's being able to fuck all night.

Carol

As an enterprising eleven-year-old, Carol went to the library in her small Oregon town to find out how to have an orgasm. At fourteen, she had an affair with a married teacher. She came out as a lesbian in college and discovered sex triads. "How I make my decisions about life is: anything that gives me multiple orgasms is worth finding out more about," says the thirty-four-year-old. Her fine ivory face is half hidden by tortoise-shell glasses. "Today, I'm very much involved in group sex. I run group sex parties, I go with my partner to SM parties, and I really love being in bed with a man and another woman." Erotic photographs and sentimental Victorian prints crowd the walls of Carol's San Francisco apartment. Nipple clamps and Mexican love charms dangle from the metal bedstead.

Three years ago, I stopped going to graduate school because I ran out of money. Restaurant work no longer seemed like a viable option. I began working at a peep show. At first, I was dancing on stage with four other hot, naked, rebellious, wild, tattooed, pierced, *crazed* women—which was delightful. We were in a small room that was completely mirrored, with a curtain for a door. On three sides were windows with mirrored glass, but eventually the glass went up, and you could see plain glass with a man's face on the other side. I was dressed very scantily, if at all, just dancing, flirting, wiggling my butt at the windows, lifting one leg so I could show them my pussy, fondling my breasts, being sexy.

I soon moved into a one-on-one booth, the thing you see advertised in red light districts: "Talk To A Real Live Nude Girl." That was my job, and I loved it. I was locked into a booth, and the guy would be on his side of the glass. He would put money in a slot, and I'd give him time on a meter: five dollars for three minutes, a hundred dollars an hour. We could hear each other through an intercom, and we could talk about anything, do anything that didn't involve us physically touching one another. One

33

of the things that surprised me was that there were men who went into peep shows to have romantic, intimate sex with the woman on the other side of the glass, including pretending that we're kissing, including endearments. What would be a very romantic fuck if you were in bed together could still happen through a pane of glass. It was amazing.

Close to half the men who came to see me in the booth had sexually divergent turn-ons. Some wanted to talk out elaborate fantasies, do dominance and submission, show me the lingerie they had on under their business suits, show me pictures of what they did with their partners at home. Ninety-five percent of these guys were married, and I'm quite sure only a fraction shared their erotic interests with their partners. I'd tell a story, or we would talk back and forth. Most often, I would masturbate, and so would he. I found that I liked watching guys jack off. It got me into a higher level of arousal: I could have eye contact, I could watch his hand on his dick, I would have all those parts of a sexual connection while I was touching myself just right. Working at the peep show, I had four hours of almost constant masturbation, two to four days a week. It made me profoundly orgasmic. It was there that I first climaxed from touching another part of my body besides my genitals. Watching and being watched, I could pick any part of my body, stroke it and orgasm.

Eventually, I quit the peep show, because I didn't like punching a time clock, and I didn't like working for a manager. But during that time, I met a man at a sex party. It was one of those "some enchanted evening" situations. I temper my sexuality by being highly romantic, and I found myself an adventurous, nasty, romantic guy. We became really close really fast. I started being able to do some sort of tantra sex with my partner: he'd be embracing me, not touching any of my sex parts, looking into my eyes intensely, and I would come. It's *connection*, not just two people rubbing on each other and being alone in the sensation. I see us as erotic equals, but most of the time he's dominant and I'm submissive. Changing that at times creates profound ripples in the usual energy. My partner has an erotic charge around cross-dressing. He's been rejected for it in the past, so it was scary for him to bring his lingerie over and dress up for me. I got to see my partner—my master, a forceful, stern top—get all fluttery

Desire

and nervous, and it was incredibly moving. The gift of somebody's vulnerability. That was also the first time I strapped on a dildo and fucked him. I had never fucked a man that way before, and I got profoundly turned on by the gender tweak. Now I see gender as a sex toy.

My notion of sex toys is pretty broad. I think latex is really sexy, and I've chosen to put rubber between me and a lot of sex behaviors. I like the moment of assertiveness that reaching over to the bedside table and pulling out a condom represents for me: "It's time to do this now." I like putting condoms on men. I think the more that the accoutrements of sex can *signal* sex, the hotter it's going to be, and the fewer problems there will be. Anybody who hasn't played with latex ought to put on a latex glove and start to understand the different kind of touches that can be conveyed. It's extremely sensual—especially with lubricants. Lubricants are the universe's *gift* to us as sexual beings.

In the last few years, my sexual response has developed so much that what used to be a difficult to achieve, one-time orgasm, can now last as a multiple for thirty minutes. My entire body undulates, and sometimes I can't stop. Orgasm is the time when my body feels the most unified, when all the cells start working together. I'm transported—I couldn't tell you where. But the transcendence is not an out-of-body experience, it's an *in*-the-body experience. A few times, sex has been so good I've burst into tears: "I never thought anybody would be here with me so much." That's vulnerability. That's superimposing this hot, sweet fuck with all the times that I was horny and alone, all the times I thought no one would ever love me. Orgasm doesn't get any better than that.

My eroticism is such now that I would gladly spend lots and lots of time on it. The only constraints are time commitments connected to having to make a living. But sex is that important to me.

Dennis

The tenth of twelve children in a close working-class family, Dennis became sexually aware at ten, the year he got his own bedroom. "I started fantasizing, having wet dreams and discovering the joys of masturbation," he says with a smile. "I remember the first time I ejaculated. That was a horrifying experience: I didn't know what the hell was going on." Thirty-three, married and a new father, Dennis is a frank, engaging man who works in a postal job and, teamed up with his wife, leads counseling workshops for engaged Catholic couples.

Ours was one of the first Filipino families to buy a house in the area. Growing up, the choices were, "Be a priest, be celibate or learn to date outside your race."

Kathleen and I met in third grade. She's Irish, from a stubborn, hard-drinking family. One day, we were playing basketball in her backyard, and she gave me a kiss on the cheek. Her mother came screaming out of the house, "Kathleen, get in the house! And *you*. I don't ever want to see *you* again!" We didn't know what had happened. She was put on restriction for weeks, and I didn't see her after that. At first we said, "We're going to fight this," but we were sixteen and couldn't. We went our separate ways but maintained a secret friendship.

I dated other girls in high school. Sex with my first girlfriend: we didn't know what the hell we were doing. All we were doing was what we saw on TV. I remember trying to penetrate her. I was so awkward. I didn't think to start with foreplay. I didn't know *why* it didn't work, but then I thought, "Let's try something else." Thanks to the porno magazines I'd read, I started to initiate oral sex, and that's when she started to loosen up and lubricate. I had her put the condom on me, and that was erotic. I remember mounting her, and it was still hard to penetrate her. Once I was in, I don't think I ever came so fast in my life. I remember talking about it afterwards, and she said, "It's like someone putting a *bread box* in you." Later, my little sister brought a friend home,

36

Desire 37

introduced her to me, and left us together. It was this woman who initiated me. She just mounted me and showed me what she did, positioning me. I could go down on her, and she'd come and come again. We had sex before school, in breaks, after school, nighttime.

In college, when I saw that I was attracting women, I started abusing that. I think a lot of it was related to the anger I felt towards guys in my fraternity who flaunted their wealth, while I was from the other side of the tracks. I was working two jobs. I couldn't afford the wool blazers or the alligator shirts. Being attractive to women was one thing these guys *couldn't* do. They could talk all uppity and have the money, but they struck out with women. I knew it drove these guys crazy: the fact that I wasn't white, and most of the sorority women were.

After college, Kathleen and I started seeing each other again, but it was still on the sly. She had to make up lies to go on dates. One day, I told her, "We can't do this. I want an honest relationship. Tell your parents you're going on a date with me." Five minutes later, she called: "Dennis, come pick me up. They're kicking me out of the house." For going on a *date* with me! Can you believe it? 1984! That next day, we went to the Catholic Church and said, "We want to get married." Her parents fought us tooth and nail: "God never meant the races to intermix." They went to the parish priest, and three weeks before the wedding, he called us and denied the wedding. I raised hell, but it didn't help. We changed parishes. Our relationship is the reason for us living.

A lot of our sex before we were married was loose and fancy-free because we were drunk. When we'd go out on dates, she'd drink me under the table. She'd drink before we'd go out, the whole time we were out, and then go home and drink. After Kathleen got kicked out, she started going to AA, and she's been sober seven years now.

For us, sex is not pumping and pistons working. It's keeping romance alive, not sexual olympics. We're very physical. We kiss and caress. When she wants to make love to me, I'm very aware of her. I know right away the first thing we're going to do is extended foreplay, and I'll perform oral sex on her—or she on me—and then we'll have intercourse. I'm receptive to her signs, and she's also receptive to mine.

Kathleen's parents finally came over to our side, and we felt that was a miracle, so we decided to put ourselves in God's hands and try to live the doctrine of the Catholic Church. We decided to stop using contraception and be open to life. We would have sex and sex and sex, but she didn't get pregnant for six years. When Kathleen became pregnant, it didn't slow down our sex drives. We continued to have oral sex and intercourse all the way through the ninth month. It was beautiful. It actually opened up a new door in our sensuality. She's very beautiful pregnant and actually glows. Since the birth, the doctor has said, "No sex for six weeks." We've been going crazy. I went back to a stash of magazines for release. But the other night, I just had to have her. I pulled out a rubber. I hadn't used a condom in seven years or longer, and I'd forgotten what it does: it desensitizes me, so I can maintain my erection for abnormal amounts of time. We had sex and loved it. She had a couple of orgasms through intercourse.

When we have sex, in the glow afterwards, I feel at peace—no matter what problems I've had at work or stress I'm under. It gives me security, it makes me feel wanted, it reinforces that I'm still an attractive, sensual being. Sex reinforces our marriage, and it really makes us feel as one. There's no feeling in the world like that moment when we're having sex. We're one person at that point.

Christopher

At age seven, Christopher realized his attraction to men made him different. Christopher is seventeen, Asian American, a bright college pre-med who plans to work in Africa. A minister's son, he came out publicly this year after discovering LYRIC, a Bay Area support group for young gays and lesbians. "My mother's reaction," he says, "is to walk around the house with the Bible and spend an hour every day praying for me."

I was fourteen. I needed to see other gay people. Somehow I got the courage to go to a porno theatre showing gay movies. I saw those guys sitting there, staring at me. I didn't understand the signals. I sat in a corner, arms crossed, head down, unable to look at the screen, too scared to move. I stayed for four hours. It was the first time that I realized what masturbation was. I went home and started doing it.

I heard about gay beaches. I had my first sexual experience there. I was wandering around, and a guy walked over to me and asked, "Do you want to jack off together?" I was so embarrassed, I blushed. It was an attractive offer: he was six-three, blond and blue-eyed, about twenty-five. I told him it was my first time, but he didn't believe me. We found a secluded place on the beach, surrounded by bushes, and he laid a blanket down. We took off our shirts, started kissing, caressing all over. That was the first time I ever kissed anyone. We took off our pants, gave each other blow jobs. He came really quick. I held out for fifteen minutes, so I felt really manly. Then I went home and took a two-hour shower, because I felt so dirty.

I thought I wasn't having sex, because it wasn't with a woman. Even though we were two naked bodies rolling around, I still thought I was a virgin. I believed when I was older, I would start liking women, and *that* would be real sex.

I went back to the porno theatres. I'd seen the routine there: you indicate your interest by resting your arm on the seat next to you. If they want you, they'll sit down. My age and ethnicity

39

make me attractive to other men. I can have my pick. In the beginning, I was stupid: I'd ask, "What's your name?" Later, I found out there's no need for verbalization. We'd do mutual masturbation. Some men tried to push my head down to give them blow jobs, but I never did it. If you really want a guy, you say, "Do you want to go to the bathroom?" It's lighter there. The stalls have no doors. A lot of times, other patrons see you walking there and follow. They're voyeurs or they want to get their hands on you, caressing your body while you're jerking off with this guy. Sometimes it turns into a group thing. I liked that people wanted me, that they found me attractive.

Men who are into Asians are called "rice queens." I used to like the Greek god type, but now I'm only attracted to the brain—I don't care about age, color or appearance. Earlier this year, I was introduced to gay bars. Even though I'm underage, I can get in, because they think we Asians all look alike. I'd go into bars with the hope of finding a relationship, not just slutting around. But that would be the only thing they wanted. The guys I've gone home with have mostly been rich professional types, so they live in really nice places with tons of Oriental antiques. We'll make small talk, kiss, get naked, hop into bed in a dark room. We'll kiss from the head down the body, sucking, taking turns. I like mutual jack-off, and I like two naked bodies tangled, rolling with wild animal passion, but I don't like giving head. It's boring. Receiving is somewhat pleasurable, but it's not heaven. There are so many other sensual spots on the body. I like to be touched all over, really gentle caresses. One time I was with a European guy, and God, those Europeans *bite*! I didn't know how to say no.

Having come out so recently, I find safe sex is the rule, not the exception, so I haven't had to change my behavior. I tested negative for HIV, and I'm going to get hepatitis B shots. To me, safe sex includes not swallowing come, not rimming, and using condoms with anal sex. The activities I like—caressing, touching, mutual masturbation—are pretty safe. I've always thought if I were dating a guy, we'd get tested together before jumping into bed. I know I'd be monogamous, and if I were with a guy, I would like to trust him. I wouldn't want to use a condom, because that would imply we were sleeping with other people.

I'm not going to do any more nights with strangers. I met Ryan

Desire

three weeks ago. He's my age, a college student, shy. We're in a group together, and we just clicked, talking about our lives, hanging out every day. He came over last night, and I really didn't expect anything. We were watching TV, sitting closer and closer, then kissing, cuddling naked in bed. We gave each other head, but neither of us came. It was solely sensual. We're going to try anal sex. I'm really curious about it, and I think it's more intimate. I feel like a virgin, because I haven't had anal sex, and society tells us that "in and out" is the only way of having hard-core sex. Still, I have a major fear of being the bottom, because it hurts, and the thought of being the top gives me performance anxiety. We're going to do this honeymoon thing, rent a motel. I want to do it.

I'd like to have sex in a pool, on a cruise yacht out at sea, in a rain forest. I'd like to rip through a man's suit. Good sex means kissing while we are doing it, different types of strokes, different hand positions, holding someone close. It's with someone I have a lot of emotional attachment to. He doesn't have to be good at kissing or sucking, but if it's the person I want, that's what matters. I've never had good sex. Last night with Ryan is as close as I've gotten.

Lissa

This thirty-three-year-old mother of two grew up in a large Catholic family so modest that sisters never changed clothes in front of each other. Lissa learned the facts of life in sixth grade from the class tart. Two years later, her parochial school introduced a parent-taught sex education course that explained reproduction but never revealed how intercourse actually took place. Today, a tall, animated figure with long brown hair, Lissa directs an AIDS service organization in rural Northern California.

In college, sex was often disappointing. Vague, gropey encounters. The real relationship began the summer I was twenty. Kevin exuded sexuality. Between us, it was almost instantaneous. Late at night after work, we'd go out to the bars, talking and talking and talking, making out. It was *fireworks*, explosions behind the eyes. There was no controlling, no saying "no", it just happened. This became a relationship. We were in *love*, and we fucked constantly. In sex with him, there was the feeling that we were trying to become one and that this was impossible. The relationship was wonderful: it was emotional, it had to do with communication, with learning from each other, with literature, politics, my being out on my own. Then my best friend stole him from me. I couldn't eat or sleep. I went on a wild rampage of fucking everyone in sight, looking for that closeness, that warmth, that hot sex. I had lost my link to adulthood. I couldn't handle it on my own, and I had no one to share it with.

It wasn't until a few years later, when I went to Europe, that my life and my adulthood started. I went to a Greek island for a weekend and ended up staying for three years. There's a strong and developed expatriate community there, people who were educated, had been all over the world, run guns, smuggled drugs. People of all ages and economic backgrounds. What they had in common was that they read books, had philosophies, ideas and talents. There was an undercurrent of sexual frenzy—pervasive, honest, open. There was an intellectual spirit and strength. It was

Desire   43

home. A painter introduced me to Lindsey. Our first night together,
he said, "You can stay over, but I have to tell you that I'm primarily
homo." And I *laughed*, because I hadn't heard the word "homo"
since grammar school. We spent the night together, and it was
lovely. The next day, he introduced me to his friend Nigel, with
whom I had a long, passionate affair . . . actually, with whom
Lindsey *and* I had a mutual affair. I remember the three of us sat
and talked about AIDS. Early 1984. Lindsey had been tested, but
it was the days before the HIV antibody test. He'd had a T-cell
count done, and they'd told him he was fine. Information about
AIDS was sketchy. Nigel and I said, "You know, we probably
have whatever causes it. Where are we going to die? Some place
warm, tropical, with cheap labor so you can hire a twelve-year-old
to fan you in your dying moments." It was a joke, but it was also
serious.

I got pregnant that summer, broke up with Lindsey and got
five marriage proposals. After I had the baby, Lindsey and I
wound up together. I remember sitting with him in the garden
one night, sipping wine, nobody around and the baby asleep.
Finally, he put it to me, "We could be a legendary love story, or
we could be nothing at all." The forging of our relationship came
step by step. It had to do with the births of our two children and
moving back to Northern California five years ago.

Once here, there was an influx of AIDS information in the
paper. Lindsey got tested for HIV and tested positive. I got tested
the next morning. The first sex we had after that, knowing that
he had HIV and I probably did too, was very intense and almost
ritualistic. Intense pain and intense intimacy. And yet it was necessary to be sexual. We needed that. I needed that. My test results
came back positive. There was a lot of dilemma and depression
for three or four months. That was four years ago, and we don't
cut a tragic figure anymore. Lindsey never did. His attitude from
the beginning was, "It's just a little microbe that wants to live.
Can we coexist?" I admire that attitude. He's more comfortable
with HIV than anyone I know and has made me more comfortable
with it.

We have educated, quasi-safe sex, meaning that we'll choose
to have oral sex, knowing the risk of infection is almost nil. The
recent studies showing that female-to-male transmission has a

0.01 risk factor makes it much easier for him to go down on me. I don't look at sex as something to be scared of, and I don't tow the public health department line, either. If you know your physical state, and you know how your teeth and your mouth are, and you know there are no open sores, I think you can make intelligent decisions on what to you is "safe sex." I'm not afraid of germs. We do use *coitus interruptus*. We use condoms. But there's no paranoia. We don't do blatantly unsafe things. There's no anal sex, not as much oral sex as there used to be, and we don't have sex during my period. We're careful, and we don't want to reinfect each other. We never made a formal agreement to be monogamous, it just sort of happened that way. And I'm not with Lindsey because of HIV. There's a lot more than that.

I don't think safe sex is a hassle. Condoms, cocks, vaginas . . . these are objects. What's really important about sex is the *connection*. It has nothing to do with where it's put or how. I find sex is getting nothing but better. Why? Because I'm older, I'm more realistic about it, I'm not trying to merge with someone. It's more of an expression of warmth, closeness, intimacy . . . and sometimes it's not; sometimes it's more erotic. To have it never the same with one person is new and different to me. Sometimes it's a quick fuck. Sometimes it's a long, drawn out, lazy stimulation thing. Sometimes it's very intense and emotional. Sometimes it's almost anonymous and there's no connection.

The type of expression that sex allows expands freedom. It creates a kind of communication that's impossible in normal, practical, everyday life. It's an intense moment, where the dishes piled in the sink don't matter. It's a freedom to communicate, a freedom to be affectionate . . . . There's this thing that happens before you start to make love: a little fear. "Do I want this? What's going to happen this time?" And somehow there's a barrier crossed or broken down, and that fear isn't there anymore. The warmth and feeling of closeness when it's over facilitates communication, whether there's talk or not. There's a bond created, an intense comfort. Good sex is honest sex, where you're *there*. It can be any number of different things: passionate, erotic, emotional, intensely intimate, rough, soft and slow. It has to be honest and present, an acknowledgment of what's happening right now.

Cooter

At fourteen, Cooter was introduced to sex by a neighbor girl in an empty garage. "I thought it was great. I felt like, 'I'm learning about life,'" he says reverently. It was the Great Depression era, and he was a black adolescent on the Gulf Coast of Mississippi. Now seventy-three and retired from forty years' work in a federal munitions plant, Cooter is planning to marry a college sweetheart, whom he recently rediscovered after a fifty-five year separation.

When I was about sixteen, I went to a big meeting the church was having, and I went to a gravel pit with this girl. I'm only five-foot-five, but she was about six feet tall. So we went out to the gravel pit and had our date, standing. I'm on tiptoe trying to reach and she's squatting down. And when the thing happened, when I really came, I passed out like somebody knocked me out. And three months later, I had a little knot in my side. My mother suggested I go see this black "doctor" who had worked around doctors but had no medical certificate. He said I had a blue ball. Venereal disease. Then my family put me through all the hell you could think about in life. At that time, if you got just plain venereal disease, you were in the hospital for seven days, and that was very expensive. Penicillin was later. My aunt sent me down to see her doctor, who was white. He examined me and laughed. All I had was a hernia. I went about seventy miles to Jackson, Mississippi to have the hernia taken out, because that was the only charity hospital for blacks. A nurse there, a black nurse, told my mother, "We'll take care of him." And she did, because I had sex with her before the operation.

I first went to college at Southern Christian Institute in Edwards, Mississippi, and we had white teachers there. My job was to clean up in the school on Mondays, when school was closed. They had a home economics teacher who was white, and I started to datin' her. There wasn't nobody in the building but she and I. Locked the doors, and nobody knew. I really felt like we were in love, but I also knew that it was death—even to be seen with

GOOD SEX

her. She knew all that, too. But all I was looking forward to was Mondays, because I knew what was going to happen Mondays.

I graduated pre-med from Tougaloo in 1942 and was drafted into military service. I was sent to Tuskegee Institute in Alabama, where I was a venereal disease control officer, teaching other black soldiers how to use protection. I had all the different prophylactic kits, showing them how to use condoms and all of that. I got used to them myself, and at my age, I still use them. I met my wife through USO in California. We got married and had two children. One of the things that made me more in love: she had been married and knew how to handle a dummy like me. She taught me more of how to really have sex. Seemed like to me she had sex more freely, her different moves, her reaction. I loved it.

I'm seventy-three now. I have regular girlfriends. I have sex maybe every two weeks and sometimes twice a week. I've always taken sex to be a physical and fun thing. More older men seem to be satisfied not having sex. They listen to somebody say, "You're old, you can't do that," and they accept that. It's planted in their mind. I think any time you find your nature not coming up, go see a doctor, find out why, see if you can be treated. I feel about sex as I feel about using my hands, my legs, my eyes: it's a part of my body that I need to be able to use as well as any other part.

The women I'm seeing are in the senior bracket—fifty-five on up. They give you as much come-on as they did when they were twenty. Personally speaking, I think most women are as sexually active as men. I wouldn't want a woman who wouldn't care for sex. That's why I always use protection. An older person, if she's having sex with me, how do I know what she had, night before last? It pays me to protect myself with her just as it would with a young woman.

Most of the things that turns women on is kinda rubbing 'em down a little. Kissing is not bad. Playing with the breasts a little bit. What mostly works for me is the same thing in return: being free, kisses, few little hugs, all of that. Feeling relaxed. Whatever problem I have, for the time it takes for sex, I can't do nothing about it anyway. As long as you're protecting yourself from any type of disease, then you can feel free. I'm a strong believer in

Desire

one kind of sex: straight sex. I don't believe in using your mouth, in a woman gettin' down, and I never did believe in gettin' down myself. Straight sex. Good sex is definitely when two people are satisfied with each other's action—before, at the time, and after sex. That's what makes it.

Sex is very individual, and that's always a fact of life. As a whole, you don't talk on that part. You react. Everybody's sex reaction is not the same, even though you're doing it the same way. The movement is different. And actually the size of the person is different: some little men my size love big womens, and some big womens love little men. I like thin women, women I can catch around. Sex brings about *more* you might say, free of talking. Being around a person freely. With words, you only go so far. In sex, you know it all.

II. SEX TALK

As some *Good Sex* interviewees lamented, there's no Berlitz for the bedroom. New and established partners bring different needs, assumptions and expectations to sexual union, a meeting enhanced by clear messages—vocal or mute—about touch, timing, safety and respect. In the sweet flux of senses, pillow talk can be crucial, yet partners are largely left to invent a common language. "Nothing describes loving sexual acts without being clinical or vulgar," complained Amanda, a young wife interviewed in this section. "The language is . . . either used in a derogatory way or it's so soft, 'making love.'" Another woman asserted, "We need a whole new language for sexuality. It's cold, medicinal, degraded and violent. It's mechanistic: women are boxes, men are rods. We need language about sex that is natural and not fearful." Sex Talk samples intimate conversation, reflections on semantics and responses to real-life mismatches in male and female arousal.

In recording more than a hundred and fifty hours of sex-centered conversation, I found that bringing forth people's natural language was a challenge, for many interview subjects were overly receptive to my inadvertent verbal cues. In numerous tête-à-têtes, the terminology I introduced—in Latin or slang—was taken up and incorporated into responses, as though my choice of words designated parameters for the discussion. This was more often true with older men, who showed greater concern about being polite, and with women, whose reticence suggested outrageous inhibition. Younger men more readily set the terms for conversation; within that group, gay and bisexual men appeared more at ease naming sex acts and describing interplay.

Open exchange promotes the vitality and expansion of language. Because sex talk mostly takes place behind closed doors, its verbal inventory is not extensive, and the vocabulary that has developed to describe erotic variations virtually hisses with value judgments. Most synonyms for sex refer to copulation, although it is just one of many slippery routes to pleasure. The labels slapped onto alternative erotic acts are often tinged with censure. "We don't always have intercourse," Amanda told me, "and how do you romanticize the phrase 'jerking someone off'? If you say 'fondling,' I think of *pedophiles*!" Additional terms that were widely used (the mechanistic misnomer "mutual masturbation" was a favorite) earned similarly bad reviews because of their negative connotations. Some people offered vague but happy suggestions: sex-play, finger-play, ass-play. Linguistically, heterosexual intercourse remains the standard for "real sex," although the act which TV evangelists so delight in calling fornication is, in reality, not accorded much honor except as a means of procreation.

New words *are* being coined or popularized, particularly by voluble subcultures. Gay-originated flowers of speech popping up throughout *Good Sex* include "rimming" and "fisting." From SM phrasemongers come "top" and "bottom," clear-cut, gender-free terms for roles in dominance and submission. SM itself remains a charged but ambiguous moniker, freely interpreted in interviews as everything from an attitude to ritualized and often painful techniques for endorphin release, sometimes linked with sex. SM's co-pilot, the dismissive phrase "vanilla sex," stretches to cover every erotic exchange outside SM's elusive border. In addition, the AIDS crisis has introduced new, hotly debated expressions, such as "safe sex" and "bodily fluids," and encouraged verbal exchange between sex-partners, including, to some extent, word games and phone sex.

Good sex is sex on your terms, and the better you're able to communicate them, the more likely your sexual satisfaction. Throughout this chapter, women and men offer helpful hints for increasing sexual fluency. As Jackie said, "Good sex is communication, talking about what you like, being able to show somebody gently, 'That's nice, but I like it better like *this*.' Simply, gently, calmly." This book documents sixty-plus ways to talk about sex— and that's just a beginning.

Ben

The year that Ben turned six, his father died, and his mother lost the bakery business and moved the family to Oakland. It was also the year that Ben remembers beginning to masturbate—in private and at afternoon Hebrew school. A poor child during the Depression, Ben made his way up the economic ladder through education. Now seventy and retired from engineering, he is a small man with gray eyes and a kind face.

I used to go to a lot of movies with my brother—mostly cowboy pictures. My concept of what life was like was built largely on movies, because there I could see how people smoked, how they drank, how they acted, their attitudes towards women and children. You never saw sex in the movies, so you wondered how that went. In the early pictures I used to see, comedies, the men's pants would fall down, and the women would faint. That was a visual stereotype of women being shocked by sex.

I relied a lot on films for cues. I wasn't stupid: I knew that these were just films, that there was a life beyond, yet the emotional impact was there subconsciously. Sex was never shown. Because of the Hayes Office requirements, they never showed a man and a woman in bed together, so there weren't any cues. Did they sleep close, did they sleep apart, did he have his arm around her? How did it feel? What's a man's role with a woman? How do you treat her? What do you do for her? I didn't know anything. I thought the man always had to take the initiative—that's directly from the movies. The man always had to pay for the dates. On my first date, we took the streetcar, went to the movies, got a hot dog and a coke afterwards. The date cost me ninety cents. I bent her over backwards and kissed her. Ridiculous, of course, but I'd learned it from the movies. I started sexual exploration with that girl. She was very responsive. Kissing, but no intercourse. I rubbed against her to orgasm, and I think she must have had an orgasm, because she was breathing very heavily.

I got discharged from the army—World War II. Then my mother

51

introduced me to my wife. She was the most beautiful woman I'd ever seen. Beautiful. When I first saw her, I was almost taken aback. Once we were married, she got me to open up sexually. This was a woman who knew so much, every facet of sex that there was. Positions, types, oral sex. Now, she never did any of these things when we were going together. But after marriage, she would have sex every day if she could. It was kind of exhausting. Sometimes she'd wake me in the middle of the night by playing around with my penis, and we'd have sex. I'd never had any experience like that. We had three daughters, and we enjoyed sex during the pregnancies. Sometimes I used to look at her and ask, "How was I ever lucky enough to get a woman like that?"

She was a manic depressive. Before we left for Israel, she went into a depressive phase and tried to kill herself, cut her wrists. One day in Israel, she killed herself. Traumatic. I take abandonment extremely hard. It's strange, though . . . . We'd had sex the night before, so it's not sex that saves the world . . . . I don't think I knew her, as I might have if we'd met in later years, when sex was not such a driving force, and we could have known each other as people rather than sexual objects. I have a hard time getting close. My wife used to complain I wouldn't talk to her during sex. For me, sex is a very involving activity, and it's hard to think. It's a totally feeling thing, very introverting. I often wondered how my wife *could* talk. I reflect sometimes on what my wife requested, and I'm sorry, because I feel I would have had better insight into her, but it's not been my experience to communicate my feelings. The strong silent male. My impression from what I've seen in movies is that men don't show emotion. Clark Gable didn't.

The gap between the sensate and the cerebral still exists for me, and my pursuit and desire in life would be to be really close to somebody and talk about our closeness. I've never talked about sex with any of the people I've gone out with. I'm going with a woman now, and sometimes I put the radio on, so I don't have to talk. I've known her twenty years, and I still don't know how she feels. It's a sexual relationship. We do mostly mutual masturbation, and she tells me what she wants, but I hardly tell her about myself, I just try to adapt. The biggest handicap in my life is that I've not been able to verbalize my feelings to somebody

Sex Talk

that I cared for. I'm seeing another woman now. With her it's not a sexual relationship, although she's very open, and we talk. So there's hope.

Nowadays, movies are very graphic. There's a much more open viewpoint on sex: they show people in bed. It's there, but I don't think they *talk* about sex any more today than the old movies did. In the porno films, they don't talk about sex either. There, the situations are bizarre, there's no talk, they just have sex. Nobody talks about it.

Guy

Bouncing on the school bus in Southern California, six-year-old Guy heard the mysterious word "intercourse," a term his parents refused to explain. "Sex was a major unspoken in my family," the thirty-three-year-old reflects. "I hated that." The son of a Chrysler auto worker, Guy is disabled by muscular dystrophy which causes extreme physical weakness and has forced him to rely on a wheelchair since the age of ten. Today a bearded man with blue eyes and salt-and-pepper hair, Guy lives with his girlfriend and works as a computer consultant.

I think because of my disability, I really do have to depend on verbalizing the things that I do. My family does not talk. We yell. We don't talk. I remember at age seven or so standing in front of the toilet, going to the bathroom. My dad was shaving, he looked down at me and said, "You know, some white stuff is gonna come out of that someday." That was it. I remember panicking a little, but I knew that I just couldn't talk with him about it. I still have trouble talking about sex. Even now with Carol, when it comes to verbalizing wants and things, I've got to work up to it. I do it, but it's always a struggle.

At thirteen, I had my first wet dream. We had just moved and were still sleeping on cots. My younger brother, age seven, woke me up. He noticed that the sheets were wet, and thought I'd pissed the bed. Dad came in, cleaned me up, but then he had to go into the front room and announce to the family that I'd had my first wet dream—which was really a *special* moment for me. It was after that that I started masturbating. I discovered that Dad had *Playboy* in his closet, and I'd get my brother to get me one, because I couldn't reach them. When I got brave, I'd go buy one. The magazines were on the ground in the magazine rack, which I couldn't reach, so I always had to ask somebody to grab me the magazine and then take it up front and pay. I had to work up my courage to ask somebody. There were always people who refused.

I started having sex because I paid for it. At twenty-one, I went to a science fiction convention in Kentucky, and the convention was a block away from a lovely section of town with lots of adult theaters. I'd never seen an X-rated movie in my life, and anything having to do with sex was immediately fascinating. I went to a movie, and I noticed there were women going up and down the aisles, leaning over and asking people to go into the back. I'm a bright boy, I figured this out. I waited there. A long time. Finally some guy came over and said, "Do you want me to get you a woman?" He waved over a woman who was incredibly old. In the back of the theater were little rooms. I couldn't fit my wheelchair through the doors. Three tries. We went to a lounge area that had a larger doorway. I didn't have a clue as to what I wanted to do. I thought I'd have her sit on top of me, but that didn't work. Finally she gave me a blow job. I came back the next night and did it again.

After college, I moved to California, because I heard it was good for the disabled. There were things called massage parlors, and so I went to those. Spent way too much money. At the time, I lived on four hundred and six bucks a month. I'd save a hundred and twenty, and that's what I'd use for sex.

Carol came out to visit me in California. We'd met at the science fiction club in college, and we'd spent enormous amounts on phone bills since. I only had one bed. She was on one side, I was on the other. I was being a gentleman, a regular Cary Grant. The second weekend, I told her I was attracted to her, and she said she was attracted to me, too. We were immobile, terrified. Then we finally had sex, probably the worst sex I had in my life. I'm amazed we had orgasms. I loved Carol, and it was just way too scary, because if this didn't work, she'd be gone. There was a lot at stake. The day after, I was so thrown by this whole thing, I made a big speech to Carol about, "I'm not sure I'm ready for any of this." The whole speech. She got a work transfer to California. One night, she came to visit me. It got late, she was going to leave, and I told her I thought I was going to die if she didn't kiss me.

We've been together nine years. When we got together, we always talked about having an open relationship. In practice, it's been a little harder than I expected. I don't think it's a simple thing to do, but then I don't think it's simple to be with just one person, either. Sex with Carol is a constant negotiation, because I always want to, and for her, it's a matter of her energy. I understand that, because in addition to her job, she also works as my attendant—getting me into bed, cooking. It's not simple to take care of me physically. No matter how we've tried to deny it, we've got a pretty traditional relationship, in that the woman does all the work and the guy doesn't do anything. I wish it was different.

Sex helps me live in my body. I spent a good portion of my life pretending that my body wasn't part of me. It was this dysfunctional thing that had nothing to do with me. I need to find a way to connect, and sex does that for me. We're great oral fans. We do mutual masturbation a lot. We don't do a lot of straight sex, partly because I come so quick. I'd much rather it take longer and play around with it more. I like making Carol feel good. I like using my mouth more than my hands, because my hands give out sooner. I like it when sex has a lot of abandon to it, when you're not worrying about how this fits into that, when you're just having a good time doing whatever you do. We talk about trying new things every now and then. It's hard for me, because I have a hard time talking about that kind of stuff. Verbalizing never gets easier. I hope it will, but it hasn't yet. I like sound, noises, enthusiasm. Words sound dumb. I do a lot of grunting and groaning and, "Oh my god! Oh my god!" I don't know why I get stuck on *that*. If I'm really, really excited, then I can maybe talk a little bit. But I have to be almost out of my mind.

Jackie

At fourteen, Jackie felt that she and her boyfriend were inventing sex, as they coupled in the shower, in cars and in the woods. "I got a master's at Berkeley and thought I'd be able to do anything. But then I found they only wanted to hire guys, even when I was better qualified," says the tawny-haired thirty-five-year-old, a former Pennsylvania farm girl. "Economically, you're fucked. You're fucked, just because you're a woman." Today, Jackie works as a prostitute in San Francisco and lives in a modest, rose-tinted apartment.

When you hit adolescence, they give you books, so I knew that girls get periods and boys ejaculate. But I thought that wet dreams were just as painful as periods, and I actually felt sorry for boys, because it could happen any time. When I found out that ejaculating was a *pleasurable* experience, I was pissed off!

What I'd learned about sex from my parents was confusing. That's why I became a sex educator. I got a job in VD prevention. It made me sex-phobic, and I went through a two-year period of celibacy. I left that job and started selling sex toys to women in home parties, and I met a guy with a Harley. I'd never used sex toys, so the distributors gave me a box full—vibrators, dildoes and lotions—and told me to go home and play. I told my boyfriend, "Look what I got from work!" We spent a weekend pulling things out of the box; I'd use one on him, then he'd use one on me. Wild. What I learned in that job was that people don't need dildoes: sex toys are communication tools, and sex is all about really good communication.

I started giving workshops on eroticizing safe sex, and then I went to a sex therapy conference and met a madam. She suggested I try prostitution, because I could still do my safe sex education and make more money. Compared to other people, I came into prostitution on a silver carpet. I worked at a house, I was trained by the madam, and the other women were fun and not competitive around sexuality. I thought it would just be one guy after another, but I've found you end up having regulars and mini-relationships with them.

What I do is sensual. I give people baths—that's safe sex. Massage them, create an experience. I sit and talk with them, have a glass of wine, make tea. I do straight sex. Clients want to have oral sex with you, they want you to have oral sex with them, maybe they want some sort of ass-play. Variety is a sexual preference. I'm very busty, very voluptuous, so I have a lot of men come on my tits. I love to watch men masturbate. With the clientele I've had, there's never been a hassle about safe sex. There are tons of ways to give a blow job where you're actually not doing it, just using lube, hands and hair. I find out if they want intercourse by talking about the condom. After a massage or oral sex, a guy'll be really hard, and I'll look at him: "Is it time for a condom yet?" That gives him the opportunity to say what he wants.

I like to fuck very few of these guys. What they call sex and what I call sex are different. They're doing stress release. They're masturbating with another person. If masturbation weren't such a big taboo in our society, men wouldn't go to prostitutes. Men go to prostitutes because they want variety and they want to jerk off, and they feel bad about touching themselves, so they need somebody to do it for them. That's the kind of sex they're having with me, not the three-hour sex you have with a lover. It's a release, not love-making. It's not the kind of sex I'd choose to have, though I'm willing to do it if I'm paid for it. For me to be satisfied and happy, an hour is not enough.

What makes sex special is the time . . . the time . . . Somebody you're willing to spend time with, somebody you want to tell your problems to and your successes to . . . I like premeditated sex. That's good sex. Not to say that spontaneous sex, where you look at each other and get hot, isn't great. But the more premeditated sex can be, the better. You or your lover sets it up, runs the bath, lights the candles, puts on the lingerie. I like that somebody cares to put that attention to it, and I like doing that for somebody else.

Good sex is communication, talking about what you like, being able to show somebody gently, "That's nice, but I like it better like *this*." Simply, gently, calmly. "I like to be kissed like this," or, "I want my ass fucked like this." Knowing what your personal requirements are, and also having the necessary lubricants, birth control and sex toys. My favorite thing is for my partner to suck and lick my entire body, then massage my entire body, making me want it, begging to be fucked. I'm very orgasmic. I can be multiply orgasmic in seven minutes. My old boyfriend and I used to see how long it took to get off together. That's the kind of game that lovers should be playing with each other: "Let's try this, let's try that." And it's really, really, really important for partners to masturbate and to show each other *how* they masturbate, because unless you're masturbating, you don't know what gets you off. You're depending on someone else to do it for you, and that's a needy place to be.

I think real intimacy comes from sleeping with somebody, not what you do sexually with them. Sleeping together and cuddling every night, paying the bills together. Partnership creates the intimacy. Good sex as part of that is great. Unfortunately, some of the people I've loved *madly* haven't sparked the greatest sexual connection. Sex is getting better. The best orgasms I've had in my entire life have been recent ones all by myself through tantra breathing. They create a feeling of being taken somewhere, a dream state, a sleep state where you're out of your body. That whole fireworks thing is *true* . . . I want to put the tantra stuff together with a partner, where we take a big chunk of time and *do* each other, with the breathing and lots of eye contact. I've just broken up with the guy I was living with. What I want now is a partnership that includes pleasing each other sexually, with an agreement that he'll try what I like, I'll try what he likes, and where it doesn't meet, we'll compromise—or hire someone to come in and do it.

Amanda

"There's a whole mystique about exotic, erotic, subservient Asian women," Amanda says cheerfully, "but I've always been a little against the grain." Her sex education began at twelve with Our Bodies, Ourselves. *In high school, when she became sexually involved with a female friend, her parents responded by leaving notes on the kitchen cupboard: "Tonight, PBS special on teens coming out." Engaged at twenty, Amanda sent out wedding invitations and felt immediate regret. The invitations came back the next day marked postage due. She left the Boston suburbs, moved to San Francisco, came out as bisexual and explored serial monogamy, including her relationship with Richard, her husband and partner of nine years. At twenty-nine, the former high school teacher is now pursuing a graduate degree in education.*

The language we use to describe sex is so hard-edged. It's either used in a derogatory way—"jerk someone off"—or it's so soft, "making love." Neither really describes what you're doing. The language bugs me. Nothing describes loving sexual acts without being clinical or vulgar. There's something to be said for reclaiming the vulgar language, but that doesn't really work, because the mainstream negative undertone is so pervasive.

Richard's probably the best lover I've ever had, sensitive and willing to listen, willing to experiment with fantasies. We learned how to talk about sex together. His bisexuality contributes to his openness, because he's already crossed some boundaries. We found each other in this world of many people, built a relationship and are lucky enough to have done that. For me, it could have been a man or a woman. For him, he's more emotionally involved with women, although his sexual fantasies are more about men.

In sex, I like things to move pretty slowly. I like a lot of foreplay. Once, we were walking in the city, and he was wearing overalls. I could reach into them and fondle him as we wandered around. By the time we actually got to sex, there had been hours of foreplay wandering the streets. When we have sex, we don't always have intercourse. We'll negotiate that: "What do you want to do?" I like it when he fondles my breasts, strokes my neck, kisses me. I'll do oral sex with him, fondle him, he'll rub against me. He'll use his hand, giving me orgasms, the tips of his fingers right above my clitoris. After nine years, he's got it *down* . . . . We're very vocal in terms of instructions, especially if something's not quite right. We don't run a verbal fantasy back and forth, but sometimes I'll ask him about his fantasies, and we'll play out a scene, one of us directing the other.

I don't think good sex is a mathematical equation: "This act plus this act equals good sex." It's more of a sense of well-being, physical release and relaxation, no doubt, no worries. We have a lot of humor. Most of the giggle sessions we have are in bed, and things happen that are so hilarious. One time, we attempted to lick chocolate fudge off each other, but it was really sticky, so it didn't come off. It was *everywhere*!

We've always had an agreement that our relationship is open, although we haven't followed up on it much. *I* have more affairs than he has, and the irony is that *he* insisted on it. When a friend came down with AIDS, we got an education fast and changed our sexual behavior. We said, "If you're going to have sex with other people, it has to be safer sex using condoms." We spent a long time worrying about it and did AIDS public education, going out and talking about it, and we took care of our friend. He died, his lover died, and another friend—an ex-lover of Richard's— died. We waited a long time to get tested for HIV, because initially there was nothing you could do if you got a positive result. Then AZT came out, we got closer to thinking about having children, got tested, came out negative. Now we use condoms pretty regularly with each other. AIDS has affected us a lot. It's affected our sexuality; maybe we don't feel quite as free to look beyond the boundary of our relationship.

It's a special relationship. Sex creates a time when the clarity of intimacy is focused. It's emotional, loving, and sometimes I burst into tears. I realize what we have together, how important that is. Often, the next day, we'll tell each other, "Thank you."

Msafiri

A slender, bearded man, Msafiri is a native San Franciscan who came out as bisexual while in an eighteen-year marriage. Now forty, he is the father of three children and works professionally as a nurse. Ten years ago, when he was claiming his bisexual identity, Msafiri was not acquainted with any other bisexual people. "I heard about the Bi Center in San Francisco," he says. "By the time I got up enough courage to go there, they were closed."

In the black community, we don't talk about sex. There's a degree of bisexual activity, but there's nobody who's up front, saying they're bi. From heterosexuals, there's some flack because, "We may be able to tolerate gays and lesbians. Maybe. But bisexuals? You are *flaunting*." People think of African Americans as liberal. It's somewhat true, but African Americans are more tolerant than liberal—not trying to impose my stuff on you, so you won't impose your stuff on me. But there's some real conservative stuff in terms of community standards: family survival, race survival, rigid definitions of masculine and feminine, AIDS phobia: "You're going to be the vector for infecting us." There are myths and confusion. It feels real shitty, because I did my early political work in the black community, and I'm part of the community. I can't leave.

I was married when I began having my male sexual experiences. A turning point was when one man I was seeing asked me to move in. It forced me to take a look at myself. I was having sex with men, but I was still identifying as heterosexual. I thought, "Am I gay? No, because I really enjoy sex with women. Well, I could be bisexual, because there are people like that around. Somewhere." I never told my wife. She found out through an intercepted letter. It was a real trauma. Zero understanding. There were attempts at reconciling the marriage, but we divorced. It generated a lot of homophobia on her part. In fact, that became a real issue in terms of custody with my sons. There was innuendo and insinuation. The court didn't buy it, but I had to fight.

I'm a sensual person. I like fingertip touching, as though my fingers were my eyes, seeing how different parts of their bodies feel. Finding sensitive areas. What do they smell like? Sound like? . . . . I really get into who this person is. That's the important part, and anything else is icing on the cake. Men feel different from women. They're harder, they're more willing to become sexual and more willing to be exploratory, for the most part. With women, sex is more emotional and sensual, and I like going down on them. My ideal situation now would be to have separate relationships with a man and a woman in my life. I want stability and safety. Emotional safety. I'm not worried about health, because I used condoms for anal and vaginal sex way before the AIDS scare, simply for hygiene and because I was not interested in a lot of little offspring.

The sexual act—penetration or whatever you're going to do—is fine and dandy, but I particularly enjoy the parts before and after. That's just as much fun. Not long ago, I was with a friend: we helped each other take off our clothes. Caressing, kissing. Facial kisses, nibbling on ears, nibbling on necks, shoulders, backs, knees—not quite erotic, but loose. We started holding each other, fondling each other, rubbing, stroking, sixty-nine. I did anal intercourse on him. I like all that.

I was with a woman friend one time. We had some dinner, went to a motel, undressed each other, lay around, a lot of touching, a lot of fondling. She said, "Lay back. You're going to relax. You're not going to do anything for five minutes." She kissed me all over, then she went down on me. I said, "Wait a minute! I'm not ready to get started so soon." She said okay, we went back to more touching. Five minutes was over. She said, "Two more minutes," and went down on me. I said, "Wait a minute!" It was kind of like a game. Later I went down on her. She said, "Hold it! You don't have a time limit. Five minutes." We played with each other, did some ass-play, finally ended up having sex a couple hours later. There was no hurry. We knew we were going to do that, but in the meantime we were having all this other fun.

People need better sex information of all kinds. That's why I do public speaking on bisexuality. When I was growing up, there was no real talk about sexuality. I remember an ROTC class: "Don't go out eatin' no pussy. Don't be pumpin' any queers." I've talked to my two oldest kids about sex, recognizing that they're going to be sexually active and there's some background I want them to have. They're seventeen and nineteen. We've talked about safe sex, but more than that: that it's okay to be sexual if you're clear on why you're being sexual. We had some talks around it, much more than I ever had. Recently, there are rap songs that talk about some outright stuff. There's one about how to give a blow job. Kids on the bus were singing it. Specifics. They were rapping *technique*!

Lani

Raised in suburban California, Lani is the daughter of a Hawaiian beauty queen and an Irish Catholic construction contractor. She was a tomboy, the only girl in elementary school who hit home runs over the fence. "As a teenager," she says, "I had my first G-spot orgasm in a car in front of my parents' house with my face on the steering wheel." Now forty-seven, Lani has been politically active in San Francisco's lesbian and bisexual communities for twenty years. In 1990, she co-edited Bi Any Other Name, *an anthology of essays on bisexual identity.*

In the fifties, all the books on sex were locked up. Adults were into spelling out words in front of children, and I got really good at memorizing spelling, then printing it out and looking it up in the dictionary. I was infuriated that I couldn't have the information. When I had kids of my own, I was determined not to hand down any of this bullshit. I forced myself to say the real words, things that made me squirm: "If you can say *carrot* you can say *vagina*."

I don't remember the first time being sexual, because it was so gradual. I was a Catholic, and I had to go to confession. French-kissing is a mortal sin. Petting is a mortal sin. It was a downhill slide from there. When my boyfriend and I started making out, we were trying everything. It was fun, we were just hot for each other: finger-fucking, fellatio, but not cunnilingus. It was about six months, gradually getting closer and closer. But I did not want to confess sexual intercourse. I had figured out an umbrella term with my friends, "impure thoughts and deeds," that would cover everything we could possibly do. But intercourse seemed bigger than "impure thoughts and deeds." The night I finally admitted to myself that we were being sexual, I took a statue of the Blessed Virgin Mary to bed. She fell out of bed, and her head broke off.

It was 1959. I was totally lucky: *coitus interruptus* and I didn't get pregnant. Used rubbers twice and it was like admitting to being sexual too much. I married my high school boyfriend when I was nineteen and had two children by age twenty-six. The sex was great and probably kept our relationship going as long as it did. I loved oral sex, but it's not *procreation* so I talked to a visiting priest about it. He said it was just *fine*.

Throughout my marriage, I always thought I was a lesbian. I was conscious of a draw towards women. My husband figured it out: "You need to leave." He really loved me. I had an apartment in six weeks and was out on my own.

I couldn't wait to go down on a woman. It was the early rush of the women's movement: everybody sleeping with everybody, because we were trying to figure out what sleeping with women was like. It was totally clumsy, awkward and hilarious. Going to bed, but—"What do we do? Maybe we make out a little bit?" I brought out a lot of women. That was my pattern. There was a level of vulnerability—theirs, which allowed for mine. I didn't believe in bisexuality. I'd never heard the word. I think it was partly the effect of Catholicism: it's black or white, right or wrong, men or women. It wasn't easy to come out as a lesbian, but it was even harder to come out as a bisexual, because at least lesbians had a movement and community.

I went up to Mendocino County and became the lesbian chef at a New Age resort. The setting was gorgeous: cabins, no electricity, organic gardens, the river. I had a six-week affair with a sixteen-year-old virgin. He was a counselor at a kids' camp, and he had wanted to lose his virginity. He had a body to die for, and he was totally attracted to me. I had an identity crisis, to say the least. Here I am, the older woman, with a wealth of information. But I also had a lot of hang-ups—shame about my body. I did not want to hand any of that down. I decided I was going to be the most sexually liberated, most evolved I could possibly be. For example, I got my period. This was pre-AIDS. I said, "We can have oral sex or not. I love going down on women when they have their periods." He went down on me and said, "You taste wonderful." Having a dialogue like that, and keeping it honest and open, that's what was so good. He still calls me.

Later that summer, Bill landed in my life. Within twenty-four hours, we were fucking our brains out. He kept saying, "Lani, you're bisexual." I'd say, "There's no such thing," and cry and cry and cry. My sex with Bill was wonderful, because of the levels on which we connected—psychic, intellectual, political. We were together five years.

Later, with my girlfriend Alice, the sex was really wonderful and the intimacy was nowhere. My experience contradicts the stereotype that women are experts at intimacy and know less about sex. Alice gets in touch with her feelings through sex. It's a survival thing for her. When I was working on my book, she'd knock on my window at two-thirty at night, we'd fuck our brains out, and she'd leave in the morning. It was great.

It's funny to talk about the difference between male and female partners, because we did a lot of the same things. What I'm realizing now is that if I've got the emotional, intellectual connections, then the physical stuff can be about the same. It's a chemistry that happens, and it's not the genitalia, not "Oo, wow, check out that basket." There's a chemistry that happens, and I don't know if it's going to be with a man or a woman. Sex to me is communication. It flows, there's trust and passion. There's giving and taking and receiving. It's beyond orgasm. It's emotional vulnerability. Fun. There's room for everything from tears to laughter. And there has to be time . . . .

Terry

Brought up as a story-teller and interpreter, Terry is a Taos Pueblo Indian from a large family in northern New Mexico. He is a psychologist specializing in treating substance abuse. With his traditional braids, slender frame and turquoise jewelry, Terry finds himself frequently propositioned by white men who mistake him for a woman. Thirty-nine, divorced and recently involved with male sex partners, he says, "The important thing is that you love, not what flesh your love is wrapped in."

Growing up with more than one language automatically makes you more flexible. You don't get stuck in, "This is right or wrong." You realize there's more than one way of seeing, more than one way of being. A lot of things that one says in English are not what one would say in a native language, because the cultures are so different. Anglo-Saxon vulgarizes things like excrement and sex, and those are simply not pejorative or dirty terms in a lot of Indian languages, because they're just natural things that you do. Indian curse words have more to do with the loss of honor than with something you do with your body.

I grew up with people who, when they were upset, said things like, "pshaw" or "oh, foot!" In my teens, when I went to see Jerry Rubin speak at Columbia University, I heard him say, "fuck this" and "fuck that." I was quite shocked, because I *read* the word but never heard anybody say it before. I was utterly fascinated by the power of that word. I remember going back home after the conference, going into the bathroom, looking in the bathroom mirror and saying, "Fuck," just to find out what it felt like in my mouth. Would anything happen? Would I change? Nothing happened, except that the word lost its power. I was disappointed.

For me, sexuality is very much connected with intimacy. I want to do it in the context of a relationship. I certainly had a strong concept of monogamy as the proper way to do things, although there was a lot of nonmonogamy in my family. Because I had watched the effects of adultery in my own family, it's not something I would ever pursue.

Sex Talk

I didn't become sexually active until I was twenty-one. There was a woman I got involved with, another graduate student. We had gone out to an Indian reservation together, and we stopped at a Mexican restaurant. It was the first time I ever had sangria. My immediate family doesn't drink. Sangria, if you're not used to drinking, tastes god-awful, but by the second or third glass it was incredibly good, and we ended up in bed together.

I enjoy a lot of sensual contact, play and laughter. My partners like that I have long hair, and I use that to brush someone, whip it across their body. I usually do a lot of massage with my partner so there's a lot of attention to the full body, not just the genitals. Two hours or more, predominantly foreplay. Like a lot of Indian men, I have relatively long nails, so my partners also enjoy being scratched gently, particularly on the ass. I enjoy playing with people's ears, giving small bites, playing with nipples. I've discovered that my nipples are erotically aroused only at a certain threshold: when someone with stubble on his chin brushes against my nipple, it's like an electric charge. Entering someone physically gives a sense of starting small and growing, like a seed. It starts at the tip of the glans, and then pushing forward, more and more of you experiences it. It grows. It goes in steps, like a dance. There's a sense of complementarity, a longing for completion; it's an arc longing to become a circle.

Orgasm has been something of a let down: "Now it's over." It signals an ending, where foreplay and pleasure are a process. You get to orgasm and you're seeing the exit you take after a wonderful vacation, and now you have to go back to the real world again. Climaxing doesn't have an overwhelming effect for me, and it doesn't linger.

Men have hit on me since I was seventeen. When I was at an AIDS conference at the Kinsey Institute three years ago—this was after my divorce—I realized that a lot of people automatically assumed I was gay. It was awkward: I'd never had any conscious feelings about being attracted to men. I thought, "I don't feel anything on an erotic level. But there's a proverb that says 'If the world calls you a donkey, it's time to bray.'"

The first male experience I had was with someone who cared about me. He was an AIDS educator, a white guy. There was no anal intercourse, just oral-genital things. I couldn't have asked for anybody more positive or romantic. But sex with him didn't change my life. That was almost a disappointment: "I don't fit in any box." Another time, I had sex with a Navajo young man, more at his instigation than mine. I thought, "It's unfortunate I'm having sex with one of our traditional enemy tribes, but maybe that's appropriate on other levels of political correctness." Not the most romantic way of getting together with someone.

I engaged in a series of non-sexual intimacies with men, still dated women, and became more acquainted with gay culture. For me, being involved in the gay community was like visiting a new tribe: "Here's a different culture, a different language that I'm trying to learn." I met a man from D.C., saw him six months later and told him, "Put me on your waiting list."

Sex creates a sense of bonding. We live with an existential sense of always being alone, prisoners in the brain cage, and the one thing you can really do with somebody is send them a message through the bars. If you don't actually unlock the cage door, at least you open a window. With so many social interactions, there are so many screens, masks and monitors: "Am I doing the right thing? Am I saying the right thing?" But with sex, that in itself holds your attention, so all those masks drop away. It's just you there with that person, entering that person, feeling connected, becoming more than each of us is individually . . . . Language is a thread of connection. My mother's native language has a certain intimacy to me. There are times I'll give a name in my language to someone I care about in order to emphasize intimacy: "This is something special that we share."

Halima

What Every Young Bride Should Know answered few of Halima's adolescent questions about sex. Black, working-class, and intent on maintaining her virginity, she practiced alternative sex techniques with high school boyfriends. At twenty-one, she took up with an older man. "I learned so much in that little room. We used to drink sake, warmed up on the radiator," she remembers. "I came away from that relationship knowing how to have fun and how to be fun." She later left New York, relocated to California, married and divorced. Now a dentist with her own practice, Halima is a small, dark woman with a glowing face and a soothing voice.

I remember when I went through puberty. My libido was as high as anything could possibly be in my life. This was the late fifties, and there were a lot of ethics and morals around sex: "You have to be a virgin when you get married"—and you *don't* get married at fifteen. Fifteen is when I became creative about sexual things, when I began looking at penises. There were two young men in my life who would let me just take a look at their anatomy, and this turned them on a whole lot. This was not petting. This was in a clinical environment. We weren't kissing and hugging and fondling each other. It was, "Let's look at each other."

Even today, the preliminaries of sex always begin with an investigation. I want to know that my partners are clean. I want to see their bathtubs unexpectedly. I want to talk about sex over dinner: how many partners they have, that this relationship is about sex. I look before I leap: I make a physical exam of a partner's body. We can make it fun, and it can become the prelude to oral sex, but I need to know where I'm going before I go there, and I am absolutely not ashamed to ask, "What's this? How long has that been there?" I don't want disease. I don't ever want to have crabs again. Now that I have all this training in the health profession, I know exactly what to look for, exactly what to do. Herpes started me on that, because herpes is forever.

71

When I was in Zimbabwe, I met a man, and we planned to rendezvous in a hotel. We got to the room, and I needed to look at him, and he was wanting to turn out the lights and be romantic. I said, "I have to look at you." He became embarrassed; he lost his erection. I finally talked him into it, and then I said, "Would you like to look at me?" He couldn't look. All he wanted was those lights out so he could do it. In and out. And I was like, "I'm not going to have any part of this 'in and out.'" He eventually took a look at me. Once he got into it, he got into it. He said, "I never looked before. I never knew what was there." He started getting really turned on by looking, probing here, moving this piece of flesh, putting his finger inside me. All these things he had felt in the dark were coming to light for the first time. Oh, then he just wanted to *marry* me. He wanted me there *forever*!

The best foreplay is a meeting of the minds, a really stimulating conversation. I like gentle sex, flesh to flesh. With men, I seek positions that will stimulate my clitoris, because that brings on my orgasm. I find I just have to take my partner, put him where I want him, and sometimes even ask him to be still until I get positioned. Men like it, because they're relieved of responsibility. Sometimes I'll use my lover's thigh or play with myself manually. Orgasm is my sexual goal, but I don't have to climax to have fun. When it happens, it's total neurological discharge, consuming my body. There isn't a part of me that doesn't respond. I wish I were multi-orgasmic, and I've been trying for *years*. It's been the *bane* of my life!

Sex is so different with men and women. I wish men were a lot less juicy. Sperm is messy stuff. Every tender encounter ends in a puddle. With women, sex is nice, and it's *clean*. And we understand one another's anatomy in ways that men can never know. I remember the first time I was with a woman. She was a lesbian, and I was living with a man. I was at her place one day, and I just had to have sex with her. I had to have her then and there. I wanted to go down on her: "Show me what to do." I had an orgasm just from touching her. She and I became lovers for two years, and that experience never ended. If I went down on her or kissed her breasts, that would be enough for me to have an orgasm. I had another woman lover after that, and sex was different with her. So calm. So beautiful. I didn't have these

Sex Talk 73

instant orgasms, hitting me like a bolt of lightning. We would just fondle one another for hours and hours and hours. For us, orgasm wasn't the primary focus: sex was a demonstration of our love.

This whole AIDS business has put a damper on sex. I have to be so much more careful than I used to be. Right now, I'm only having sex with one man. He's an older, married man. I feel safe with him, because I know he sleeps with me and his wife only. I trust him, he's an honest man, and we have agreed to tell each other when we're going to introduce somebody else into our relationships. With him, I have early morning sex, which I love. He'll call me, "Can I come over?" I'll say "yes" and leave the front door unlatched. He'll slip into bed, and sometimes I don't wake up at all. Sometimes, I just get on top. I like going down on him, so sometimes, half awake and half asleep, I'll feel my way down him.

I love the sensual part of sex. I wish sensuality was in every part of my life, and I find the only time I can really have it is in sexual encounters. Being over forty now, I know my libido has taken another rise. I feel like I'm headed back to teenhood, and I'm not sure I'm interested in going there again.

Jay

As a Hawaiian teenager hanging out on the beach with groups of friends, Jay side-stepped the awkwardness of high school dating. His family, a European and American Indian mix, made sure he got a good sex education. "It started off, I'd sneak books out of my parents' library and hide what I was reading under the mattress," he recalls. "And then things showed up under the mattress that I hadn't put there." In the seventies, Jay made his first sexual proposition to a stranger at an EST training, had an open marriage, and enjoyed group sex and sexuality workshops. Now a stout forty-two-year-old with small hands and large gray eyes, Jay lives with a striking young woman a few blocks from the beach in San Francisco.

At the end of my first year in college, I eloped with my girlfriend. We did the whole thing: she passed me her suitcase out of her bedroom window, climbed out. We flew from Honolulu to Hollywood. Early '68. I was nineteen. It was just electric. We drove north, and I was so busy talking to her over my shoulder, I ran a stop sign, got a ticket for it. We were living together, totally in love; we weren't trying to sneak something. Nobody was going to come and interrupt us. It wasn't, "Get her home by curfew." There had been a couple times before we eloped, like, "Whose house can we borrow? Whose parents are away?" Your friends are outside in the other room standing guard. Is somebody's mom going to come home? Are the cops going to come shine the flashlight in the car, chase us off Submarine Ridge?

A lot of people do that for a long time. I think a lot of men are really trained into premature ejaculation. You gotta masturbate before you get caught. You gotta get it in and get it done before you get caught. Most people grow up having to sneak sex. And if you're going to get caught, you get out of danger quick. Men are trained to be conquerors and victors. That sports training overlaps: if you're shooting hoops, the faster you can get the ball through the net, the better it is. But men don't want to get caught, don't want to get accused. There's incredible pressure to get off.

74

Sex Talk 75

My best orgasms are when I take my time. I can focus on my partner's pleasure, shift from a stroke that's incredible for her to one that's incredible for me, get up to the edge and *back down*. I don't have to come at the first urge. I can pause, relax, take a break. The longer it takes, the bigger the rush. It's really in a man's best interest to take his time. I've had a couple women be startled by the dramatic, cataclysmic nature of my orgasms. We're not going *uh uh uh*. We're talking about suns exploding and galaxies being born—never mind the earth moving!

A number of my lovers have been preorgasmic before we got together. Either they'd never had an orgasm, or they'd never had it with another person. What they needed was more time. They needed men to not be in a hurry, to recognize that this is an enjoyable journey. By asking verbally or exploring, I find out what my partner responds to. I don't just find the hot button and push it. Sexuality is not limited to the genitals; we've got a big canvas here. If she comes in the first five minutes, okay, but she's had five minutes of pleasure. If it takes her an hour, she's had an hour's worth of pleasure. And if she doesn't come, she's still had an hour's worth of pleasure.

Straight men and women don't talk about sex. They're busy playing the game of getting some and giving some, rather than sharing some. There's this cat and mouse game. But they played so many games to get into bed that they're not straight about what they'd like. There are positional preferences people never discover, or never share with their partners. There are women who are going, "Show me what you can do." 'Scuse me, are we in this together? What do *you* like?

No man wants to feel sexually incompetent. Joking with our buddies, we're all studs. It is real difficult for a man to admit any kind of problem or dysfunction, any kind of ignorance or lack of experience. You don't want to get shit from a woman for being a lousy lover. You don't want to get nagged or harassed—or cut off. I've had a few times where I wouldn't get erect or it would take some time. Luckily, I had understanding partners, and I knew that it could happen. I was uncomfortable with it—challenged *my* self-image. But worrying's going to make it worse. My sexuality is not limited to my penis. There are things I can do to pleasure my partner, to get her off, without sticking it in her.

Sometimes I've gotten more consoling than I needed: "Oh, you poor dear." No, I know how tired I am, how distracted. Sometimes I've said, "Well, that's it." And other times, I've said, "Let me take care of you," and the erection would come back.

Great sex involves the whole person. It's a mental exploration, discovery, wonder. It's an emotional connection. I've had the experience where two hearts became one: there's only us here, and *us* is a single entity. We are so trapped in these bodies. It's a delightful irony, an incredible piece of design work in the universe, that the way to get out of your body is to get into it—and get into somebody else's. It's best when you connect physically, emotionally, mentally and spiritually. But hey: three out of four ain't bad. Two out of four ain't bad.

I'm not out looking as actively as I used to. I notice beautiful women, sexual women, women I'm attracted to—and those three sets are not congruent. I'm always prepared for safe sex. I keep a supply of rubbers. In the six months Shelley and I have been together, we haven't been with anybody else, so I don't find safe sex necessary. If I were going to step out, play with somebody else, it would depend on who I was with, how well I knew her, how well I could trust what she'd say. It's not as much fun with a rubber, but it's better than nothing. There's that saying: "Son, the worst sex I ever had was wonderful."

Paula

It was a copy of Peyton Place *that ignited eight-year-old Paula's interest in masturbation. Growing up in a small town in Minnesota, she found the paperback at her grandmother's house and passed it on to her sister with carefully marked passages. As a teenager, Paula had spontaneous orgasms while necking—climaxes she concealed—and first engaged in intercourse as a send-off to a boyfriend bound for Vietnam. She married at twenty and divorced a few years later. "I was allowing my husband to use me," she says, "and he was oblivious to what was going on. During sex, I'd grit my teeth and clench my fists." A serene, graceful woman at thirty-nine, Paula works as a massage practitioner at a hot springs resort and lives with her lover Crosby, a carpenter with whom she has been sexually involved for a year and a half.*

That achy feeling that comes when you're really turned on, I had that quite a bit when I was young. Later, when it was okay to have intercourse, something switched. It's taken me years to get to where I've been able to enjoy it and not be afraid of somebody in me, thrusting in me. In my earlier years, if I was just necking, there was no pressure to be open to the guy, which allowed me to be very open. But with intercourse, it was all of a sudden: Oh, my God, I have to be turned on, I have to be wet, I have to be open to receive this man inside of me. So I reverted to the quiet coming on my own, and I didn't want to share it. It may have been a kind of warped logic—that if they knew I came, they would think they had made me come, which gave them more power. And I was afraid of their power.

I had my first orgasm with a man inside me about five years ago. Now with my lover Crosby, desire's very strong: "I want to feel you in me." It surprises me; it's so new to be so open. With him, I've had immeasurably wonderful times. The best is when there's a sharing and blending, a weaving back and forth of initiating actions. One time, we were making love and I felt like an animal, a cat. Not *like* an animal: I realized that I *am* an animal, and we are mating here. It was so primal . . . . I really get into licking my partner, even more so than kissing all over the body. I love being licked just having someone's head nuzzle up to me. Clitoral licking. Playing with my breasts, and little tweaks. Sometimes a firm hold on me gives me a feeling of pleasure, a feeling of a man's sexual power. When he's really into his power—holding me, moving me—I don't come. It's only when I put myself in control that I'll come. Now it's moving more to where I'll allow myself to come when he's in control. That's the next step.

We'll do it in the car, on trips, on empty highways. He'll be driving, and I'll be sucking on him or he'll be playing with me. I've had orgasms while I've been driving. He can tell when I'm getting turned on because I start speeding up. I accelerate. Last year, when we took our holiday, we'd just stop at the side of the road, and do it there in the car. There was one place we stopped in the desert, a little oasis. The grass was pretty tall; you could tell that some other animals had been there, resting. We put the blanket down. He stalked me like an animal, outside, naked, with nobody around.

I can go on for a while, if he wants to come and hasn't yet. Lots of times he waits for me, lots of times he doesn't even come at all. That's a whole thing with the Tao perspective on love, that a man should only come once out of every ten love-making sessions. To refrain from that and save it. That's nice, because I know sex is not just for him to get off. In the past, I was this object, and guys were having sex so they could get off, and that was it. That's not Crosby's motivation. He's also there to please me, and he really enjoys it when I have an orgasm. He's delighted by it. And when he comes, there's a delight that I feel.

When I climax, he loves it, he loves me expressing it. It turns him on. It's not a male power trip, which I'd thought it was in the past. Sometimes when I masturbate, I can go two, three rounds with myself, but I don't do that with a man. One time and that's about it. I've asked myself why that is. As it is, he can be in me for an hour, doing all sorts of different positions and staying on that edge for a long, long time. We'll come up to a peak, not reaching orgasm but, "Stop, stop, stop!" We lie very still until that subsides, then continue, and it can go on for a couple of hours, back and forth like that. At this point in time, I don't go on to a second orgasm, I just play to that edge with the first one. Being on the edge is more exciting, more pleasurable in a way than actually having an orgasm. I postpone my climax as long as I can to maintain that pleasure.

One of the things that got me hung up in a way was thinking that sex had to be a spiritual experience. Having sex with God. With my lover, it becomes more spiritual the more primal it is. I'm becoming a lot more comfortable with the assertiveness of a man. In the past, I wouldn't assert myself, and when the man did, I'd back off. Now I'm allowing myself to receive and enjoy it: "Do your stuff with me, I'm right here to do what you want." Because I know now that I can have control. Sometimes when I'm not turned on, I panic that it's never going to happen again— panic because finally I'm coming into a new sense of sexuality, and I want it to be there. Part of me wants to be turned on all the time.

Anthony

When Anthony's mother died in childbirth, his father took over raising the family. His was an Italian working-class household that never again included adult women. "I never got a concept of the traditional sex roles," says the Chicago-born psychologist, now a bearded forty-seven-year-old. "Our babysitters were frequently widowers, my father's retired male friends from the Bowery, where he came from. Tough, fragile men. Tough guys who would cry at the drop of a hat." Married to his partner of twenty years, Anthony is active in the men's groups inspired by poet Robert Bly.

In high school, I was less than a sexual celebrity. When I was eighteen, I was four-feet-eleven, had braces, zits and stuttered. Not a pretty picture. I was somewhat fatalistic in those days: "If I don't get bigger, I can always join the circus." I didn't grow till my first year of college. Then I started working out and making up for lost time. I came back home a foot taller and much more manly; everything about me had changed. My sister's friends were going, "Gee, is that your brother?" I had two reactions. I was terribly flattered by it, and I was just enraged: "You bitches! How I *longed* for you. I felt so inadequate, and you used to laugh at me. And now because I fit your vision of what a man is, I'm more acceptable to you."

I got married at twenty-one, but I was unhappy in my marriage. I had an affair with an older woman which went on for several years. She really educated me sexually. I learned how to talk to women in a different way, to ask a woman what she liked and how she liked it. I certainly learned how to make *love* . . . going more slowly, overcoming whatever inhibitions I had. I remember once she went down on me, and I came in her mouth, and she came up and kissed me and put my come back in my mouth. She just looked at me: "Now swallow it. If it's good enough for me, it's good enough for you."

In the early seventies, I was out of my marriage, into graduate school. The temper of the times was exploratory, avant-garde, provocative, risk-taking: "You ought to be able to accept everything." I experimented a lot, which in part translated to having every social disease known to man *multiple* times . . . although I've tested negative for AIDS. I experimented with group sex, swapping, open relationships, same sex experiences. I would get in some of these avant-garde situations, and I'd find it wasn't my scene. Sometimes I was in bed with people I didn't particularly want, but I wound up there to prove something to myself. It taught me about my limitations. For instance, I'd have a terrible time getting an erection in group sex scenes. I went to my therapist, and he laughed and said, "Congratulations! Your mind and your body are working together. Maybe you ought to listen to your body: you're putting it in places it doesn't want to be." And it took me a few more years to really pay attention to that, to understand that one of my conditions for sex was more privacy.

I don't have the same urgency to copulate now that I did ten years ago. How much of that is physiological and how much comes from being more selective is hard to say. Today, sex can be an expression of love, procreation, recreation, a way to hurt the other person, a way to reconnect after a fight. You can't separate it from passion, and you can't separate passion from anger, from sensuality. I think one of the secrets of being a good lover is first finding out what the other person likes, then telling them what you like. And preferably, you don't do that in bed. Preferably, you do that over a cup of coffee later: "You know when you did this or that to me? I really liked it. Do you want me to try that with you?" So good sex has to do with openness, with trust, with a sense of humor. I think we make sex deadly serious, and that has a way of killing spontaneity. I'd much rather have it be fun. First and foremost, it ought to be fun. You can love the person. More importantly to me, I really need to like the person. My wife and I, we've grown to like each other. She's not only my lover, she's my mate. We're very well tuned in to each other's bodies, and there's a comfort with that. We're much more playful. I don't think we have the same kind of wild abandonment that we did twenty years ago—although we have our moments.

Sex is like the mortar that holds the brick wall together. It's the communication, the recognition that we have something unique here that is friendship but goes beyond friendship. I see sex as a bonding, a reaffirmation of our connectedness, a grounding of our connection. I enjoy the connectedness of a one-on-one relationship. Philosophically, I take issue with the concept of monogamy, and ostensibly our relationship is open. On paper it's still open. But given that my wife and I work full time, have a kid and a home . . . well, I call it monogamy by default.

I have clients who tell me they lack sexual passion in their lives, spontaneity, quality relationships . . . . Probably the most prevalent sexual dysfunction these days is the lack of desire. I think it's a function of a lot of people working very hard. One income doesn't go as far as it used to, so you've got two people working now—often very hard. We've gone from about a thirty-eight hour work week to a forty-seven or forty-eight hour workweek. People have less time for leisure. Time when you're rested, time when you're not preoccupied with all the bills, the worries. Time in which you could potentially have a quality relationship, including sex. I'm more fortunate than some people because my wife and I are both psychologists and work in private practice, and we can orchestrate our own hours. We choose not to work one day a week, and we figure out at the beginning of the year what that costs us. On the day that we don't go to work, we'll take a walk, sit in a little coffee house, read the paper and talk. We'll go to a matinee in the afternoon. We'll have sex in the afternoon. That's great . . . . People on their deathbeds don't say, "I wish I'd worked an extra ten hours a week. I would have *gotten* the Flubbo account." They say, "I wish I'd spent more time with the ones I love." I don't want to have that regret.

III. FE/MALE TROUBLE

Mother Nature shapes us into two basic bundles, male and female, but she has little to do with postpartum notions about masculinity and femininity. Fashioned instead by social norms, gender types are a kind of intricate cultural bric-a-brac, a collection of beliefs about power and personality. In this country, the emphasis on boy-girl differences starts early, with amniocentesis screening, pink and blue baby blankets and perky jingles about "sugar and spice" versus "snails and puppy-dog tails." Some people find the twin-pack of gender roles a cramped container for the human spirit. Fe/Male Trouble investigates gender variations through interviews with men and women who sidle into "the opposite sex." Their stories make puzzles of the seemingly simple pronouns "he" and "she."

This chapter's gender-benders firmly believe in the boy-girl division. They just find themselves on both sides of it. In many cases, cross-dressing supplies the passport to the hidden persona. "I can be Janet at the drop of a dime—but most people don't realize it unless I'm dressed that way," said David, who even got a credit card in Janet's name for her shopping sprees. Cross-dressing is most often associated with men, but it's not just a boy ploy. As women in this chapter demonstrate, female gender-bending pushes far past the accepted androgyny of jeans and Jockey for Her. "Cross-dressing can be assertive, and it can be sexual," said Cybelle, for whom donning a suit and fedora cues the emergence of a male persona. "I get very orgasmic . . . . As Cybelle, my sexual feelings are more diffused, more generalized, more erotic. When I'm Alan, it is all in the cock, all in my groin."

83

Numerous interviews mention changes in sexual response. Richard, a female-to-male transsexual, discovered that the routine multiple orgasms he'd experienced as a woman evolved, post-surgery, into single climaxes. "Now I need at least ten minutes in-between, and I can't do more than two of them without rest," he remarked. "And it does happen that I'll come too fast." Shannon, who is part way through a male-to-female transsexual shift, found, "I'm becoming multiorgasmic without even getting an erection. It bypasses the whole male sexuality . . . . Now when I get turned on, it's a glow-on, not a hard-on."

Gender is no predictor of mating habits. Fe/Male Trouble's nine interviews wriggle free from facile conclusions about gender identity and sexual orientation. Consider the ad that Shannon placed in a personals column: "Until recently lesbian, preoperative, male-to-female transsexual seeks open-minded straight man . . . ." Such complications wreak havoc with the mainstream heterosexual imperative, "Adam and Eve, not Adam and Steve." Even so, parts of the gender-warp community are more than a bit queasy about homosexuality. As Andy, a pretty transvestite, said, "A lot of guys who do drag are homophobic and want an A+ wife who'll buy clothes for them or take them out on the town dressed up." In another interview, a married cross-dresser observed that his wife is afraid of the lesbian aspect of their relationship when he slips into girlish garb.

Tracking down gender-benders willing to talk was a challenge, as many are considerably closeted. Even hotline volunteers were shy. Nearly all my contacts used cross-gendered pseudonyms. Calling them up, I'd find Roxanne was a baritone, Rachel a bass, Mark an alto. The cautious responses were certainly justified. Those who openly cross the gender line risk scapegoating and sometimes ruthless walloping towards assimilation. Men reported taunting, threats at knife point, and lifelong fear of disclosure that might lead to job loss. One woman told of being chased by a group of queer-bashing skinheads who mistook her for a gay man. As Richard commented ruefully, "The society prizes individualism, but there's no room for individuals."

In reflecting on these anecdotes about the nature of manliness and womanliness, I find myself thinking that gender serves as a kind of mundane update on sacred archetypes of yore, those exalted ideals that are not realizable in the fretful course of daily life. For all of us, in the cross-over camp or not, attempts to become "the total woman" or the he-man equivalent inevitably result in approximations. These nine commentaries from the cusp of gender urge serious consideration of sex-role identity and present gender-tweaking as a mighty exercise in self-determination. But the interviews also propose a more playful approach to the diversions of boy-girl display. "I learned a lot of my butchness from women," Tede, a former drag queen, said with a humorous glint. "I'd go to gay bars, and the bull dykes would buy me drinks and practice their chivalry. We knew we were playing roles, but we were playing the parts of the roles we found pleasant."

David

*David's long face shows his southern European ancestry. Forty-five
and a postal worker, he recently founded a transvestite support
group in his suburban community, a short jog from San Francisco.
He has cross-dressed consistently since age twelve, and he remembers yanking little girls' clothes off a laundry line and trying them
on when he was three. An ex-Bostonian, David sported jeans and
a black leather jacket for this interview.*

I spent twenty years in the military, stationed in the Pacific and
in the States. At age twenty, I got married to a girl from my
home town, and the marriage lasted five years. I was afraid to
tell her about my cross-dressing, because I was afraid of losing
my job, getting bounced out. "A security risk." My first wife
never knew. Nobody knew. I was so deep in the closet I couldn't
see the door.

I went to Japan, and we started divorce proceedings. Six months
later, I went down into one of the notorious bar districts in
Yokohama and met this extremely beautiful young lady. She did
things to me . . . whoa! Physically, sexually, psychologically . . . .
To have a long, relaxing bath, to have someone wash you, bathe
you, dry you, and just lie in bed and enjoy the sensuality of each
other, without having to get it on two seconds after you've closed
the door. Hot and frantic, on occasion, is nice, but so is this: to
spend the better part of a night slowly building, exploring each
other's erogenous zones, enjoying the sensuality of the moment.
I saw her a few times—she disappeared, and nobody knew where
she was—but I think it opened up the door to understanding
sensuality.

I met my present wife, Kumiko, through a friend. She worked
at a Japanese snack bar. After three or four nights, I asked if I
could walk her home. She looked at me and rather emphatically
said, "No." That was twenty years ago . . . . I was still very
much in the closet. It wasn't until six months before I retired from
the military that I started acquiring some clothes. I was finally

Fe/Male Trouble

coming to the end of a long road, and I was looking forward to major changes in lifestyle, jobs, careers. I was thinking, "Now I can learn to deal with an issue I've lived with for so long but not understood." The day I retired, I came out of the closet—to myself, anyway. I went to see a psychiatrist, four times altogether. That answered a lot of questions. The light went on: "You mean there's all kinds of people who do this?" Somewhere in that time frame, I told my wife. Her major concern was, "Where is it going to stop? Is it going to progress to hormones and sex changes? What's going to happen to me?" It took a lot of getting used to on her part. At first it was tolerance, then acceptance, then having fun. About four years ago, I started to really have fun with it and be able to enjoy my feminine side, Janet.

I can be Janet at the drop of a dime—but most people don't realize it unless I'm dressed that way. Being Janet is more comfortable, more natural. You lose that male, macho pressure to perform that's always there. I think it's an ease of understanding other people, being much more empathetic, less likely to look for a quick fix to a problem, thinking things through. It's fun to dress up, to let your feminine side run amuck at times. With women, in a lot of instances, it's easier to present Janet than David. You can have a roomful of women socializing, and if one man walks in, the walls go up. If Janet walks in—even if they *know* about me—the walls don't seem to go up. It allows me freer access to their feelings. And mine. I feel like Janet is who I should be all the time. Unfortunately, a lot of the world won't let us be that way. Society won't. That's been my thought, "Why do I have to explain that there's David and Janet? Why can't I be in between—or Janet all the time?"

The essence of femininity is an intangible thing. You're hoping you can capture that feeling when you see a woman that you know in your mind's eye is a true woman. To capture the moment of how she feels, her movements, her body language. For me, now that I've come to understand what this is all about, there's no fear of experiencing a softer, feminine side. That's not an issue. If you're secure in yourself and know who you are, you don't feel threatened by letting your feminine side out. The experience of being able to totally be yourself, free of any inhibitions or societal constraints—real or imagined—can allow you to reach a level of consciousness that transcends sexuality. Those moments being rare, sexuality can reaffirm it.

My wife is my only partner. No dogs, cats, sheep, boys, other girls. Absolutely not. I'm not given to that at all. Sometimes Kumiko is turned on to Janet. When it's part of our sex life, it's playful fun, "Let's do something different." One of those times, with Janet as Janet, I remember doing a very slow, sensuous kind of teasing all over the body, from the toe all the way to the nape of the neck. Fingers, lips, just teasing the entire body. Then starting at the nipples, working down rather slowly. Working down to the vaginal area, to the more sensitive parts of a woman's body. Taking time. Letting her build, her desire, to the point where she is ready for me—not just a case of "Mr. Happy's ready." She has a Ms. Happy, too. That kind of thing as Janet is fun. By the same token, it's fun when Janet's in nylons and a teddy, having the same things done to her. The slow, sensuous sex is much more enjoyable. There is a different kind of feeling as Janet, more psychological than physical.

When Janet's Janet, she's on the bottom. There are times that David's on bottom, or we'll be sitting up, facing each other, or doing it "doggie style," or standing up. The kitchen table, the kitchen counter. Intercourse is just part of sex. You can have really sensuous movements without actually having penetration: sensitive moments, tender caressing, just holding each other . . . the feel of each other's closeness, remembering things from the past . . . the smell of her hair, the smell of her body . . . cuddling in bed on a rainy day and not wanting to get out, because you're so comfortable . . . a semi-dream state. Good sex is having so much fun with it that you hope it won't end. Unfortunately it usually does, whether in orgasm or sheer exhaustion.

Mark

Mark is a pale young woman with cropped hair and a large bunch of keys swinging from her hip. Raised in an upper middle-class family in Manhattan and London, she says that her early incest experiences strongly shaped her sexuality. Mark came out as a lesbian at nineteen and a few years later discovered sadomasochism in a rural, small town romance. Till recently, she has been involved in a long-term nonmonogamous relationship with an ex-stripper, "the goddess incarnate." Professionally, Mark works as a counselor.

I consider myself ninety percent male and ninety percent female. My identification is basically as a gay leather topman who happens to be into girls. Femme females get me hot. I always wanted to be a boy growing up, 'cause then I could pee standing up and fuck women. Then the day came I realized I could do both.

I have several dildoes. I have one I consider my cock, seven inches by an inch and a half. It packs easily. I wear it a lot. I designed a harness that I can wear without discomfort. Then I have a bigger dick, eight inches, for women who like things bigger. Just having this monster thing in my pants is amusing. I use condoms. Always have. Easy clean up. I think a woman going down on a dildo is totally hot. It's very much about dominance and submission. And to watch someone deep throat it is hot as fucking hell. The first time my ex did it, I thought I was going to come. To have someone licking it in my pants, pulling it out, holding it, putting a condom on it . . . . *And* there are occasionally people who remember that there's a clit behind it, and they work it with their hands, too.

Receiving vaginal intercourse is low on my list of things to do on a Saturday night. Anal's really hot for me. Vaginal, I'll get scared or disconnected. But I don't get penetrated a lot. That's a real trust thing for me—although one woman fucked the living shit out of me and made me come. 1984. She fucked my cunt, shoved her fingers up my ass, worked my clit. I don't know *what* she did, but she made me come. And in all the time my ex and I were together, she made me come three times.

I could never deal with the heterosexual model: male dominant, female underneath. The potential for violence in the dynamic was just too much for me. I'm not particularly interested in being submissive to start with, but I'm not interested in being submissive to a Neanderthal. Some men interest me physically, but I'm not into interrelating with them, being penetrated, dominated. I like gay leathermen: they have a lot of sexual energy, but it's aimed at other men. The universe is my top and carries a very big stick, and I don't need anyone to hurt me. I like to receive gentle touch. Kissing, touching, lying together. Flesh to flesh is one of the most satisfying things for me, when I can lie down and breathe and tuck my head into someone. Just to hold and be held. I was hanging out with someone yesterday. She had long dark hair. I just brushed her hair.

I like putting my hand inside someone. Latex-covered. I like fucking a lot. I'm very sexually connected to my cock. I wish it would come. One of my favorite sex positions is lying on my back with someone sitting on top of me. I like being gone down on, although the need for latex has made it less fun. I've never been that into going down on other people, so latex has made that a non-interesting act. Although I've discovered if someone's *shaved* the latex just gets wet and *sticks*. I like oral stuff: licking, sucking, chewing, and I love to bite. Most of the time, my partner is not bringing me to orgasm. I get off by using a vibrator on my clit. And being held and kissed while that's happening. I love being kissed while I'm coming. I test for HIV every six months. I've been negative three out of three times. It's really hard to look at sex with no body-fluid contact. Gloves are easy; it's the oral sex thing that's hard.

I tend to be into connecting with the individual I'm with, finding out what she likes, saying what I like and finding where the intersection is. If there's something I really want to do, and you *don't* want to do it, there are plenty of people out there who are interested. So there's no reason for me to push you. Likewise, if you want me to do something I don't want to do, then you can fuck off. That's why I do SM: it's about consent. Consent makes stuff very easy. If both say "yes," it's yes. If either says "no," then it's no. If one says, "I'm not sure" or "I don't know," it's no. Anything but "Yeah, let's go!" is no.

Last weekend, I was playing with a friend. She's a great submissive, a masochist. You take a crop and hit her, she gets wet. We'd been fucking, and she asked me to cane her. Afterwards, she got up and climbed up on my cock. That's response! She has pierced labia. At three A.M., I made a comment about locking her up the next day. She wanted me to do it right away. So I got out a great big padlock, made sure I had the key, and locked up her labia. The lock was heavy, but just small enough that it didn't rest on the sheets when she was lying on her back. That got her totally insane, and we kissed, moved and made noise for another hour.

I really like marking someone. It's sort of a temporary ownership thing: "She's wearing my marks." It's about having a connection, and I like the marks aesthetically. If my partner gets into it, then for a period of time she belongs to me. No matter how many partners she has out in the world, there's a part of her that's mine, and there's a part of me that's hers.

Good sex: where the connection works between two people, where they have a good time and are slightly different when they come out than when they went in. A magic, a chemistry, an energy. It doesn't matter whether you have a whip in your hand, or a glove on your hand, or you're sitting across the room from each other, not even touching. Or, you're three thousand miles apart on a phone line. In the last few years, I've probably played with or fucked fifty or more people. But there's only one woman with whom it's been *right* on all the different levels: fantasies, physical, emotional, intellectual. You just don't find that every day.

Tede

A self-described Southern belle, Tede was a plump, lonely boy from a working-class, church-going Florida family. He left home and became a transvestite. "Gender identity, sexuality and even sexual orientation is a constantly evolving thing," the bearded forty-year-old observes cheerfully. "It's a reaction to the world around you and a powerful presence in your life that forms the world around you." Today, Tede works at a San Francisco bookstore and lives with his long-time lover.

Before I came out and found out about feminism and gay liberation, I saw two models offered to me, the macho man and the feminine woman. Men created violence and had a need to control the environment around them, even though they never seemed able to understand it. Women seemed to understand their environment but had no power to control it. I took the identity of the female side, because I suffered male violence, being a fat child and considered a sissy. I found more acceptance from little girls and adult women, who explained life to me. I came out in Boston at age twenty, and a month later I was living in drag. I did that for three years.

Straight people thought I was a woman. My daytime look was Joan Crawford. I used to shave my chest and stomach, but I was a feminist, so I *wouldn't* shave my legs. I worked in factories as a woman for a dollar-eighty an hour. Then I was hustling: I could make two hundred bucks a night giving blow jobs in cars. I wore a woman's fifties motorcycle jacket, black hot pants, black fishnets and boots. I had long hair. A fierce femme. I didn't involve my sexuality with it. It's a violent lifestyle: there's a lot of guilt for the men picking up hustlers. They don't want to admit they want to do it with a man, so they do it with a man who looks like a woman. That gets weird, and I got into dangerous situations. Also, I was organizing the drag prostitutes. My hustling partner got killed by the Mafia, who controlled the whole Boston bar and prostitution scene. I got raped by two mafiosi and almost injected with heroin. As they say, it takes balls to be a drag queen.

Back then I was more into anal sex. Anally, I'm more of a top, and orally I'm more of a bottom. I generally like to seduce. God created men to be fucked: prostate stimulation makes the orgasm more intense, makes the ejaculation stronger. It's like warp speed in *Star Trek*. I've been with my lover seven **and** a half years, and I'm his first male lover. At first, we had unprotected anal sex: "We're in love, so that will protect us." Stupid. We never made a conscious decision to stop having anal sex, but then it stopped happening, and now we do it maybe once a year. Even without talking about it, AIDS can put a damper on sex. I used to really like rimming, and I've seen videos where guys do it using Saran Wrap, but I'd feel like I was sucking on a packed *lunch* or something! With my lover now, we're mainly monogamous. The relationship fits me so well: I feel loved and validated and still have a lot of space to do what I want. When we make love, it's oral. I like long love-making sessions. Sensuous kissing, affection, talking, taking breaks. Coming isn't the most important part, and I like to put off having orgasms, since I may *look* good in drag, but I can't have multiple orgasms.

These days, I'm mostly beating off by myself, wearing out the VCR. Sometimes I watch videos of fucking and get misty-eyed and a hard-on, because I did enjoy fucking my partners. I still have wandering eyes, and I go to the bear parties—that's a gay aesthetic: big men, older men, men with beards, hairy chests. They're once a month, and my boyfriend and I alternate going. I mainly perform oral sex, or have it performed on me, without condoms, without anyone coming in an orifice. Occasionally, I've seen people there engaging in unprotected anal sex, and that generally bums me out enough that I leave. I feel sad, because here are these brothers of mine doing something proven to be dangerous. That boy's having fun right now, but he could be getting AIDS or spreading it. In the early eighties, I used to go to Buena Vista Park and enjoyed the intrigue of going through the bushes under the full moon, meeting people, watching people, but the actual sex wasn't that all that intense for me, because finding out about a person gets me more sexually interested.

The sexual connection is a whole other level of intimacy. Our concepts about what turns us on are developed in such secrecy that anonymous sex is almost easier. But being able to be intimate and care about somebody, to know that person very well and still be turned on to them after years . . . that breaks through those feelings that sexuality is something you have to keep to yourself. It helps bring unity to my life. Making love feels like casting a circle and being within that circle. Whether you're alone, with another person, or in a sex club, that's the only world that exists. In everything else I do, I'm very conscious that there's a world around me. In sex, I feel transported to another plane—where to, I don't know. But it's exciting, it's hot.

Sex is the greatest opiate: I definitely prefer sex to getting drunk or drugged out of my mind. I'd much rather get sexed out of my mind. It's a great tranquilizer. Also, auto-sexuality—masturbation—is something I do for myself. It's not to please anybody, to fit in anywhere, to *be* something for somebody else. It's about the only thing I do to completely please myself. There's a spiritual connection, because it's part of me no one can ever know. I can share it, show it, talk about it, but I can never fully verbalize it, and so in a way, it's my own mysteries.

Drag isn't part of my sexuality anymore. I'm proud of being a drag queen and glad I did it, but the context changed, and I evolved away from it. I started doing drag just in theater, and then I stopped doing theater. I got tired of being treated like a woman: men pinching your ass, grabbing you, your body somehow theirs as social property. I didn't like that. Still, I find that the more masculine I look, the more femme I am in bed. I just can't leave well enough alone! It's funny: when I was more femme, I was meeting more masculine men who wanted to be bottoms . . . . Today, I feel much more at home with myself. Not just myself: I feel much more at home with the world. There's more diversity now, whether it's bisexuality, or gender identity, or more mainstream people bringing their sexual beings a little more out of the closet.

Vaughn

Into her adolescent years, Vaughn was often mistaken for a boy. Today, she considers herself androgynous. An attractive woman who wears her dark hair in a punky cut, she alternates between a male and female presentation, but never mixes the two. Vaughn works as a computer programmer and lives in a small apartment decorated with posters of Noh masks and female bodybuilders.

I was sexual with men in my twenties, mostly to find out what it was about. I had one boyfriend who was very warm and rich in feeling—the best lover I'd ever had. We had sex, and afterwards I caught myself going into a depression: "I want to do what *you* did."

In the seventies, I was fascinated with lesbians, whom I mistakenly saw as sort of men-women. I wondered, "Am I a lesbian?" But I didn't feel any sexual attraction. In college, I became infatuated with a professor—a total butch, though married. Then it was, "Am I a lesbian? Of *course!*" I decided to start with a clean slate and find out what I liked sexually and what I didn't. I found I didn't like vaginal stuff: I could come, have orgasms, but afterwards I didn't feel this was it. My breasts were a distraction, my vagina was a distraction . . . . The first time I tried a dildo on a woman, it was like, "*Hallelujah!*" I was jumping with joy. I even wanted to smoke a cigarette, and I don't smoke.

I read about surgery and hormones, and I started taking male hormones. My voice dropped a bit, I got a mustache and facial hair, so I shave every day. My period didn't change at all. I didn't want to be completely masculine; I wanted to be right in the middle and do both. The hormones make the clit grow, and they shift the sexual sensation. It feels more precise, more phallic, more directed. It fits the way I think. Vaginal orgasms are more vague and spread-out. I feel better if I use a dildo: it rubs against my clit, and the phallic orgasm is more releasing for me.

Six months after coming out, I realized I was attracted to gay men—as a man, not a woman. I tried to link in with gay men, but it wasn't too easy. It was a dream and a wishful wanting to be closer. It's the way they talk, that slight flirtatiousness, their sensitivity, their secret rapport. They care about how they look, they're into cocks, they like masculinity. I love the ones who are masculine-looking with a touch of effeminacy. I like to think about being fucked and fucking them. My favorite fantasy is that we have one cock . . . . I met a guy and told him I wanted to explore gay sex. I was in therapy at the time and actually hired him as a surrogate. It was nice . . . he fucked me in the ass, told me I was a faggot, I used a dildo on him. Later, I learned about AIDS, and I haven't been sexual since, except with one woman. There's still a longing in me for a relationship with a gay man—a buddy and a fuck-buddy. There's a man at work who is driving me crazy. I get teeny little orgasms standing next to him, but I don't know what I'd want to do with him at home.

To me maleness is a certain physical feeling and sense of myself as being male looking—a flat chest, bristles on my face, being sexual with a dildo cock. It's not postures or different behavior. It's not about how I'm seen by others, but how I see myself. I wanted a masculine chest. As soon as I read there was surgery for it, I wanted my breasts reduced. I did it eight years ago. I was going to get tattooed to cover up the scars, but they're minimal. Everybody told me not to, but I've never had regrets. I'm a guy, and I'm a girl: my nipples stick out enough that they're visible through a silk shirt. Most of my friends think I'm on my way to being a guy, but I don't want to give up being female. I just want both. I'm not going to delete my history, give up the way I've learned to be in the world . . . . And being a girl is *fun* too. Ninety-nine percent of the reactions I get are, "You can't be in both places." To me, it's like being bisexual: fifteen years ago, it wasn't a possibility; you were either a lesbian or straight.

I like women who are feminine, delicate, able to see me as a male. My last girlfriend was bisexual, and she loved to be fucked. I wanted her to say, "Stop, stop!" like in high school, but she could never say no. I liked taking her clothes off slowly, her stroking my face, sneaking on the dildo. I'd rub her with my hand, kiss her breasts, have her whisper things in my ear, "You're such a good man. Your cock's so big." The traditional things. Fucking her, slow and deeper, listening to her come in that high

Fe/Male Trouble

voice. I'd come, too. A real physical thrill was holding her down. Consensual struggle. Driven . . . . Good sex is pleasure while you're doing it and relief afterwards. You get a sense of reaffirmation. There is a sense of accomplishment, too: you've taken care of a need you have as an adult, as a human being, and you've taken care of someone else.

I'm much more comfortable being ambiguous to other people and whole to myself than I would be trying to fit into a category. No matter how I think about it, I can't squeeze myself into being called a woman; I'd have to be called a man if I were being sexual. In bed, I do boy, not girl. I have some fear around ambiguity, mostly about how people will respond if I go to a job interview, for example. If the world loved it more, I would do it more. I *love* it. It used to be very, very stressful. But now I feel I'm just going to stand my ground.

Being in-between is a place where I can be genuine, where I don't have to be concerned with my grooming or presentation. I see more people bending towards androgyny, so attitudes might be changing. It's so easy to read the psychiatric literature and go, "Oh, this must be sick." And then I see Michael Jackson, and I feel great. If he can do it, so can I.

Cybelle

For Cybelle, clothes indeed make the man. At age twelve, she bought her first boy's tie and learned to knot a four-in-hand. "My first invisible playmate was a little boy: I'd go back and forth between being a little girl and being him. I always felt I was both," says the slender brunette, who works as a corporate secretary. Now forty and identifying as bisexual, Cybelle has been happily married for more than fifteen years.

In the seventies, I moved to Southern California from the Midwest. My first jobs, just to pull money together, were working as a go-go dancer and art-class model. I felt fine about posing nude, and I love costumes. I met my husband, Larry. He's a painter. We had a basic, normal sex life, with some fantasy role-playing through costuming as artist and model. He introduced me to fetishistic lingerie and leather boots, erotic dress, all girl stuff. He taught me how to use make-up. As a model, I got totally into this femme thing, big-time make-up and hair. Then I took a part-time job on weekends as a taxi dancer for about four years. This continued my super feminine role—the mini skirts, fishnet stockings, the stiletto heels that you could hardly walk in, lots of make-up. At the dance hall, you got regular customers who fantasized that you were their girlfriend. Men told me their dreams, their frustrations and hopes, their out-and-out sexual fantasies. Most didn't dance. They called it grinding. Kind of gross.

Five years after leaving L.A., Larry was becoming more and more aware of being a cross-dresser. He realized he'd sublimated it through me and other models—dressing up women the way he wanted to be dressed. I like it when Larry cross-dresses. When he first started doing it, I wasn't sure. His cross-dressing led to the rediscovery of *my* male side, which has been there since childhood. One night, I went to a party cross-dressed as an escort to my husband, and a part of me that had been sleeping for years came back, stronger than ever, with thoughts and feelings of its own. I started getting in touch with this part of myself by cross-dressing more often, putting on a mustache, looking like a guy. The more I did this, the happier I got. Now I become Alan by dressing, putting a dildo in my pants, doing different things with my hair, putting on a mustache. Then, all I have to do is look in the mirror, and he's there, ready to go out.

Alan is a lot younger than I am, because he was suppressed for a long time, ten or fifteen years. When I become Alan, I have more energy, I can dance longer, I look and feel younger. I tend to walk like a mafia person from the movies. Alan's a T-and-A man: when I look at women's magazines, *I'm* just looking at the clothes, but Alan's looking at the *women*. I've always been a visual person. I've read somewhere that's a male thing—that men are more visual, especially with sexual cues. When I'm Alan, I see women as being even more beautiful. I don't know if women realize how beautiful they are . . . . Alan is crazed about women. As Cybelle, I'm not jumping up and down about them, because I *am* a woman. I know what this is. For Alan, it's like, "There's a different species, and aren't they great!"

Larry is my primary partner. We basically have a continuation of the sex life we've always had, where I'm in charge—meaning that I initiate sex—and we do it when we're both in the mood. One change: the male part of myself fell for the female part of my husband, all dressed up as his persona Debra. Now a large part of our sex life is relating as Alan and Debra—or sometimes Cybelle and Debra. We have fantasy play there, too, though Debra as a she-male doesn't screw me. We tried that once and didn't like it . . . . As Cybelle, my sexual feelings are more diffused, more generalized, more erotic. When I'm Alan, it is all in the cock, all in my groin.

I feel more primitive, and I don't know if it's really how men feel or just my interpretation . . . . As Alan, I love to be cock-teased and dominated by Debra. Alan doesn't actually *fuck* Debra, probably because Debra's not a real woman and doesn't go for anal sex. Debra's very narcissistic: she gets turned on by looking at herself in the mirror. I'll help her get off. Sex now is equally intercourse and manual: I jerk Debra off, or she jerks herself off while I watch. We're both voyeurs, of each other and ourselves.

I think good sex is any kind of sex that makes you as an individual—either by yourself or with a partner—feel whole and good about yourself. And, if you're with a partner, makes them feel good, too. Some of the most extreme happinesses I've had are in the fantasy games that we've played as Alan and Debra: Debra making Alan come while she watches . . . . In the past, fantasy games between Cybelle and Larry, where a supposedly strange man would walk in the door, and they would play a game together that would end up in intercourse . . . . Long ago, when I was working in the dance hall, Larry'd pick me up afterwards at two in the morning. He'd pick me up; I'd be a hooker, and he'd pay me. For me, it was a continuation of the prostitution fantasy of the dance hall—which I never carried out—but with somebody I really loved and cared about. For him, he was picking up the hooker of his dreams who just *happened* to look like his wife.

In the last year, Alan has started going to girly shows. That's kind of a balance to when I used to dance for men. He's had a couple of lap dancers. He has a very realistic dildo, and he packs it in his pants and goes to the peep shows. Little private booths, and the girls can kind of see him, but only from the waist up. So he watches them and masturbates. Alan realizes deep down he's part of me, but I give this part of my personality free rein so that he's autonomous, with his own little life. So he thinks he's a straight man, and that the dildo is really his cock. The action of jerking off is a visual turn-on for Alan, but physically it's the back of the dildo that's stimulating my body, my clit, which gets me off. One night, the girls could tell what he was doing and got excited, two of them performing even more, making love in his window. It was a give-and-take through the window: he was performing for them, and they were performing for him. At the end, he pulled the dildo out of his pants and waved it in the air. He wrote to one of the girls, and they started going out. She's been very supportive . . . . She gave Alan his only blow job. He felt funny about it, because he's a submissive man and felt it was demeaning to his partner, even though she was hot to do it. I guess he knows that as a woman, I don't like doing that either. Putting myself in that position, I feel subjugated.

In the work world, I'm definitely Cybelle. But at the office, I often wear a vest and a tie, and sometimes I wear a whole man's suit, with the wing tips and the tie—even though I'm very feminine in appearance, wear make-up and women's jewelry. The reactions are interesting. I get cruised by the closet lesbians, especially when I wear a tie. Some of them don't know I'm married, and they probably think I'm a lesbian because I'm wearing a tie. Some of the very straight women can hardly look at me on days when I wear suits. They're scared; even though they know I'm married, they think I'm probably cruising them. And I had this fear myself years ago as a "straight woman" when I didn't know what lesbians were like, and you get these *rumors* about lesbians going for straight women . . . . As far as men's reactions to my suits, most of the younger ones smile and think it's interesting. The gay men in the office *like* it. Where I get the weird looks or actual challenges are from the older corporate executives, because for some reason I'm in competition with them because I'm wearing a suit and tie. It's all nonverbal: looks of disdain or disgust, not getting in the elevator because I'm getting in.

I feel I'm bi-gendered. Sometimes I feel like I have female anatomy: breasts, cunt, periods, a soft voice. Other times, I feel I don't have a cunt anymore. I have a cock, facial hair and a different hormonal structure. When I was dressing up frequently as Alan, I actually stopped having my periods for a while. Then one day I put on fingernail polish and a dress, and my period came within twenty-four hours . . . . As far as gender, what it is to be masculine or feminine, it's just a feeling inside you. Subtle. It's anatomy—or the anatomy that you feel you have.

Andy

A former high school jock from the California suburbs, Andy has been taken with erotic cross-dressing since age nine, when his mother's negligee, stolen from the laundry hamper, brought him to unexpected levels of arousal. It was a private pleasure—sometimes shared with lovers—pursued with great ambivalence till ten years ago. Now forty, slender and long-haired, Andy works as a computer processor and writes about his transvestite experiences and his female persona, Selena.

I like the woman I become. Selena is very pretty. She doesn't have one style of dressing or one personality. She's playful, passionate, intense. She's not a bitch. Andy can be uptight, but Selena is loose, open, accepting of other people's ways. She's friendly, both a giver and a taker. She's fetishistic, with classic fetishes like high heels, latex clothing, leather, slickers—that's those yellow rubber raincoats, a British fantasy. I am fascinated by corsets, and I like pretty tight bondage. Selena blossoms once I start putting the clothes on.

Clothes put me into my body. A bra can do that, a girdle, a corset, a slip, stockings. It's a body rush, intensity. Mind and cock combination. There's a giddiness, especially if I've got some new clothes. It's like taking a journey into another world, getting myself totally sensitized. One of the more intense experiences is to get dressed in a latex dress that's tight and beautiful. I'll put on a corset with garter straps, stockings, heels, the dress, long gloves, go to the bed and lie back. I'll take my leather hood and put that over my face. Put the mouth gag in and the eye blinds. The leather on my face is soft and erotic. My face is being turned on, my whole body's being turned on. It's an orgy of senses. It's a perfect place to be for a time. I know I've got a body then, and I don't always know that in daily life unless I'm hurting. The pleasure overwhelms my daily aggravations.

That's a private erotic experience. It's even better when I'm with someone I'm in tune with, when we're making love. I feel

Fe/Male Trouble

that's the ultimate thing, when you're with someone, male or female. I still do not know how to be with a woman in a relationship. There are too many mysteries and barriers. In the past, I felt like I was always asking for more in the sexual area than women wanted. I didn't like having to ask to be sexual. With men, you don't have to ask.

I have partners I see on a regular basis, but maybe only once or twice a month. Men in their forties and fifties who are not macho, who can ultimately be vulnerable, who can touch and be playful. Married, with seemingly almost no sex life. White men, black men, who usually discovered their interest in transvestitism when they were in the service overseas. Most identify as heterosexual or don't say what they are. I like it when they say they're bisexual. I think a dick to a dick is bisexual, and I wish more people would own up to bisexuality.

To me, the best times are when someone's really into touching and kissing for a long time. Maybe we don't even touch genitals for fifteen minutes. The old high school kiss—which I didn't do in high school. I like a man to be sweet and gentle, I like him to care about me, and I like a flow. Good sex usually has a beginning, middle, and end, with a sense of building up, like a story you play out. You are *immersed* in the here and now. The energy is going back and forth. You're feeling it together, and you're in tune. There's a lot of passion.

I'll generally make things happen, because I tend to be more experienced. I get turned on by turning someone else on, and the sensation of using my mouth and tongue is highly erotic. I like sucking nipples. I've discovered a lot of men are desperate to have someone suck their nipples, though they may never say it. If one of us is getting too turned on, we might slow down, go back to kissing and touching. I like licking balls, licking thighs. Then cock-sucking: slow, easy, pressure without teeth. At some point, we might do some fucking. Sometimes it's the most wonderful thing in the world. That's the time I feel "like a woman"— that's a fantasy in my mind—but having a man inside me in that way is wonderful. Sometimes it hurts; other times it feels good but not wonderful. I have a big mirror on the side of my bed, and I like to watch it happening.

I like building up together, which I can ride out for three hours with a guy, and I've learned to completely control my orgasms. So we have time to play out different scenarios, get so much more into the touch, spend time talking. I'm amazed at what men reveal when they're vulnerable, how unsatisfied they are not just with their *sex* lives, but with their lives. They want to break out of their strait jackets, and I'm somebody they can do that with.

It helps that I can pass. Most heterosexual transvestites don't look very good. Still, they can look in a mirror and see beauty, the way an anorexic girl can look in a mirror and see fat. But most of them, like me, didn't start out doing it to look good, but because it feels good. I've learned to revel in being a sex object, especially since I have control over it, as many women don't. I'm not tied to being Selena: I can do it just for myself and the few people I see sexually. I take care of myself in the world wearing male clothes ninety-nine percent of the time. I like playing the role of the giver, the lover, the maid, the submissive. Because I was brought up in the fifties, there's still a part of me that stereotypes all that as a female head trip. Being "the perfect woman" is a lark. I'm a guy, and it's fun to turn things around by playing out the classic femme role and turning on a "real guy." Parts of me feel more womanly than manly, but a sex change seems so radical that I can't picture it. My thing has always been trying to get the best of both worlds.

Diane

Dancing was sinful to Diane's rigid Protestant family, Pennsylvania mill workers. She married at twenty. "I decided I was going to be a virgin when I married. I would give in to the church and my family up to that point, and after that I would be my own person," she says with soft-voiced resolution. Now forty-six, a delicate woman with ash brown hair, Diane works as a technical writer and lives with her second husband, Daniel, in a suburban stucco bungalow.

D aniel was the first person I'd met who was so easy to be with. Things worked without effort. We'd both had a lot of adventures—he'd served in Vietnam; he'd worked on the Alaska pipeline. We had normal sex for two or three years. Then one time, he was polishing my nails and talking about how lucky women were to be able to wear soft, sensuous clothing. I had a dress from the forties, clingy rayon that feels good to your skin. "Here," I said, "put it on." He was excited by that. A few weeks later, he said, "Maybe I'm a transvestite." I said, "Oh no. You just like to wear women's clothing."

At first it was fascinating. I thought he looked stunning as a woman. He has a very interesting face: the bone structure is male, but he has huge eyes and long eyelashes, beautiful with mascara. We did have fun for quite some time creating this person, and we never forgot who he really was. He knew he was a man, I knew he was a man, and we never got that mixed up. I never feared he was homosexual or wanted a sex change, and that's become confirmed over the years. He just likes the sexual turn-on that dressing up gives him. I found I could live with it, because we had so many things going for us in the relationship. The cross-dressing didn't interfere. Daniel is interesting, provocative, entertaining, and caring in every way. He tries hard to be a good and lenient mate, because he knows he's asking a lot of me. I respect him. And the key to our relationship is that we can always laugh at the absurdities of what we do.

At first, his transvestitism prompted me to get in touch with my femininity—wearing more make-up, leather mini-skirts, high heels, just being as pretty as I could be. But now I think sexuality comes from within; it's not how you're dressed. Daniel made me appreciate how much I do enjoy being a woman, and how I take for granted all the freedoms I have to dress the way I please, in different colors, different styles and moods.

Sexually, he started wanting me to dominate him, but we're both milk-toast submissives. We'd still have a normal sex life, trying to balance his need to be dominated with my need for equality, a give-and-take kind of love. Where I'm most successful at being dominant is telling him stories while he masturbates. I come up with creative scenarios: things for him to do, pretend things, fantasies about me being made love to by somebody else. Leading him in masturbatory sessions, I'm watching him enjoy himself, and that's a loving thing to do, but it's not sexually fulfilling for me. For three or four years, I was doing it because I loved him, to please him. Then I started looking at my own needs.

I met another transvestite in his female persona. Jeff . . . or Jenny. It was almost like I had another girlfriend. It's so refreshing to be talking to a man but feel that you're talking to a woman. One day I went to a party, and there he was, dressed as his male self. My heart *leapt*. To find that my girlfriend was actually this handsome *guy* . . . . Daniel said, "Do what you have to do. Just don't leave me."

For the first time in my life, I really became turned on to a man in a woman's dress. That surprised me. With Daniel, I've been slightly repulsed by making love with this overtly sexual, slutty-looking woman. But with Jenny, it was kind of sisterly, comfortable, emotional. We were so alike, so attuned. When we'd be talking over a cup of coffee, there was an aura of sensuality. It usually stopped short of sex. But when we did get sexual, there was something exciting about being with this woman, a pretty redhead who'd lift up her skirts, and there was this wonderful cock. A woman with a penis . . . . Kissing another person with lipstick on, breathing feminine perfume, the tactile feel of two people in feminine clothing, and then being able to go up her skirt and find this erection. Kissing his neck. Her neck. It was erotic to me: a man with a very masculine job, and for me to

have him completely in my hands and pleasure him as a *woman*
. . . . That relationship went on for three years, painfully off and
on. He wanted to get married, but I didn't want to leave Daniel.

I loved Daniel more than ever, but sex between us still wasn't
the way I wanted it to be. With his encouragement, I became
lovers with another man six months ago. For Daniel, my going
out and coming back, tormenting him with stories of being made
love to, is very exciting. It's a continuation of the sex stories that
I've been telling him for years, but now the stories are true.

With my lover, everything that I wanted is there. With him,
it's reciprocal love-making. Plain old-fashioned fucking. Tenderness and care, kissing and touching. I like how he turns me over,
this way and that way, and I feel he could do *anything* he wanted.
Then there are times I'll take control and get on top of him, and
he likes that . . . . Intercourse is the key thing for me: I feel
incomplete without being penetrated. I don't necessarily have an
orgasm—that's not the important thing. The pleasure is in entering
me. I could just be entered over and over. That experience of
being taken is exquisite. It causes me to gasp every time. It's kind
of a surrender, a gasp at my lover's strength, a thrill at the hardness
of his cock.

Good sex is wordless, speechless, thoughtless. It's when you
lose your mind and get into pure sensation. In merging with
another person, it's the closest feeling of connectedness that you
can have. It's a temporary loss of being alone. For me, it has to
be penetration. I have to be entered. The physical union. Being
thrilled at this . . . .

When you're in a relationship with somebody who's not clearly
male or female, you have to be pretty open to just enjoying the
sensuality as it exists. For me, what's lacking with Daniel is the
mystical merging I've been talking about. I like the differences—
the masculine energy and my own feminine energy. Not that those
dynamics make the best kind of marriage, but sexually the oppo-
sition is good.

If I had known that I really crave the male-female dichotomy,
maybe I wouldn't have gotten involved with a transvestite. However, I would have missed eight wonderful years—and hopefully
an eternity—with Daniel, and I don't regret exploring all these
gray areas with him. When people are so rigid—"Men have to

be men, and women have to be women"—they're missing out on wonderful experiences with the way things are. Everybody wants things to be black or white. I'm trying to live in between. Why *can't* there be men who feel more comfortable living in the female gender, and why *can't* they keep their penises if they want to? Why do we have to conform to society's definitions? I think I have relationships because people bring out different parts of me, different elements, and I want to see who I am with this person. It's a way of getting to know myself.

Shannon

Playing both sides seemed to come naturally to Shannon, a red-head from central Massachusetts. "I remember in war games as a kid, there was an element of, 'What if you suddenly realized you belonged on the other side?'" says the thirty-one-year-old. "What if you defected to the 'bad guy' side, which would be your 'good side'?" Close to completing a sex-change from male to female, Shannon lives in her Oakland art studio.

When I was growing up, my father was off in his shop, a metallic environment with an acrid smell from metal-cutting blades and welding. I hated it there. It was too harsh. My mom was one tough-house character, the disciplinarian with the leather strap, and she could be merciless. A part of my growing up was screaming for softness. Like any little being, I just wanted some big old arms around me: "Here's a safe little spot for you. We'll keep the world at bay and let you get strong." I had to be strong from the start, and I always wanted a resting place.

I was a virgin till nineteen and met a woman who was two years older and quite a nymphomaniac. Wonderful. In a year and a half, we covered just about everything: bondage, SM, shaving each other, master/slave. She was the first one I came out to with my cross-dressing, and she was real open to it. In my next long-term relationship with yet another kinky woman, who *loved* to fuck, I got into being cross-dressed for sex. It would soften my persona—a gorgeous feeling. I ended up having sex as a woman: two orgasms, separate from ejaculation, wave-like, prolonged, satisfying at every level. Once I glimpsed the intensity of the female-to-female connection, there was no going back. It opened up Pandora's box. When I thought through the logical progression, I saw that I would become a woman. That was scary. It took me six years to come around and be open to it. We all want to be loved and accepted. What kind of creature would this make me?

Now I have this radical body to play in, with the softness of a woman and the strength of a man . . . female fat and male musculature . . . difference without separation. The real me is the umbrella being behind the two roles. When I orgasm, I don't ejaculate any more, and because of my hormone treatments, the scrotal sack is about gone. I still get a full erection, and at times spontaneous erections. Sometimes my dick is embarrassing: I see myself as a woman, so what the fuck is this thing doing here? My external genitalia don't represent my androgynous balance. For me, a vagina does. It represents my receptivity, the knowing of me within. I see the genital surgery very much as a reshaping. Other people cringe, "What about the pain?" It's only physical pain. I've been through so much, with all the electrolysis and the psycho-emotional anguish of knowing that I was so far from home. The other side of that pain is as c.ose as I'll get to home . . . . I've been between the trapeze bars for a long time. A long time.

I have a lifetime's desire in my female side, which never got to be a young girl or woman. I've had more partners in the last three years than in my whole life before—women who are everything from pretty dykey to quite femme. I've had some amazing sexual experiences. At a safe sex party, I met a dyke, who asked me if I'd come to talk or fuck. Next thing I knew, she was pushing me back on a couch and lying on top of me. We kept our clothes on, we got off together, and I never knew if she figured out that I wasn't a natural-born woman. Then I was seeing this one woman—a real fifty-fifty bisexual. We ended up on my bed, playing around, and she said, "I don't know what to *do* with you." Here's a person who's totally comfortable playing with men *and* women, and yet . . . and yet . . . she didn't know what to do. It stopped her cold.

I wanted to have sex with a woman *as* a woman: sex from the female side, which is about feeling and nuance and gray area, less defined and so free to merge. I met a woman who was pretty out there sexually. She's bisexual and makes a living as a prostitute. We got together for brunch, and while we were waiting in line, I said, "I'm in need of serious de-virginizing and wondered if you'd like to participate in a ritual." She just cracked up, "That's a new one!" We got together. It was wonderful because she was able to engage me emotionally and connect sexually. She's so used to initiating with clients, she just started making the moves. Physically it was playful: we were like kittens tumbling around. No power play, very much a dance. Animal. Instinctive.

More often than not, when I'm having female-to-female sex, I'm multiorgasmic without getting an erection. It bypasses the whole male sexuality. It's rubbing groins together, full body contact, emotional interplay, eye contact, feeling *present* with each other. The connection isn't so genitally oriented—though I can still have penis-oriented, male sex, centered in the groin, the hot spot. When I'm having sex as a woman, my whole body is attuned, and my sense of touch becomes more acute. With the male orgasm, there's this drive: "Satisfy *this*. Get this *off*." Now when I get turned on, it's a glow-on, not a hard-on.

Amidst all of this radical change, I'm really sort of old-fashioned: I'm monogamous, I love to develop the depth of a connection, and I love sexuality as a tool to explore. Good sex for me is physical communication between people who see their bodies as a source of pleasure, who love their bodies and each other's, two allies coming together and empowering a union. Good sex has a lot to do with the merging of energies. It's not the merging that comes from the male side: wanting to envelope, control, have power over. It's communion, rapture, physical delight, equality. Transcending the physical through the physical. The kind of orgasm that goes beyond physical stimulation and *flies* on its own. It has so much to do with that willingness to merge, to create something greater than the sum of its parts, to make magic together. That kind of good sex requires emotional safety and communication on a moment-to-moment basis, in sex and out.

Recently, I find that I would really like to explore being with a man. I actually wrote an ad for the personals. What I'm looking for is a guy who's glad he's a guy, gentle, emotional, basically straight, but really interested in someone with a female take on things. Good God, I'm looking for Mr. Right! I would be very amused to hold down the girl side of a relationship. Hanging out with a guy brings out my femme side: I feel softer, cuter, lighter, and gentler when there's somebody holding down the boy role. A man is going to expect me to be more femme, to wear make-up and maybe even a skirt. Except that I have a penis, I have a beautiful female body, and I want to play my girl-body against the man's. I haven't set out to become socially accepted as a girl; being straight almost isn't kinky enough for me. I'd just like to check it out.

Richard

At two, she refused to wear dresses. In school, she went for wood shop and found refuge in androgyny. Today, Richard is a transsexual, a small, brown-haired man with a mustache. Now forty-two, he works at a Silicon Valley software company and lives in a tidy condominium, brightened with photos of the daughter he raised with his ex-lover.

My sense of self was never female. I didn't hate my body, but it wasn't *me*. People teased me in high school and said things like, "queer," but I had no idea what they were talking about. I knew I was not like the boys, and I was not like the girls. It wasn't just sex. It was gender, too. I looked very androgynous. I would get beat up on the street, because people don't like to see something they can't understand. I've had incidents in public bathrooms where a woman would be insulted by my presence there, and I would raise the pitch of my voice and be demure, trying to make things smooth. At one restaurant, a woman went and got her boyfriend, a big, burly truck driver kind of guy. They stood in the front of the restaurant and screamed, "*That! That* was in the bathroom! That's the *thing* that was in the bathroom!"

In my college years, I got involved in the lesbian community in Portland. I thought I would finally find some place to fit in, but I also got a lot of shit from lesbians about being too male-identified. It was just the way I held my beer. I met a woman who was attractive and interested in me. The first time we made love, she said, "I don't know how to tell you this, but I feel like I was just with a man." And I said, "I don't know how to tell you this, but I think you were." Our relationship lasted fourteen years. One morning looking in the mirror, I tried to imagine myself as a fifty-year-old woman, and I couldn't see anything there. Nothing. No future. I got scared, and then I tried to imagine myself as a fifty-year-old man, and there I was. Then I really got scared, because I thought, "I know what this means: I'm going to have to do something."

Fe/Male Trouble

I got into a sexual dysphoria program and started taking hormones. Hormones put you through puberty: I got stronger, my voice started to break. Testosterone really does increase your libido. A week after the first injection, I woke up with a hard-on that would not quit. We had a marvelous session of love-making. The next night, we did it again. That was the last time we had sex. We woke up the next morning, and she said, "Don't ask to have sex with me, and if you want to save this relationship, you'll get us a counselor." We found a counselor, and the first thing out of my lover's mouth was, "Everything I've ever hated about you was your maleness. Now that your body is starting to change, I can't overlook it." She left me, and I was devastated.

My body was continually changing. Hormones cause the clit to grow, and if it gets large enough, they don't do a major phalloplasty, a surgical procedure which is expensive, very risky and not terribly satisfying. They can do another procedure that doesn't remove or cover up the clitoris but makes it into your penis. That's what I have. It's an inch and a half long when it's erect. Not very big, but it works and it's me. A few months after my lower surgery, I met a woman who was very interested in me. I was reluctant to get involved, but she was persuasive. When I finally did relent and hop in the sack with her, it was terrific. This woman is absolutely carnal. She loves everything about sex. She was surprised at how much she enjoyed my tiny cock. This is a woman with vast sexual experience, and she says that she's never felt so female as she has with me. I had been afraid that no one would ever love me again, that no woman would want my genitalia anywhere near her. It's been an incredible relief to find that my fears were unfounded.

We have a spectacular sex life. The dynamic between us is extraordinarily powerful. Sometimes we'll do straight missionary position, sometimes she'll sit on top of my cock, sometimes I'll use my hand and finger-fuck her, sometimes I'll wear a dildo. I love it when she sucks me off. My own sexual gratification in this body is much more intense and satisfying than it ever has been before, and every time I have an orgasm, it reaffirms that. I like the feeling of getting hard and larger, and my whole body gets hard. It's like a dream: you just get bigger and bigger and bigger, and then it releases, releases in spasms. I feel a full body orgasm, but it's very cock-centered.

Sex is a vehicle to let go of everything, a permission to be with yourself. It's a separation from space and time. When you really lose yourself and you're having really good sex, when you're really *with* your partner, trying all these different positions, and you're not goal-oriented, then sex is completely releasing. There's no time to think about anything else. It's the here and now, and that's all there is. Nothing else matters. Good sex involves people who are comfortable with themselves, enjoying themselves and each other, unconcerned with anything outside of their mutual pleasure. There's an intellectual component, a physical component, an emotional component. There has to be an element of trust and surrender. I don't think you have to have an orgasm to have good sex, though it's certainly nice. And I guess you can have good sex by yourself. I wouldn't want to exclude masturbation.

In virtually every aspect of my life, including sexuality, I am now fully expressive of myself. It's a multifaceted transition. As a man, I can walk into adult bookstores more easily, but I have new problems: it's not acceptable for me to display emotion or to show interest in little children. Also, I've had the experience of walking behind a woman on the street and seeing her look back at me in fear. I hate it. And after twenty-five years in the gay scene, it's weird to be heterosexual . . . . But it's an ongoing process: I've only been in this life for three years, and I have a lot more transition and experience to go through. Because of all the exploration I've done, I feel more able to be a human being, to be with another human being and share those things. It's pretty powerful.

IV. MIXED MEDIA

"I like mixed media in sex," said Sybil, a professional dominatrix. "I like complicated people, complicated art and complicated sex. Sex is one of the most profound ways of discovering who we can be." This chapter considers various artful techniques for cranking up the erotic voltage as a means of disclosing the innermost self. "In a role-play, *surrendering* means totally putting myself in somebody else's hands. It's such a releasing experience," Pamela explained. "I'm totally myself, free of any kind of bullshit. To break through to that is really difficult."

Those featured in this assortment of personal narratives do not snap on the *bustier* or draw forth the blindfold to serve a partner or add mail-order zest to lackluster relationships. Rather, the guise is assumed in order to reveal an aspect of the *wearer's* erotic nature and make a direct, risky bid for positive recognition from a sex partner. Acceptance from that partner communicates respect and serves as an erotic mirror for the one exposed and vulnerable. Such affirmation can be profound and indeed fundamental to many kinds of sexual interaction, but especially those which deliberately toy with breaking taboos. "Things society considers illegal we can play-act as adults: a little boy and his mother, a little girl and her daddy," noted Morgan, for whom sexual theatre combines transgression with the long-lost fun of childhood make-believe. "Adopting a persona provides me with the ability to sidestep the daily roles . . . . Part of what it's about is distracting myself from the rational mind, so I can be sensual and sexual.

Dressing up signals desire, a readiness to be naughty, and conscious separation from the demands of the work world and chore wheel. Detailed erotic preparation and display extends the time devoted to sexual engagement. As one man put it, "Better than half the fun is the so-called stalking of a partner: the first impression, the build-up, the anticipation." A woman described ten hours absorbed in training a partner how to serve her a glass of wine.

For some, assuming roles in sex play liberates them from self-censure and shame. In this chapter, Mishell described a brief affair in which she discovered that bondage games allowed her to banish deep-seated Catholic guilt. Shame—or escaping it—may also be a factor in sadomasochism's ritualized interactions; for example, the eminent Kinsey Institute for Research in Sex, Gender and Reproduction defines SM as behavior involving punishment for lust. Mixed Media presents several thoughtful interviews on SM role-play. They praise the highs of escalated sensation, and they emphasize the necessity for a sober and studied approach to body manipulations. Sybil, whose work includes "SM 101" lectures to sex therapists, told me that suburban bondage fads alarmed her, because inexperience could prove lethal.

Those contributing interviews to this chapter maintain that they are not dependent on SM or fetish clothes to reach orgasmic ecstasy. In different ways, they each describe an animated psychic atmosphere embellished with props and fantasy figures, but the symbols are not an end in themselves. The accoutrements—from femme silks to butch strappings—constitute steps in a staircase that spirals to a vista, and it is the view from the heights that has meaning. "I explore my own sexuality and practice things at levels that other people dream of," reflected Jack. "I feel privileged to be living a life that is really my own."

Kris

The oldest daughter of a Midwestern Methodist "family of the year," this never-married single mother lives in a Berkeley cottage overflowing with books, flowers and animals. At forty-nine, Kris is a charismatic talk show host. Sexually active, she has in recent years kept intimacy at bay through long distance relationships and a three-year affair with a married man. "I like brutal sex, fierce sex, and I like tender sex, loving sex," she muses. "But right now, I'm reassessing my relationships with men."

When I was twelve or so, there was the reading of some novel about the life of Christ which involved Mary Magdalene with which I was much taken. And I remember dressing up as I assumed she must have—because she had been a prostitute and a dancer—and dancing up in the attic for my younger brothers and sister. That felt very sexy to me, and it felt very sexy to *them* too. They went running downstairs and told my parents. My father came up the stairs, and I jumped into bed—it was very hot, August in Illinois—and I pulled the covers up to here. He said, "What are you doing?" I said I was taking a nap.

Letting people see me, that's a turn-on. And you don't just let anybody see you. Some of it's a turn-on whether the other person's going to accept it or not. Sometimes that's not necessary, you're just going to do it anyway. I like that part of myself—I mean, sometimes it could be described as stupidity, but sometimes it's courage, too. It's a desire to be known.

Trying to know myself is what sex is good for, because I don't really feel that I know myself all that well—or it's a constant struggle. Sex makes me confident of the value of my impulses; I don't have to constantly edit myself. I feel very powerful, and it's a true power, very calming. I'm just more relaxed about my whole life, because sex reminds me that I know how to love and I know how to be loved. That's very difficult for me. It's **much** easier to love than to be loved, and it's very affirming to let yourself be known or be seen. That's what it's about.

I am willing to expose myself to things, to show that *this* is really me. It's not just something I'm doing because somebody else wants me to. I felt many things in my childhood had to do with what my parents wanted or expected. I'm still trying to figure out what *I* want and what *I* expect.

I had a boyfriend with whom I had sex that was very physical and very exciting, almost violent, but it never went where I wanted it to go. Afterwards, I'd be exhausted, but I wouldn't feel like I'd gotten to know him any better or that he wanted to get to know me any better. It was more like shadow-boxing, like gymnastics— and I'm enough of a jock that I do enjoy that part of sex, too. I just *know* it's good for my circulation. That's good sex, but there's also deep sex. What it gets you to is the unique combination of the souls, not necessarily the body or the physical technique.

I think of my strong points as being natural and accepting. Not pretentious—although I do have little costumes. I like to do that part, too. I've got lots of lingerie and stuff. There are times I don't want to do any of that dressing up, and there are people who aren't interested in it. My current lover likes all that stuff, and I don't know if I'd be into it if he weren't. But I do enjoy it. I like costumes and make-up. I like to be able to put it on and take it off. I don't want to feel that I have to be anything all the time. I like wearing stockings with seams and garter belts—and in my real life, when do I get to wear that? I don't even want to. Why would one?

There are places and times you can be other things than you are every day, and that's fun. I don't know how it affects the sex. I mean, we like to have mirrors and candles, and I love this fantasy that I can't quite get my lover interested in. He's too shy, when it gets right down to it. I keep wanting to videotape us, to set up cameras all around. I like the eroticism, wanting to see what I look like, or what it looks like, or what we look like. Because to see that passion . . . . I'm a visually-oriented person. And I think that's what I like about black men, too, the difference. I remember when I was seeing this guy who was nicknamed Blue because he was so black. We used to sit and look at ourselves in the mirror, because the contrast was so stark. I loved it, because I could see myself and see him, and both of us were very distinct and clear. And we were both there.

Different lovers will do different things, and I've never really asked them to do anything. I just figure whatever they want to do is fine with me, that they should express themselves. That was the gift: they would let me see them; they would be vulnerable. And some of it, too, is letting me love them. Sex is taking care of somebody. It's not about getting off or letting them get off, like you're counting, adding up or keeping score. I feel with this current romance that the sex is incredibly intense, and I don't know if on film it would even look like we were alive. But it's some other country. I've seen the landscape. I've seen the colors. There's some meeting . . . of something that doesn't even have a physical form. It's really wonderful. It happens through sex. I don't think there's been that kind of meeting other ways.

Mishell

As a little girl, Mishell kept a copy of The Happy Hooker *hidden in her doll house. "Someday," she told her twin sister, "we'll have to know about this stuff." Catholic and working-class, Mishell grew up in a California industrial town, made livelier by teen adventures into drugs and gay bars. At twenty, she tried out intercourse while parked in a public parking lot. Now thirty, red-headed Mishell is a cosmetologist.*

Almost without exception, guys will be like, "So, you have a *twin*?" You can feel it, the unspoken question in the air. They may not ask you right then and there, but eventually it's, "Could the three of us get together?" I think it's so stupid. I mean, sure we're identical twins, but she's a member of my family. I'm not attracted to her in that way. I've had men whisper things to me while I'm having sex with them: "I'm pretending I'm fucking your sister," or "Maybe you're playing with your sister." It fills me with a homicidal rage. I'm a *person*. We're not the same person with two different addresses. I feel like men should want to be with me and me only. I'm not just a convenient receptacle for perverse desires. And neither is my sister. Don't you go near her!

We were dressed alike as kids. I had to struggle so hard to forge my own identity. To this day, that's part of the reason I can't stand being considered part of a couple, because I feel like I really have to establish myself as an individual. I still struggle with it, especially when people say, "God, you guys look so much alike!" or I run into my sister's friends on the street and have to get out my identification.

I was with this guy for four years. Sex was our primary form of communication, because otherwise we just talked baby talk. I am not kidding. Then we became drug addicts. We used heroin, smoking it and snorting it. We went for a full year without having sex at all, and I didn't even really think about it at the time. He used to ask me, "Do you still find me attractive?" And I'd say,

120

Mixed Media   121

"Uh huh. Turn the channel." With heroin, you're not thinking about doing the wild thing. You're more worried where you're going to get the drugs from. You could maybe have a romantic, Platonic, lip-service-type love affair—which I think would be great. It would be nice to be in love with someone and be in love with his mind. I guess I'm kind of Gothic in my views.

Initially, drugs helped me feel bright, attractive and on the edge. They also put me in situations that I would not have been in otherwise. For example, I met this guy at a party. He was sort of a big guy, not that attractive but with this wise guy sense of humor that I've always liked. I went home with him. He was living in a warehouse space, and there was all this wild stuff lying around: pieces of leather, pieces of clothing, a prayer stall in one corner. We did some drugs and were drinking and talking. I decided to take a shower, and he gave me a fur coat, turned it inside out and said, "I want you to put this on." Actually, he came into the bathroom before I finished, dried me off and put the coat on. It felt really nice next to the skin.

He had restraints on his bed. He set up a scenario: the rich heiress and the kidnaper. Rip-away clothes. He played with me with a vibrator, and we had sex after that. I liked fucking him. He seemed like someone I could trust: honest, gentle, funny. We always talked about things before we got going. I stayed for three days. In that time, I discovered all kinds of roles and characters within, parts of myself that made me powerful and that I'd never really known before. And it was provocative and freeing to be submissive, because I could free myself from any deep-seated guilt: "He had me tied up, so I just *couldn't* get away." At the end, he put leather manacles on me and left the house. I slipped out, got my clothes and left, thinking, "Can't stay here forever. Mom and Dad are going to be wondering where I am." I left him my name and phone number, and we had an affair that went on for three months. Even though it didn't last very long, I still thought of him often and called him up when I got drunk.

Good sex involves a certain amount of fantasy, understanding, humor. There has to be trust, and you have to be able to talk to the person. I've had raunchy sex in the back seat of my Datsun—oh so cramped. Just lustful. Sex in the bathtub is slippery and fun. Masturbation is something I've explored a lot. It's generally underrated . . . . I have some fond memories of some of the wild, bizarre situations I got into, but now my whole concept of intimacy is so different. It is scary these days to consider intimacy without drugs. AIDS has really clarified things, because I do want to be involved in a relationship, and it has certainly made men more willing to use the dreaded *commitment* word. I'm worried about AIDS, although I've been tested twice and both tests came back negative. It really has changed my choice of partners, because I used to look to drug users or people hanging out. A couple of my lovers have been bisexual, and now I probably wouldn't choose them as my partners—or I'd be safer in my procedures. I have a serious stock of condoms now, so I'm ready for any eventuality. I'm ready to be involved with someone caring, tender, someone I can trust—about his past and about treating me with respect. I believe it can happen.

Steven

After leaving a sexually dissatisfying marriage, Steven began to scout the sexual terrain through swingers' parties and different kinds of couplings. A small man with dark, curly hair, who calls sex "a path to unboundedness," Steven has been involved in a nonmonogamous relationship with his girlfriend Elena for eight years.

Control's a big issue for men. It's part of the training, to always be in control. So to get down into the kind of sex where you're just *gone* is difficult for men. I think a lot of men search for ways to be sexual and maintain control at the same time. But for me, sex is an arena to investigate going out of control. That's what I like to do: to create a safe context, trip out and *go*. I think a lot of guys are afraid of that. When you go out of control, it brings up all the shame stuff again. Who knows what you'll do? "If I let my sexuality go, I'll grab every woman on the street. I'll end up slobbering with my cock walking." Because it's so bottled up.

Elena and I started setting aside weekend time for sex dates, a deliberate time and a sometimes-fabricated context for how we're going to do sex. One time we set up a scene where we pretended that we didn't know each other. I went to a bar, and I was sitting there, talking with all the guys . . . . Elena shows up, all decked out, low-cut blouse, short skirt, the whole routine. Everybody in the bar is looking at her. And *this* is a woman who doesn't think she's attractive, because she's heavier than women are supposed to be. She comes over and strikes up a conversation. We dance with each other, dance real sexy. I had my van parked outside, with a mattress in it. We fucked in the van. We had made a deal beforehand that we weren't going to drop our roles until we were actually back home. So it was hot. We had made up personas: different names, different jobs. We had a tremendous time, having sex in the van. We exchanged phone numbers and promised to call each other. I walked her to her car. And then

123

we met when we came home. It was wonderful.

One weekend, I was Elena's servant: "Just say what you want. I'm here for your pleasure." It was fun. Another time, we reversed it—not a slave, because that wasn't the image, but a servant. I told her how I wanted her to dress, make-up, everything. This was all for me, just for what pleased me. So she was off dressing, and I was suddenly terrified, because I realized I didn't know what I wanted. The notion that this was all for me—that it was okay that it was all for me—blew my whole scene. I decided I wanted to be taken care of. I wanted to be bathed or massaged. We set up a massage table, and I directed her. She leaned over me, and her breasts touched my face. Gradually, I could let myself say, "Lean over further," and I started playing with her body, and she started getting turned on.

It evolved into this scene where I was touching her, and she was getting turned on and getting into being turned on. I said, "Wait a second. You're not getting turned on for *your* pleasure, but for my pleasure. Because it's exciting for *me*." Every time it would slip over and she would get more excited, I would say, "No, this is for me." I told her that she couldn't come, and I got into turning her on more and more but not letting her come. The tension grew and grew and grew. Finally, I wasn't touching her, and she was standing with her legs wide apart, and I said, "Now you can come." She just *came*. Flooded the floor, without moving, without being touched. Just there because I wanted her to.

It was amazing. When we settled down, we looked at each other: "Where are we? What was that? What in the world do we do from here?" We had been doing extended sex dates every weekend, and we didn't do another one for about two months. The experience went so deep, we ended up in a place so new, that it made us cautious about doing it again. It took time to integrate it all. There was a sense, "If I go way out there, I won't be able to come back. I'll die. Whatever force of order is holding the cells of the body together will *dissolve*, and I'll become a puddle of protoplasm, and I'll die. Whatever organizing force life is, I'll transcend that." It's that sense of ultimate chaos. It's the journey to Ixtlan. Once you take the journey, can you go home again? Yes and no. Everything has changed, because you've done what you've done. I live for times like that.

Paris

As a child in Los Angeles, Paris read her brother's dirty books by flashlight under the covers, "and I just knew I was going to try these things." An African American with honey-colored hair and skin, Paris takes a frank and open approach to sex, from one-night stands to outdoor frolics beneath Fourth of July fireworks. "I've never dated anybody who wasn't black," she notes. "I have what they call a masculine approach to sex: it's to be done, it should be good, and you should do it as much as you want." At thirty-nine, Paris is an artist who supports herself working in a hospital lab.

I get really freestyle when I'm in bed with somebody—I don't hold back anything. In my twenties, I had one close friend who I experimented with. With him, I discovered my own sexuality: my limits, what I could take, how much I liked it. I had him tie me up and turn me upside down and take me. We'd do it in the phone booth, in the car. He was really into baths, so we'd sit in the tub for hours by candlelight. He awakened me. I learned that if you treat sex as a totally selfish act, you'll both have a good time, just tearing each other apart. Selfishness means participating, being there, building the chemistry. If you think, "I'm here to please this other person," you'll shortchange yourself.

Twelve years ago, I met the guy I live with today. When I tried to do the kinky stuff, he didn't want any part of it. I'd put on sexy underwear, and he'd say, "What do you have *that* on for?" He inhibited me. He's a road manager for a musician, travels on the road and has groupies. From the letters he's getting, he has a kinky, wild time with these girls, but he doesn't want to do that with me. He wants to keep me on another level. The women he sleeps with on the road are all white, the ones he has the hot sex with. Now why can't he come home and have wild sex with me? He's very affectionate, but when it comes to sex, it's almost mechanical, as though it isn't an important part of the relationship. Five years into the relationship, I made the decision to have affairs, because I needed that kinky spice in my life. It took me a year of thinking about it to actually do it.

Two years ago, I started having an affair with this guy who's thirteen years younger than me. I met my match when I met him. He'll do everything and is good at everything. He reeks sex. One night, he tied me up and blindfolded me. Then he shaved me really slowly, talking to me through the whole thing. I'll never do that again—it itches too much growing out—but at the time it was *erotic*. We've had sex outdoors countless times, over and over again, because he can go all night long.

I like my lover to stick his hands in my mouth, in any little hole. I used to get into the food items, but now I like hot tubs. Sometimes he just kisses me for fifteen minutes in the hot, hot water. We get into golden showers, peeing on each other. That's a real turn-on. He's a verbal person: he tells you what he's doing, what he wants to do, what he's going to do. So I am able to respond, which is something I never shared with a lover before. I never had a verbal, open sexual relationship. If we only have an hour together, he'll say, "We've got a half-hour for sex, fifteen minutes for talk time, and then fifteen more minutes for a quick one." Sex time *includes* talk time. He's a great sexual partner because he's a great communicator.

Intercourse has never been the way to get me off, but there's nothing like penetration. If the person gives you head and gets you off, or plays with you and gets you off, still the ultimate is going inside. If I like a guy, and he smells real good, I enjoy giving head immensely. I like him to come in my mouth. I like to see a guy go crazy through sex, losing his mind. Sometimes their eyes roll back in their heads, and they're just drooling. That's a total turn-on. For me, orgasm starts from the physical, but it's your sense of freedom that allows it to go wherever it's going to go. If I really love the person, it's a lot more intense.

I work in a hospital blood lab, so I'm exposed to AIDS every single day. If I get it, it'll probably be through work, not sex. I've had a free sex life, and it's hard for me to change those habits. I have a tendency to live on the edge anyway. The man I live with increases my risk, because he's always out, and he won't wear condoms with me or with other people.

My lover's not seeing anyone besides me. He's a young guy,

Mixed Media

not really together, and so I know I need to break it off, but I can't cut the sex part loose. I really would like to have a nice relationship with somebody who's hard-working, has his life together, and then have wild sex with *him*. All the women I know want a hot number for their husband. But then the men I know talk about, "This girl, she's wild in bed," but they would never marry her. I don't want to sit on the couch with somebody and watch him get a big stomach, and that's the end of sex. Sex should be an everyday part of the relationship, like eating or sleeping. It's a method of communicating, a closeness, a comfort that you find with another person. When you're with a lover—even a temporary lover—you have that sense of intimacy, warmness, that *best friend* feeling. You're totally yourself and let it all hang out with that person. They know you like nobody else.

Bill

Raised in a blue-collar Michigan town, Bill is a soft-spoken man with white hair and owlish glasses. "When I was growing up, what I figured out was straight, missionary-position sex," he says, "but I always had different ideas and feelings, which I now know are kinky." Fifty years old and in his second marriage, Bill and his wife Judy are involved in threesomes with two different women. Bill recently quit a computer job to sail to the South Pacific with Judy, and they live on their boat in the San Francisco Bay.

People think there's a line you step over and all of a sudden you're a pervert. I've tried to define that little line and found out it doesn't exist. I like sex in threes and fours. I like to be touched all over my body by one or more people at a time. Stroking, squeezing, some pain. As for SM, there's no sexual arousal there for me. I think kinky people will try anything once. They may decide they don't like what they find, but they tried it.

After we got married, Judy and I began to look around and find different lifestyles: sex with multiple partners, group sex, same-sex involvement. What we were looking for in the beginning was a third person to share a life. We're still looking. That person could be male or female, though it seems easier to find females. One woman we were seeing for a while enjoyed being tied on the bed, arms and legs spread out. No inhibitions. She liked to look into your eyes when she was coming. She'd want to be fucked, "I want your cock. I want it now." It brought out the "top" in me: having that control was pleasurable, making someone do what you want, seeing her move, seeing her enjoy it.

Women dressing up with a harness and a dildo really works. That's a tremendous turn on. The look of a cock hanging off of a woman—even if it's a dildo, the look is still there. It's fun to get down and suck the cock. The smell of leather and pussy together is *wonderful*. The excitement of having both genders together . . . I fell in love briefly with a transvestite. I found myself wanting to reach under her dress and feel her cock. I

128

Mixed Media

wanted both. I could see one and couldn't see the other, but they were both *right* there . . . things being veiled, revealed . . . . What's exciting is the unknown. What does someone look like with their clothes off? What's the coloring of her vagina? What's his cock look like? Women's nipples. Men's nipples. Rings through them.

Bisexuality with men . . . there's more to it than being sexual. It's a general feeling and acceptance of men as people rather than someone to watch baseball with. Someone you can talk to about problems, get support from, experience a closeness that doesn't have to come out in a sexual medium. It would be nice to have sex with men—fucking sex, but it's just too scary. Because of AIDS. I'm afraid of that. I'd much rather get into a contact of touching rather than fucking. It's happened in group situations. There was a group of us fooling around on a picnic table on Mount Diablo one night. Three men and two women. After a while, I forgot the women were there and was just touching the men, holding their cocks, holding their balls. The only intercourse that took place was between one man and one woman. I managed to get my finger in her vagina while he was fucking her, and I could stimulate the end of his cock—and her clit at the same time with my thumb. A woman was sucking on my cock, and I almost didn't know she was there, my concentration was so much on what was going on with the other two.

For Judy and me, our main way of being sexual is just the two of us, not a group thing. Now that we're not working, we find we have a lot more time for sex. We'll wake up at six o'clock in the morning, make love, go to sleep, wake up and do it again, sometimes all morning long. We'll fantasize about fucking somebody else: "I want to see this person do this to you." Or, "I'm going to fuck your ass now"—*doing* none of that, but talking about it. Lately, she will masturbate me and fuck my ass with a finger or two. Lubricated fingers, latex gloves. Doesn't everyone have Crisco next to the bed? We hold each other and touch. A lot of oral sex. Vibrators. Masturbating ourselves, together. She's one of those women who can have one orgasm after another. Occasionally I try to count and *lose* count. If she tells me when she's starting to come, that turns me on more, and we will more than likely have an orgasm together or very close. Coming together is more powerful, more intense, longer. And also you can collapse together . . . . Good sex is mutual enjoyment, mutual fulfillment. You want to do it again.

We were out sailing the other day, and I said, "I think it would be nice if you started sucking the captain's cock right now." Out on the bay. She did, after looking around. Two miles from anything, but you still look around.

Carolan

Three-year-old Carolan loved her father, a World War II Canadian Air Force pilot. "When he was killed, it was like God left me," she says. "From that time forth, I kept the connection to my divinity through my sexuality." In Calgary, she managed a boutique specializing in sexual and sensual supplies. In California, she launched a business in "pleasure parties," women's coffee klatsches where sexual wares were displayed and discussed. Now a blue-eyed forty-nine-year-old with four grown children, Carolan leads women's workshops on spirituality and—occasionally—sexuality.

Probably the most erotic experiences of my life were as a teenager making out in the back seat of a car, because I was so armored with girdles and nylons, and it was so much fun playing the game of seeing if he could get into my pants. For me, the build-up is better than the intercourse. It still is. I got pregnant at fifteen. It was a classic fifties situation. We didn't know about birth control. There was no possibility of abortion. I thought if I wiped the semen out with Kleenex, I wouldn't get pregnant. The secrecy, the shame, having my mother call me a slut: that really made it difficult for me as a woman to trust my desire. I'm still struggling with how to trust a man and let him give me pleasure.

I got married at nineteen. Sex disintegrated into this two-minute thing. I didn't know about my body, the clitoris, how orgasm happened, and yet I had a lot of desire and sexual energy. Finally, when I was twenty-eight, I learned how to masturbate to orgasm: I was sitting in a dentist's office with my little toddlers, swinging my legs, reading *Time*, suddenly building up this enormous heat and pressure and *pow*! I just grabbed the kids, went home and sat on the edge of my bed for two weeks until my thighs were so sore I couldn't move. I learned to have orgasms by crossing my legs.

Receiving pleasure is tough for me: laying back, letting go, being given orgasms, being treated royally. I can give *myself* pleasure endlessly: bubble baths, reading erotic literature, using my vibrator and having twenty-five orgasms in a row. Not having an orgasm, holding that edge, riding the wave of pleasure while I'm stimulating myself. Sometimes I lie down on my vibrator, sometimes I lie on my back, sometimes I lie on my side, sometimes I dress up in lingerie and get real raunchy with myself. I love doing it when my lover Nick calls. We'll talk on the phone and masturbate. Masturbation is part of my lifestyle.

I don't have a lot of orgasms with Nick when we're making love. I feel like my orgasms are mine, and I spend my time with them myself, much more than I do with him. But I'm interested in changing that. Playing with him, sometimes I really like to be bitten, have my nipples twisted, be roughly taken, pulled down and taken quickly. Sometimes I like to be played with and tantalized for hours. Laughter's important. I love that he talks to me. Sometimes what I'd like—and we don't do a lot of—is tenderness. Sweet, sweet, tender kisses, this melting feeling that you both have, that you're merging into each other.

Sex is much better if you build up to it. All day, preferably. Sometimes I'll dress up in my Merry Widow corsets and wear them underneath my clothes. With a former partner, I was into dressing up as a little girl, in kilts and knee-socks. I love wearing a strap-on dildo and fucking a man from behind. I think that's really erotic. Men love it: it facilitates the intensity of their orgasms. And I feel really powerful, in control, sexy. Toys are really fun: blindfolds expand your senses. Fur mitts, feathers, massage. Tying each other up. Tantalizing each other . . . . I used to think you should say, "Put your hand here, touch me this way." But that isn't the way some people respond—men especially. With Nick, as soon as anybody starts telling him what to do, he shuts down. Sometimes fantasies work well. He's all in his fantasy about me and another women, and I say, "Well, what she *really* wants you to do is this." That way he comes around to it.

My sexuality was my identity for a long time. I remember when I was a teenager, thinking, "What these guys want is somebody that's good in bed, so I'll be good in bed." I became very "good in bed" and put a lot of creativity into my sexuality, but it was about how to *give* pleasure, not how to receive it. A

Mixed Media

common thread that I see with women—including me—is that we don't trust our lust. We don't own it and say, "This is *my* desire. What do I want to do with it? This is *my* body. What do I want to do with it? It isn't my partner that turns me on or gives me an orgasm. It's me." As women, we've got to respect our passionate, lusty nature. I still struggle with that, even after being in the sex toy business for fifteen years and listening to tens of thousands of women.

What I've realized is that it was longing that took me down the road of sexual experimentation. When I got to a certain point, I found that what I was longing for wasn't there. It isn't in how many ways you can fuck somebody. My longing is to come back to my divine source, through a sexual connection with a partner. I'm not saying I just want sex to be spiritual. I love lusty fucking: yesterday morning, we fucked in the living room, up and down the stairs, up on the kitchen counter. To me, sex is a mystery, but one I've mastered to some extent. Now I want to master *relationship*.

Pamela

"We equate good looks with good sex. That's what the advertisements have done to us," says blue-eyed Pamela, a former homecoming queen from Nebraska. "I have a beautiful face, but my body is not one that automatically qualifies for beautiful because of my disability." Stricken by polio as a toddler, she grew up as "the cute kid on crutches" in the care of an alcoholic father who molested her till she was twenty. Now a video producer and performance artist, this wheelchair-driving forty-two-year-old inhabits a snug Berkeley apartment garnished with collages of commercial beauty—female body builders and lingerie models.

When I was a teenager, I felt very, very lonely. I wasn't dating. The first man who ever admired me was killed in Vietnam. I had a stepmother, and I remember overhearing her mother say, "Poor Pammy, she just doesn't understand that no decent man is ever going to be interested in her." I think a lot of the reason I did so much experimenting—once I became sexual—was that I had gone through such a lonely period, I didn't want to let an opportunity go by. I would rarely turn down a chance to have sex. When I realized that being alone was better than being in some relationships, I began to be able to say no.

With my husband, it was lust at first sight. We had very, very good sex. That's probably the reason the marriage lasted six years. We would role play a lot: we lived in a house heated with a wood stove, so there was the fantasy of the woodsman delivering the wood, and I didn't have the money to pay for it. Oh, what could I *do* to pay for it? We'd do things like tie beads on a string, insert them anally and slowly pull them out. One time for Christmas, he gave me a paraffin mold of his cock—a dildo exactly shaped like his cock. He said making it was a little painful.

I'm now with a man in a nonmonogamous relationship, and we've been together for a little over three years. We're both bisexuals, but we're mainly active with the opposite sex. With men, sometimes I like just a good hard fuck. Short experiences. With women, I like intensity, being sensual and building gradually to

Mixed Media 135

an intense level. With both, I like an element of hardness, but not to the degree of pain. I like to be on the edge: to have my breasts squeezed, my nipples bit, to know that the threat is there. I like to role play. Not hard-core SM . . . surface SM. I've played with being tied up, peed on, verbally humiliated. I don't like pain. Most of the time I've been the submissive, and it's a real rush, because I can reach levels of orgasm in unique ways through total surrender. All my inhibitions are also surrendered, and I reach levels of climax I can't access other ways.

We come from a repressed society, and we buy into a lot of "shoulds" and "shouldn'ts." We're so taught to be polite: "This is the way you walk. This is the way you talk. Don't drool." So rigid, so controlled, so afraid of getting out of control . . . . You go to a rock concert, and people are hardly *moving* because they're afraid of what other people will think of them. Even though I'm very open sexually, I have a lot of blocks, too: always worrying about pleasing my partner or my own need to get pleased. All my life, I've had to be so together—to figure everything out, have it organized. So in SM, playing the submissive role, where nothing is relevant but what this other person *tells* me is relevant, creates such a high, such a rush. A good dominant won't push me on things to make me bolt but will help me get to that high. It's so orgasmic. You release all the programming you've gotten, and you're at the core of who you are.

SM is an accent. It's not the main thing I do. There's a temptation to make it more important, but it tends to cloud up a relationship. I don't do SM with my boyfriend, because I'm working on an intimate relationship with him, and I've found that kind of sex interfering with my ability to get intimate. With somebody you're just having sex with, it's easier to define yourself as a dominant or submissive. I haven't done a lot of successful dominance, but I would love to. It's more like, "Do this . . . uh, if you want to." I feel that dominance would help me. I've spent so much of my life being passive—manipulating people, but in a sweet way. It would be a contrast to my co-dependent behavior and maybe healing for me. But it's hard to find partners who really want to be submissive. They say they do.

Nonmonogamy works for me. It's nice to have a relationship where I have fun, sensual, free sex, and at the same time have the freedom to go out and have a wild, electric fling. Very rarely in a committed relationship do I get that total abandonment—except when I'm ovulating. Then it's, "I want fuck now. *Quick.*" Intense craving comes over me. If I could use a telephone pole, I probably would. I'm multi-orgasmic, mostly vaginally. My most frequent orgasm would be clitoral, which I rarely reach with men, often reach with women and almost always reach with myself. Plus, I've perfected this wonderful ability to orgasm without touching myself. It started one day on the BART train when I was ovulating, and I felt myself throbbing. I started running a fantasy in my mind and discovered I could bring myself to orgasm. The only trouble with a public place is you have to control your breathing.

I don't want to limit my animal drives. I don't feel any moral or social problem with that, but there is a physical risk today because of AIDS. As far as safe sex goes, I'm enjoying phone sex, mutual masturbation. With one guy I'm having a fling with, we only have phone sex. I will not have intercourse with a partner who has not been tested for HIV. Anal sex is definitely out. Oral sex is a real dilemma. With men, my solution so far has been to not orally take in the head of the penis . . . . My partner uses condoms with other people. I'm allergic to rubbers, and I used to rely on animal skin condoms, but they're not barriers to the AIDS virus. So a male partner needs to wear two condoms—the rubber one first and then the animal skin one over it . . . . I mourn the loss of the zipless fuck. The hardest dilemma for me is whether I should be using safe sex in my fantasies. I feel guilty if I don't!

The quality of sex I'm having is higher today, though it's less frequent. My sexuality is less proscribed by society. I've been in intensive counseling for incest, I'm working on intimacy, I've had a lot of positive sexual experience, and I don't feel I need to prove anything anymore. I shape my sexuality now, whereas before it was shaped for me. In good sex, you're in sync with your partner. Your timing is right. If you both want a brief encounter, that can be good sex. Or if you both want a nice long evening together, that can be good sex. You can be very natural with each other, you can ask for what you want, you know your partner will ask for what he or she wants. And most of the time, you're willing to grant those requests.

Morgan

Morgan found pleasures in pubescent circle-jerks, transvestism and masturbating with condoms filched from an older brother's stash. "They were simple rubbers with a paper band around them, like on a roll of hundred dollar bills. No muss, no fuss, just instant clean-up," says the thirty-eight-year-old Californian, casually attired in penny loafers, jeans and plaid. He has revived those early practices as part of his wide-ranging safe sex activities. A lean man with red-brown hair, Morgan works as a chiropractor.

The male role is not confining. It's limitless, but it's just the male role. The penultimate role, the warrior, I've done: I was in the military and killed. I spent ten years as a truck driver. I've done construction work. I was a husband, part of a het couple, slipping into middle America, that furtive, scared group of people. I understand what it is to be a man, and I understand the rituals: to camp, cook, live in the woods with nothing but a sharp knife. I know how to do those things, and they're fun, but other things are fun, too.

In this society, adults are not supposed to play. We're supposed to work, to be consumers. One of the things that lies at the core of who I am is that I want to go play. Adopting a persona provides me with the ability to sidestep the daily roles. I can become the daddy, the little boy, the little girl. I can fall into these characters and play at them in an adult way—a sexual way. I can really learn what *grovel* means and get off on it. What does virginity mean, and how many times can we recreate it? I can be the blushing bride, the proud groom—or the jockey, for that matter. There are aspects of all those characters in us.

At fourteen, I discovered two things at the same time: sex with women and cross-dressing. I found myself involved with a young woman who said, "Here, try these." I tried on a pair of her panties, and we rubbed around on the bed with each other and necked. We didn't have intercourse, but I had a really hot orgasm, and so did she. I got turned on to wearing panties. I ordered stuff

137

from the Sears catalogue and had it delivered to her house, and we'd play dress-up. I thought I was all alone, the only boy in the world who did this. Then I talked to one of my friends, and he was buying tight, silky drawers through weight-lifting catalogues. I was seventeen when I saw my first Fredericks catalogue, and I knew that stuff wasn't for women.

With lingerie, I like the feel of the fabrics, the transgressional aspect of it. Even with my six-foot-two, two hundred-pound body, I like the look of it. I like the feeling of being nasty, and the responses of people who find it hot. It's an interesting concept that these are women's clothes—*I* bought them; they're *mine*. And yet it explores an aspect of feminine nature. I don't know that I can understand what being female is . . . . I know that when I'm on my back being fucked by somebody with a strap-on, I don't think of myself as a woman. I think of myself as a man in hot drag being fucked. When I'm *able* to think . . . .

In an erotic context, my butch role would be playing Daddy, playing the masculine savior-hero, taking the position of physical power, being rough-and-tumble and throwing somebody against a wall, playing slap-around, restraining someone. Force and physical power. In SM, I can be butch from the other end: having someone push me around as a *man*, removing my physical power and yet still being male. But I can also be a woman, a slut, a princess—Lord knows I can do a queen! I can make up my own characters, play those roles, do the things most people only do in a sedate way on Halloween.

With my girlfriend, there's a level of intimacy that I've never had with anybody I can name. In previous love relationships, the feeling has flashed and faded. With her, it's stuck. We're adventurous, and we explore romance as deeply as we possibly can. Many would say we're hypersexual perverts. We've explored Kundalini, tantra, shower sex, public sex and you-name-it nasty. Most of my drag is at her house now—about forty or fifty pounds of lingerie. I have two or three times that in leather and latex, and several shipping boxes of toys.

Face-to-face intercourse happens to be one of the most romantic, deep, atavistic things that I can do, but it doesn't get me off. I like to masturbate, put things in my ass and play with toys. I especially like shower-play: "If you'll wash it, I'll lick it." I like

Mixed Media

slow, long, hot, wet sex things. I like being fucked and fucking. Tongues, toes, fingers. Cuddling, romantic holding, kissing . . . . Kissing is oral sex. Hands in me and on me. All of those are good sex. I enjoy fisting, having *large* things put into me, the sense of pressure, the sense of connection. Even through a latex glove, it's very connected, very centering. And something *that* large and alive coming out of me—and this is sheer envy on my part—is as near as I can get to giving birth.

Orgasm is many different things. Coming takes me away from the cares of the world, through joy and intimacy. There's a sense of being all-powerful: it wouldn't matter, at the moment of orgasm, if I died. It takes me out of the earth, in touch with the universe. It can take me there, or to that place where I want to kneel on the bathroom floor while somebody fucks me from behind: "Just *use* me." I know that feeling of being so hot I'm drooling.

In 1979, there was a lot of disease going around, and I had friends who were worried about hepatitis. I stopped having sex with men, but not with women. In 1981, I heard about safer sex. That got my attention. That meant I could go back to all the things I like to do: masturbating with condoms, playing with vibrators, expressing myself in drag around other people, sitting on a couch and kissing somebody for hours till my heart wants to break out of my chest. A few years ago, I started doing volunteer work for safe sex parties, being a monitor and a model for safe sex. I can show people how to have a good, hot, sexy time without swapping body fluids. I do it from a playful standpoint, a public health standpoint. And I do it because it feels good. You can find me coated in lace, latex, lube, leather . . . . It's like a playhouse now.

Sybil

A tall forty-two-year-old with henna-red hair, Sybil works as a professional dominant. Her work space includes an elaborate SM dungeon dripping in restraints and a cozy fantasy room stocked with costumes and baby toys. Sybil was born in a Massachusetts mill town. She was an outspoken, passionate child in a family of hard-working New Englanders who did not express emotions. Sybil entered the sex industry at twenty and found that stripping suited her dramatic disposition.

I liked everything about burlesque dancing. I loved the autonomy, the travel, the pretty clothes, the partying. Good wages. This was from 1968 to 1980, an era where strippers were well-paid, had choreographed acts and beautiful costumes. I had several acts: a cowboy act, a little girl act, a slinky siren act, a biker act, a baby-oil and powder act. As I reached thirty, dancing was changing, and what I loved about it was going away. More and more, you were being required to sit and rub on the men in the audience, get your clothes off *much* faster and do a gynecological spread, crawl up and down the runway on your hands and knees and show your cunt for money. To me, this was not what burlesque and stripping was about. The word was strip *tease*. Anybody can put their legs into a V. To tease takes talent. Naughty, but not designed to get the guy off. Now they want bunny beaver. Eighteen-year-olds, not real women.

I started to go to college, because I could see the handwriting on the wall. I had decided to be a dental hygienist. I couldn't really understand *why* I wanted to be a dental hygienist, but years later, after being in the SM world a long time, I figured it out: "I'm in a uniform, they're not. I'm standing up, they're lying down. I'm doing painful things to them for their own good. This is so *me*."

In 1983, I went to work as a professional dominant in training. I was submissive to the mistress and, under her instruction, dominant over the clients. It was a great way to learn. At first it was

Mixed Media

hard for me to assume the dominant role, to take that first jump and say, "I'm in charge!" That's changed with practice. I learned that I liked SM from both sides—I liked intense sensation. There had been times in traditional sex—intercourse, vanilla sex, whatever you want to call it—where my mind would wander, where gentle touch wasn't enough to focus me. That's not true in SM. You are *present* because the sensation keeps you in your body. I also liked the trappings, because I'm a theatrical girl. So I loved the costumes, I loved being dressed or dressing somebody else exactly the way I wanted. I found I could be turned on for a whole day, not come, not have sex and not be in love. It was remarkable for me to separate love and sex.

I entered into the world of sexual theater. In my professional work I cann myself a "fantasy facilitator," because I support people's fantasies coming to life. I'm in charge, but I provide a service. I have three areas of specialty. One is gender, a lot of cross-dressing. That is where I teach men how to walk, how to sit, how to put on make-up, how to create a figure and how to be receptive sexually, how not to be the initiator. Then the SM clients are interested in being whipped, cropped, caned, paddled, getting nipple work, cock and ball work. Some are masochistic without being submissive: they just want the sensation. For others, the sensation is a tool by which they surrender. With SM, there's a point where the sensation builds up to such a degree that you let go inside and *fly*. The third group of clients are submissives. They want to serve, clean my house, polish my boots. They want to be controlled by me mentally. It's a release from everyday pressures. So I have a lot of very high-powered executives—it's the classic scenario, but true—who are not necessarily interested in getting off. What they want is to have their minds stop.

I enjoy taking people's power away from them in the outside world and finding out what power they have that's innate. I like taking away their clothes, their responsibility, controlling their mind, meaning that they have to speak a certain way, can only speak with my permission, have to ask my permission to pee, eat, drink and move. This provides a wonderful container for a person to let go and not be in charge. And it's hypnotic for both us. Very erotic. What I find sexy is the intimacy of trust: their willingness to be so vulnerable means they trust me a good deal.

I like to dress them up in a way that appeals to me, to bring out what is hidden: a little girl, a grown woman, a sexual priest. That takes time and intuition, but I've got tons of clothes and lots of rope, make-up and masks. I've never had oral, anal or vaginal sex with my clients, and I don't masturbate them. That's illegal. Some of my clients masturbate themselves under my instruction. That's not illegal.

In my personal life, as opposed to my professional work, I'm currently with my life partner, and I'm very, *very* happy. We've been together three and a half years, and we keep falling in love . . . . I love to kiss. I *love* to kiss. I love to bite necks and leave hickeys. I'm also a sadist, and it's not about damage or anger; it's about intensity. The more you're turned on, the more sensation you like. I like starting out medium: I'm in charge, and I like having my cunt eaten exactly the way I want, having fingers used on me, being fucked just the way I want, and from a dominant perspective. Taking a person on a pleasure journey can be a dominant act. Domination does not have to mean it's painful, nasty or unpleasant. I'm simply being the initiator. It can be fucking, sucking, giving head. It's not about clothes or body position, it's about my *attitude*: telling him how to do it, to slow down, slapping his ass, biting his neck, "No, you can't come. I have to come one more time."

Good sex for me is no longer rubbing two parts together. It's good communication, but even more than that, good sex is about consciousness, being awake, knowing what I like. In our society, we are not supposed to talk about sex. The people who do have a fuller relationship. Sex is full of the stuff we have in our fantasy worlds. In my lover's face, I see the child come and go, the girl come and go, the orphan, the warrior, the mother, the magician. Sex is a body language and a mental game in which are many hidden parts of ourselves, and if we don't share that, we don't share parts of ourselves. When you do share it, you bring all the rest of you to the relationship. You bring a kind of physical intimacy and emotional intimacy. It takes me very close to my partner. There have been times I could not tell if I was me or him. The envelope of my individuality blurs, and I lose track of that, and it's incredibly intimate. Time stops in that moment, and I feel like I'm just love. I don't have a name, I don't have a job, worries go away, everything stops, and there's just love. If one could say sex is *for* something, I would say it could be for that.

But I also think sex is just plain for fun, and I don't want to be high-minded about it. There's nothing wrong with sex for sex's sake. It can be a transcendental experience, a lot of fun, a release of tension. Sex is a lot more complicated than we know. It has many, many functions—and it's not just to make babies. I think we're only starting to learn what sex is for. Sex is for what you make it, as long as it's consensual. You're only limited by your imagination.

Jack

Jack grew up a fair-haired sissy, a lonely child who often contemplated suicide. At fifteen, he had his first conversation about being gay with a man he tracked down through a gay newspaper. That night, Jack's father said he was worried to see his son look so happy. In college, Jack became interested in SM through reading The Story of O *and finding himself identifying strongly with the central character. Today, at thirty-six, Jack is part of the San Francisco leather scene and works as a writer and Episcopal lay minister.*

S adist. I dislike the term used to imply brutality, the whole idea that a sadist is an evil, vicious person, or that a masochist is a totally sick puppy. I prefer the term sadomasochist, and it's a real interesting thing about SM: people who are into it call it SM, and people who aren't call it S *and* M. I'm into SM. It's one thing. I enjoy top and bottom. I get a certain amount of validation and strengthening when I get a really good whipping. I feel a tremendous amount of validation and strength when I give a good whipping. There is a very deep bond that exists—however ephemeral—with my partner. The best part of that strength is being able to nurture: I'm giving somebody something that he wants, that he needs.

The whole notion that sex is a matter of putting a penis inside a cunt . . . well, if that's all there is, let's keep dancing. It's a whole body experience. I can feel incredible waves of pleasure, joy, and eroticism in my throat, in my ass, along my thighs, in my ankles, anywhere. Sex is a full-body experience. The real joy is in being with another person, and the physical charge is anywhere in the body. And this *obsession* with genital sexuality, well, that's a relatively small part of the whole picture.

Guys who are afraid to have their asses touched are missing out on a tremendous amount of pleasure. The direct stimulation of the prostate is just exquisite. I think a lot of guys experience their sexuality outside of themselves—I'm talking about men in

Mixed Media 145

general. If a man is fucking a woman or another man, then what's going on is outside of his own body, and he's just entering into the ass or vagina. But when a guy's taking it inside himself, you just feel it *within*. And you're *filled* with pleasure, you're *filled* with the sensations. It waves all through you, and it's just fabulous, just wonderful.

I was really eager to explore the feelings connected to SM, but I had no idea what I was doing or where I was going. Terrified. So I went down to a leather bar, and as I'm walking up to the bar, I see two big burly guys in black leather jackets, chaps, boots, black leather hats, dripping chains. These big, heavy-duty leathermen are discussing *antiques*. So the leather bar is not so frightening and butch as I thought. Now where do I really find out about this SM stuff? I went to a bathhouse called the Slot, a real sleaze palace. The action was not too shocking, not too different, until I started going down on this guy, and he's not getting hard. I just work, work, work, and he's not getting hard. All of a sudden he starts pissing in my mouth. I pulled away, I got up, I ran to the bathroom, washed out my mouth, got my clothes, got home, rinsed and gargled, rinsed and gargled—I don't know how many times. I got in my own bed and thought, "Well, lots of guys do it. It wasn't really that bad, I was just shocked. I'll give it another try." I went back to the Slot, got soaked, loved it.

One of the things about being an adventurer is that you find yourself in situations that are not always pleasant. The whole business of adventure is risk taking. If you don't risk, you don't gain, and you have to be willing to lose in order to win.

Mostly I enjoy bondage, whipping, paddling, spanking, various forms of pain. I love electricity. Almost anything I do as a top I do as a bottom. It's important to experience something from both sides to really understand what it's about, and I would not do to someone else anything that I'm not willing to have done to me. I want to be able to empathize with my partner. That's a very important part of the intimacy. I like a paddle. Doesn't matter which side of it I'm on . . . . Candle wax, cock and ball bondage and weights—with piercings, there's a lot more you can do with weights. I have some permanent piercings, done professionally.

If we're getting into space that is especially risky—either physically or psychologically—we do what's called a "safe word." When I'm introducing the safe word, I'll say, "The safe word is *mercy*. If you say no, I'll say yes. If you say stop, I'm gonna go. If you say easy, I'm gonna beat you harder. If you beg for me to stop, I'm gonna pound you a lot harder. If you say mercy, I'll let you go, and I'll ease off on you. Now what's the safe word, boy? Good boy. Don't say it again until you mean it." And very rarely do we have to use it.

Sex brings me to myself and it's also very transcendent. There is a point where I feel at one with the universe, and I feel that much more as a bottom than as a top. Not by degree, but it's easier to achieve. When I'm a bottom, and the endorphins take over, and there's a really good master who's got me right where I need to be, there's this merging of the universe, this transcendence. It's a matter of being totally and completely there with another person. A moment of perfection. There are all sorts of different ways that can happen . . . . I enjoy SM, but I don't have to do it all the time. I also enjoy vanilla sex. It doesn't get me to the same place, but I don't always want to go there. What I can feel with vanilla sex can be very wonderful. Cherishing, gentle, wonderfully good. Intense, but a different kind of intensity. Sex does not have one goal, one purpose. There are times I love the open abandon of certain group scenes. There are times I like the intense personal sharing when I'm having sex with a friend, somebody I do love, somebody I trust at a lot of levels. At other times, I love the adventure and exploration of anonymous sex. Good sex happens when the partners are paying good attention to each other, when they truly care about each other—whether they've just met or been friends and lovers for many, many years. The universality of good sex is empathy, attentiveness and caring, and everything revolves around that.

V. SEXUAL HEALING

Ringing up potential interview candidates, I found that frank discussions about sex opened the floodgates to reports of physical and psychological violation. The deluge was disturbing, though the individual stories were often hopeful and resolute. "I'm damned if I'm going to let it wreck my life," declared one woman. "I'm very sexual with my partner. I still want to have a good time, and I love sex." Those sentiments echo throughout Sexual Healing's ten interviews. These are vibrant self-portraits, different from the victim images framed by tabloid TV, where abuse survivors are readily granted expertise on bad sex and compulsion. But these are women and men with plenty to say about *positive* sexuality. They cannot be so quickly dismissed.

In some instances, I sought out this chapter's contributors for their insights into the complexities of the healing process. Others who appear in these pages did not actually disclose their assault issues up-front. Maya, for example, took an upbeat, bubbly approach to sex in her advance interview by phone, although she wept through much of the subsequent conversation recorded at her kitchen table. Several other interviews with young people, which are not included, suggested unrecognized traumatic episodes. For example, a celibate twenty-two-year-old maintained that she had no memory of her childhood. Yet she did recall her parents virtually training her sister to be the slut they condemned, her own fear of enraging her father by bringing home male schoolmates, and her adolescent longing to be an angel, "because angels don't have sex."

The interviewees presented here frequently took an optimistic tone, but they never simplified the process of recovery. Each is a personal exploration. Some commentaries, especially from those working with counselors, emphasized gains in communication skills and success in securing personal boundaries. Barbara accentuated the reawakening of sensory pleasure. Rachel shared her hopes for healthier relationships and described a renewed sense of self.

In these stories, traditional sex roles add to the damage—particularly the social sanction given to male aggression and female submission. David, looking back at beliefs that shaped his once-abusive behavior, explained, "It's part of the man's role to be in control and never ask . . . . If I never hear 'No,' then it's up to me to experiment and see how far I can get." Women described survival patterns conditioned by abuse: passivity, flirtation, provocative behavior, the automatic dip and sway of acquiescence. "Daddy set me up to be the perfect rape victim," Veronica stated with bright bitterness. Later, she added, "I think a lot of men have to be educated not to be perpetrators and to touch in a loving way, not a grabbing, using way. There were times when my fiancé touched me that felt like a perpetrator-type touch, but I've worked on sharing my feelings, and he's working on changing his behavior."

Veronica earns her living in prostitution, which she described as an avenue for her to explore the still explosive issues of consent and control. Body-based adjuncts to more conventional forms of therapy appear in two other interviews. Cathie, an SM enthusiast, teamed up with a man to redefine daddy-daughter roles. "He was a catalyst for me, a dominant man who helped me," she said. "He listened to me when I talked about my abuse. He made me feel safe." The physical practice of martial arts has boosted Judy's self-esteem and assertiveness. "And that goes right into claiming how I am sexually," she said firmly, "which means saying what I want and what makes me feel good, instead of just pleasing the other person or being passive."

Never simple, sexual self-determination is one of the hearty demands ringing throughout this chapter. In ten very different interviews, Sexual Healing captures brief moments in extensive struggles to dispel ghosts and possess the present. "During my childhood abuse, I used to just mentally vanish from the room," one woman told me. "Now, good sex is *being*, staying there and feeling it all the way through. In recent years, I've been able to claim sex on my own terms and not ever doubt it again."

Barbara

As a child in rural Minnesota, Barbara often fell asleep at her school desk, weary from nighttime vigilance against molestation. She married young and had two children by age twenty-one. A quiet, passionate woman, Barbara has actively pursued recovery from early sexual abuse through therapy, self-awareness and public speaking. At thirty-eight, the former social worker now makes her living as an independent construction contractor. She lives with her lover and is helping raise an infant grandson.

Most of my stuff stems from being abused, being victimized, being manipulated, and knowing shame. I had three older brothers, all sexually abusive from the time I was five years old. They also abused each other and my sisters. As a youngster, it was my brothers and neighborhood boys playing games. They'd take over, wouldn't let me out of the room. I was the only girl. These boys were three or four years older, so I obviously wasn't going to beat them up. Penetration didn't take place till I was seven. I told my mother. She believes that whatever men or boys do, you're supposed to be available to them.

I knew that if I got a boyfriend, my brothers would leave me alone. That was their message to me. I got married at seventeen to get out of the house. This guy seemed like my friend. I thought I was going to be married for the rest of my life, but it wasn't a healthy relationship. There was abuse, battering. My husband was pretty good sexually, but it was always around his needs, when he wanted it. I was submissive. I was the pleasure piece.

I had always been attracted to women. The fond memories of childhood are the ones associated with me being a lesbian: sexual relationships with my girlfriends at camp—not abusive, very mutual. I had a girlfriend from the time I was twelve on. My safest and most enjoyable sexual experiences were with women. During my marriage, which lasted six years, I met a woman who knocked my socks off. I told her, she freaked out, somehow we got together, I got divorced. She and I were together for four years. It was fantastic: sex became a giving and taking relationship, an opportunity to feel the nurturing that could go on between two people.

My current girlfriend Catherine and I have been together eight years. She's also an incest survivor. With her, sex starts with a lot of touching, sometimes massage with heated oil. Rubbing of shoulders, arms, fingers and palms. Maybe a bath and washing my lover's hair. If we move into a sexual place, it's by finding those stimulating parts on the body. Touching my breasts, touching my nipples with her tongue or hands. Deep kisses . . . . I try not to lose contact with my lover's face or breasts—because it's easy coming from an incest background to detach from the body, and I want to make sure that her toes are still there, and her knees are okay, and her arms are still with me. Is she making noises? Slow movements? If I feel a lot of wetness, I know I can go further, stroking her outer lips slowly or fast.

My legs and groin aren't as conscious as my breasts. My clitoris does not like to be touched directly, but to the side. My inner lips: I don't know if I feel sensitivity. Sensation on the outer part of my lips registers in my thighs and alerts the groin, the uterus. I'm not always ready to be entered right away. I want it to be slow . . . . If she sucks on my nipples, my vagina swells and lubricates. When I feel that stimulation from breast to pelvis, and they're *one*, that's when I want Catherine to enter me. Sometimes with one finger, sometimes with two, sometimes with a latex glove and lubrication, entering me with a fist. To me, orgasms and climaxes are different things. When I have a climax, it's centered . . . around the clitoris or just in the vagina. In orgasm, my whole body responds, not just the walls of my vagina. My toes tingle, my knees shake, the flow goes through my whole body.

Together we create a bond, so there's a lot of nurturing involved, an extra reaching out, paying attention to each other's feelings, to how my body's reacting to her touching or our movement. I'm on the same awareness level as my partner, which creates this energy that intensifies the orgasm or climax. My skin warms, my veins open. I'm sensing my partner and her pleasure at the same time. Good sex is that concentration never getting broken, just exploding—even to a higher plane. It doesn't dissipate after orgasm. It's an interaction between two people where you're touching each other's souls. You've touched the body, your genitals,

Sexual Healing

your breasts, your lips—every part of your body is tingling, and it lasts a minimum of three hours.

Who I am as a lesbian doesn't mean I wouldn't have sexual desire for a man. I take an androgynous approach: I'm interested in the *person*. There are things I remember about being with a man that I like: penetration, the rubbing part of it, the feel of the penis in my vagina, filling it up. The one thing I didn't like was the ejaculation, the feeling of sperm. It interfered with my own lubrication and felt intrusive. Today, if I decided to be with a man, I'd ask him to pull out before ejaculating—or, in this day and age, definitely to use a condom. At this point in time, penetration comes to me in a lot of different ways. I went and bought a dildo. I used it for a while and it was *awful!* I ended up throwing the fucker away. I didn't use it with a partner—just an individual sexual thing. I live out more fantasies and experiment more on my own, and I fantasize about many women caressing my body.

I have been lesbian longer now than I have been heterosexual. It's so cool. People say, "It's just a phase, coming out of an abusive relationship. When she finds a nice, nurturing man, she'll be herself again." My mother and brothers cling to that idea. Well, I've been myself all along. Had I had the life of some of the young women I've met who got to come out in high school, I probably would not have had those terrible ten years in my life. *That* was my phase.

Luke

In the midst of New York City, Luke's childhood world was tiny, made up only of his mother's seething, silent house and his school across the street. Black and middle-class, he spent his teen years in social isolation at a Massachusetts boarding school, where he learned the fundamentals of sex from books. At thirty-two, he left New York and moved West. "I came to California to change myself, starting from ground zero," he says. "I did my damnedest to stop mistreating women, being mean, narrow, unwilling to fully consider the other person. And I tried to give up fear of emotional entanglement." A lean, elongated man, Luke is a poet and mental health counselor.

I'm a person approaching sex from not knowing. I think about myself being chronologically fifty-four and feeling somewhat younger and not knowing what to do with that. I want a good partnership with a good woman, whatever format that would take, and yet I don't want to make that a be-all and end-all. I've gone through a long period of time in my life where I feel like a ghost, where I'm not responsive to anything, hardly responsive to myself. I can go from motion to motion to motion, wondering why. I don't think I helped myself too much, drinking everything I could get my hands on up until six years ago.

At eighteen, I got involved with a woman, and that was quite an awakening. The importance of erotic sensation, the closeness, sweetness, warmth. That something like this would exist in my life was totally beyond my ken. It was an introduction to another world. I probably experienced as much erotic sensation with her in those three years as any time since, even with very little sexual intercourse at all. Streaming feelings, streaming sensation, all through the body. We had oral sex and most erotic practices short of fucking. When she broke up with me, I went into a depressive fugue.

I did not know what to do, not having any inkling whatsoever about human communication, about the content of relatedness.

152

Sexual Healing

It ain't all that hard to cut into a woman, but what am I doing this for? The criteria for engaging in sexual behavior is sometimes elusive to me. Friendliness is important, feeling that a woman is a friend. I would have to feel the possibility of some kind of intimacy before sex. Casual or recreational sex, I've never been there, although I've had periods in my life that I could call semi-promiscuous. Parties, bars, the New York art scene. I was moving around, politically and socially involved. Some nights, I'd just make a phone call to a woman I'd see three to four times a year. Another evening, just walk out to the corner bar and hit it off with someone. Just before turning thirty, I decided to give up warped male conquest consciousness. Politically and philosophically, it didn't seem to fit with what I was feeling.

If I'm comfortable, I'm a pretty hands-on person. I like body to body, a lot of moistness, affection. Not necessarily verbal, unless it's real, or unless you want to call all noises verbal. At one time I would have been quite the opposite, "This is not a saying thing, this is a doing thing." I like sound, surface sensation, sensation inside—when things are going good, you can feel it through your whole nervous system. Sometimes oral sex, mutual oral sex, sex without sex: rubbing arms, nuzzling, kissing. Fucking, I definitely prefer slow and long to anything furious. The only positions out of the ordinary would be side to side, if a woman was lying down and had one leg under me and one leg on the shoulder. That can be reversed, too. I've gotten into mild bondage, all kinds of so-called fetishistic practices: a woman dressing as a man and me dressing as a woman. There's all kinds of drama and ritual to doing things. Dressing each other, playing with each other while dressing. One time, doing sixty-nine, both of us wearing pantyhose. You can slice pantyhose open.

Early morning fucking, especially if you're both working. Somehow, just waking up responsively with one another. You just end up getting into nice, slow, sweet fucking, and yet in the back of your mind, there's *time* to be made. That charges the being together, but you're also deferring decision-making. Oral sex with taste—not just oral-genital sex, but rubbing each other with syrup and licking it off. It's like taking time, taking time. Time is important here. I was with a woman who would want to take a midday break from work, come home and just cut, where that would never occur to me. I wouldn't be responsive, wouldn't even be *open*.

Good sex is where I feel comfortably affectionate and I'm communicating that, physically and maybe verbally. And something of that order is coming back to me. Times when there ain't nothing else on my mind, nothing bothering me. It's not necessarily orgasmic.

After my last bad relationship with a good woman, I got emotionally washed out. I thought, "I'm going to go home, and I may just stay home, because I ain't getting no satisfaction no motherfucking matter. If I do *nothing* I can't feel worse." I'm really quite in a quandary at this point in my life about what I'm going to do. I don't run the streets no more. I don't hang out no more. I have limited contact with women who might be good erotic partners, good life partners, or any combination of the two. And a big thing: in the age of AIDS, I would tend more to keep my dick in my pants. Never did like condoms. I felt that long before any kind of AIDS thing. Mostly I counted on women to use birth control. AIDS just brought home, "Hey, Luke, you've got to look at this."

Veronica

College helped Veronica flee a desolate childhood in the Oregon backwoods. She graduated with honors, found low paid, pink-collar employment and two years ago left a sales job to work as a call girl. Recently engaged, Veronica shares an empty, immaculate apartment with two pampered cats. "I've always thought it's a real burden to be a woman in today's society," reflects the blonde thirty-one-year-old, shaking her head. "Men are cool when they fuck, but women somehow lose status for having sex and enjoying it."

We did not go to public school. We studied a correspondence course at home. My father said the reason he kept me out of public school was to keep me away from sex education, because it was a communist plot to overthrow the United States. I didn't have a sex education other than my father fondling me, talking nasty to me, taking nude pictures of me, showing me dirty magazines. We spent five and a half years in a little tiny travel trailer, ready to leave in the night, because he was afraid the school board was going to put us in jail. My mother was sick all the time and distracted; she couldn't remember what she'd said five minutes before. My father collected guns, and he liked locks and bright lights and practiced karate. Until fourteen years of age, I was only allowed to be two places: at home or with my father. It was like growing up in prison. My fiancé spent some time in prison, and he's the only one I've ever felt really understood what my childhood was like.

Because of my experiences with my father, I equated love with sex and didn't know how to distinguish them. At seventeen, I went out with a boy from church. We had lousy sex: no foreplay, it hurt, I didn't bleed and so he questioned my virginity. The second time I had sex, it was with a man who gave me gonorrhea. With the third guy, we were necking in a car, and it was the first time I was starting to get into it. Then he asked, "Do you do this with everybody?" And I remember feeling my heart sink: he was going to have sex with me and invalidate it at the same time. At

155

eighteen, I went out with an attractive older man, and he fingered me in the front seat of his pick-up truck. That was my first orgasm. It was a wonderful sensation and the first sexual encounter where a man wasn't gratifying himself. He was giving me pleasure. That was the first time I thought maybe sex was for women.

I moved to California. I finally started coming alive and fell in love with a man at work. Adrian. There was a lot of co-dependency, drug addiction, alcohol addiction, but it was the most feeling I'd had for anybody in my life. We got real involved with cocaine, and our relationship turned extremely violent: he tried strangling me, I stabbed him with scissors. It was hell on earth. After two years, I got sober and left him. I started having great sex. It began when I incorporated my spirituality with my sexuality. I started focusing on my twelve-step program and working on my feelings. I was in incest therapy for a couple years. I had several affairs in my twelve-step group. It got to a point where I was afraid to walk into a meeting, because there'd be four or five men I'd had sex with all sitting there next to each other. I met a male stripper, a black guy, and fell very much in love. When I was with him, I became very aware of my bisexuality, and it was a painful thing for me, because I realized I wasn't going to be able to pretend it wasn't there anymore. I'd gone to the Mitchell Brothers to look into working there as a stripper, but it didn't pay well enough, and lap-dancing reminded me too much of what my father used to like. But while I was there, I watched a girl do her little dance in the altar room. I got hot flashes and heart palpitations and gave her every dollar I had. I remember crying that night, "I'm not straight, I'm never going to be straight." My boyfriend said, "You do whatever you have to, and I'm with you all the way." Shortly after, someone introduced me to Heather. Then I was on top of the world: I had a girlfriend, a boyfriend and good sex with both.

Through Heather, I got into prostitution. I do it for the money, but beyond that, prostitution has really given me an avenue to resolve some incest issues, to be able to say yes and no, to be in charge and in control. I have strict boundaries, and nobody does anything that I don't want them to now. I do straight sex, oral sex and hand jobs. Fifty minutes. I don't allow my clients to kiss me above the neck. I use lots of nonoxynol-9 and don't worry about my own lubrication. The things I focus on are having strong

Sexual Healing

vaginal muscles to make my clients come quicker and prevent them from getting too deep inside me, because that would make me feel too vulnerable. I fake orgasms. I don't practice my sexuality with my clients: I provide a sexual service, allowing them to express *their* sexuality. Everything I do is safe. I use latex gloves, latex condoms and nonoxynol-9. I don't handle any bodily fluids except saliva, and I make clients wash their hands after they've handled their own condoms. A lot of clients would like you to fall in love, give them extra time for free, date them. So you're constantly reaffirming the boundaries.

Adrian got sober, and we reconnected three months ago. Much to my shock, I was still in love with him, and I felt all these feelings coming back. We're engaged. The best sexual interaction I've ever had was four weeks ago with him. I'd been on vacation in England for two weeks, during which I didn't have any contact with clients, so I was able to bring a lot of my barriers down. I came home; he picked me up at the airport. We started kissing. It was like kissing and coming, with no focus on sex acts or what we were doing, just on *being* together. My body was alive with sensation, and yet I didn't feel there were barriers between our bodies. For a moment, it was as if we were one person, having the same orgasm at the same time. What I learned from that was that some of the best sexual experiences are gifts that you have to be open to receive, rather than prizes that you go trying to chase.

I feel good sex for me today is a spiritual and intimate connection with one person, and I'm directing all my energy towards my lover. It's important to know what your needs are; mine come and go with age and circumstance, and I try to honor that. Good sex takes time, intimacy, trust. It contributes to the relationship and becomes an integral part of it. That's the kind of sex I'm not going to get in a motel room, where I might have this ass-kicking orgasm. I'm glad people want to pay for sex, because I get my rent paid, but it's unfortunate that people think they're going to find so many answers in paid-for sex. People come to me aching for human contact: a hug, a smile, the warmth of a touch. And there's such a focus on sex in this society that people are trying to meet every need they have through their genitals. Sex is just sex. Love-making is entirely different: it's falling, letting go, floating, being vulnerable, tapping into what's innocent and pure about you and your lover. It makes me feel at one with myself, my lover, my God, the universe.

David

As a ten-year-old in a Connecticut home where sex was never mentioned, David was molested by his sister. "It started out as a game. She's six years older, so we played the game by her rules," the tall, gray-haired man says quietly. In his teens, he was sexually abused by his sister's husband, an abrasive alcoholic. Today, David is in a court-ordered therapy program following arrest for molesting his daughter. Forty-six and married for the third time, he is a mild-mannered man who works in the Silicon Valley computer industry.

To me, the best part of sex is afterwards, the feeling later on, a certain amount of euphoria. The rest of the world disappears, and it's just the two of us. I can see this picture of myself running, taking twenty foot leaps, almost flying, not touching the ground, airborne, a free spirit. Nothing has an attachment to me. The world goes away. There's been a lot of times where I'm under stress, where I wish I could just disappear. I don't know how to fix all the stuff I'm into, somebody's trying to put the screws to me, nail me down, and if I could just chop all those strings and fly, I wouldn't have to worry about looking back. Free of obstacles. A bloom set loose that floats and keeps on going and going, and it looks like it's going to float forever.

For many years, the only way to have that really intense feeling was to have sex, to do something physical to express a feeling towards another person or get something from another person. I could say, "I've got an hour for lunch. Let's go to bed," but I couldn't say, "Can we have a cup of coffee? There's something I want to talk about." It was always difficult to say what I liked in bed. "I hope she does this, because it turns me on," but it was never okay to ask. And if she told me what she wanted, I experienced it as a judgment call: "Apparently I've been doing it the wrong way for years." Never direct. It's part of the man's role: in control and never asking. When I was a kid going to the drive-in, I had the car, so I was in charge. It was, "Let's push the limits and see how far I can go. Is it going to take three dates or three

Sexual Healing

minutes to make this happen?" I used to deal in fantasies, because not being direct, I didn't know what was going on. So I tried to second-guess things and wasted a lot of time.

I had three children with my second wife. After the divorce, I didn't see my children for three years. We had problems with rules: the rules were a lot easier at Mom's house than mine, and it wasn't okay for me to confront people or set boundaries. I didn't like what was going on, so that was it. They couldn't come over any more. I didn't answer the door, I didn't answer the phone, I didn't do anything with anybody. Then the children sort of showed up one night for dinner and just never went home. My daughter was fifteen. Here was a young woman who had a sincere interest in me. She'd say, "How are you feeling today?" I took that to mean: this is small talk, the lead-in to something more. That was the fantasy I was in. She used do things like make me coffee in the morning or bring me a glass of wine at night, the things you'd expect a wife to do. She was doing these things to be nice, and I'm hoping that there's more: you bring me coffee in bed and I'm wondering where this is going to go. What I needed was an adult to talk to, someone to help relieve some of the stress I was going through. One evening, I came home, and she came into the bedroom and gave me a hug. I couldn't let go. I was crying in her arms.

We started going to adult functions together. She became my date. She never said no. We'd curl up in the same chair and watch television. I finally got to the point where I was sleeping with her—not having sex, but getting the warmth and closeness, like the after-feeling of sex. In the middle of the night one night, I molested her. What I wanted was more of that feeling, where the rest of the world disappears. She woke up and just looked at me, and I could tell by the look I'd done something terrible. As a man, the unwritten rules say it's okay to put my arm around you—and how far can I go before the wall goes up and the answer is "No"? And if I never hear "No," then it's up to me to experiment and see how far I can get. From a man's standpoint, if it's okay to hold her hand, sit in the same chair, curl up next to her and go to sleep, I guess that means there's an open invitation to whatever's next. And there wasn't . . . . The next morning, she moved out. I dismissed it till I got a call from the police department.

I've been in therapy about a year and a half. I met my wife through the counseling program, and we got together four months ago. There's only one day we haven't been together. For the first time, I feel like I'm alive. Neither one of us felt we had to give up ourselves to be part of the relationship, and both of us have gone through good times and bad without either one of us leaving. To me, the best part of sex is still the feeling afterwards. What I've found with my wife is that we can arrive at that same point without having to do anything physically, without having to have rip-roaring sex or multiple orgasms. Sex is something we can do without a goal in mind. I can go to bed with my wife and do something with her sexually without reaching orgasm myself. Either one of us can do that. And that's okay, because we can have the feeling without having sex.

Good sex is something that's enjoyable for both partners. I guess I believe that nice guys should finish last. It's okay to play out some fantasies without doing anything threatening or harmful to someone. My wife told me, "If you wake up in the middle of the night, and you're in the mood, it's okay." That kind of conversation is something I wouldn't have had before. There are some cautions. I have to be up-front and direct more than before, because my wife was molested as a child. I would feel terrible if I made her feel uncomfortable. I have to be direct in identifying boundaries—what's okay, what's not okay. I can't just experiment, I have to ask. Sex has a place, a different meaning. It's still physical and feels good, but the manipulative aspect is gone.

Judy

Growing up in a redneck town in the Colorado mountains, sandy-haired Judy started kissing boys when she was five. Later, adolescent groping in cars intrigued and frightened her. She says, "A lot of my sexual contact was when I was drunk, because I started drinking when I was thirteen years old. I didn't have sober sex till I was twenty-five." A beautiful woman at thirty-one, Judy divides her time between teaching martial arts, performing in a dance troupe, and practicing Buddhist meditation at a Zen center. She shares a sunny Oakland apartment with a lap cat and a dog named Miracle.

When I was eight years old, I had an incredible passion for horses, and so did my parents' best friend. He supported my riding career—I showed jumping horses. He was kind of a surrogate father. I spent more time with him than anyone else in my family, because we did a lot of traveling with the horses. There were things I have come to call incest: innuendo and emotional game-playing. He owned my favorite horse, and I was always under the threat of losing the horse. He had an incredible way of making me feel tenuous in the world.

One of the messages I got from that experience was that your sexuality determines your worth. At seventeen, I was driving drunk one night, taking a friend home. I had an accident and broke my neck, which paralyzed me from the chest down. My boyfriend left me, ostensibly because he thought sex wouldn't be any good anymore. That was a real message for me. I absolutely shut down. I couldn't bear the thought of being sexual, but I couldn't bear the thought of not being sexual, either.

As a college student, I transferred to Berkeley to get away from ghosts and find out who I was. I got involved with a disabled guy, and that was a wonderful experience—not in terms of emotions and interpersonal dynamics. I do a lot of, "Come close, get away! Come close, get away!" Typical incest stuff. But it was wonderful because I didn't have to try to explain my disability.

There was real understanding of each other. I hadn't been sexual since I'd gotten hurt, and that relationship let me get in touch with that aspect of myself again.

I ended up leaving him because I wanted to be with women. When I moved to Berkeley, I didn't know what a lesbian *was* although I can remember being incredibly in love with my women friends in Colorado. My best friend in college: I remember us lying in bed one night and her saying, "I wish one of us was a man." Those feelings were there, but I didn't know there was an option. In Berkeley, I fell in love with a woman. Later, I had a series of flings with able-bodied women. Some good, some awful. One of the most sensual, erotic times I ever had was with a woman I had a short fling with. She came over one night. We lit candles. She brushed my hair, and we were looking at each other in a mirror, with a total sense of timelessness and spacelessness and this incredible sense of connection in that mirror.

Disabled people are taught to dissociate from the body and to use our minds to succeed. That's what happened with me, but I couldn't figure out how to succeed with my mind, because I've always been a body-oriented person. I can talk a blue streak, but that's not who I *am*. So the first nine years of my disability were excruciating. Then I happened to luck into some people who said, "Let's figure out how you can use your body." I started working out more, dancing, doing martial arts, moving. I've reclaimed a lot of my own independence—getting myself in and out of bed, driving. The biggest block has been getting over my idea of the *right* way to do things: "If you can't do it absolutely the best, don't do it." Here I am, a disabled woman trying to figure out my way in the world, my movement, my way of being. A lot of my martial arts work has been about learning to be assertive, being aware, knowing how to carry myself through the world. And that goes right into claiming how I am sexually: saying what I want and what makes me feel good, instead of just pleasing the other person or being passive. I think it also comes down to caring who I'm with. I don't like being single these days, and I could pick up some jerk, but that's not what I want out of a sexual relationship.

I was with my last lover for two years. She's very sexual, and I really learned to like sex with her. She was in love with me and into exploring, and she was great about my disability. Those early stages of relationships . . . you can barely get through the front door, and next thing you know you're on the living room floor or doing it in the kitchen . . . . What I learned with her was I could tap into body memory. The medical profession tells me I'm not supposed to feel anything in my body, but I have sensation and feelings all the time. I like touching, contact. I have a really sensitive neck area, so when I'm with somebody, I'm usually covered with hickeys. I can spend hours kissing. Hours. I love going down on women. At one time, I thought, "Oo, I don't know if I could do that. It could be kind of weird." But it's wonderful. I like being penetrated—not dildoes. Fingers. It taps something in me that's primal. I like to play around with bondage, being held down, that feeling of being taken, swept away. It's such a relief to get out of this world and swept into another plane.

I'd say I'm orgasmic, probably in a different way than most people think about it. I don't know if it's in my body or my mind. I think there's too much emphasis on orgasm. Sex is more than body sensation. I experience a build up, blood rushing, blood pressure going up, tingling, but mostly for me, it's that connection with someone else, that merging. It's like being held in space. Being present, being right there. It takes me a lot more into my emotions, into my body in the same way that dance and martial arts do, but deeper. I always feel much more creative and alive when I'm in love. I love being in love, going around with your cunt throbbing for days on end, just feeling like you're not going to be able to stand it for one more minute. I love playing with that line, "Oh my God, I can't stand it any longer. Take me, take me!"

I believe we're all sexual beings. That's our birthright. What I've realized is that I'm an artist, and to be creative and to be in the world, one has to own one's sexuality. I've had to re-own that, just to be in the world the way I am.

Cathie

A twenty-nine-year-old preschool teacher, Cathie grew up in a Latino and Italian San Francisco household in the company of her mother's gay male friends. She mimicked their conquest attitude towards sex and at eighteen determined to pick up ten men. Her first vaginal orgasm was with the ninth partner on a bench under a freeway. A vivacious, heavy-set blonde, Cathie notes wryly, "People say you have to be thin to have sex. But getting laid is not the trick, being in a relationship is the trick. The only advantage skinny women have is more offers." Four years ago, she met her husband Chris through a personals ad and found love at first sight. As newlyweds, they initially set aside Monday nights to act out fantasies: sex in the car, sex on the beach, nude photography, spanking.

One night, Chris and I trotted out to a "play party," which is where people are in a big space practicing SM together, and we just sat there with our mouths open. It was a sexual genesis: we were both getting hot, and we left to fuck in the car. We dove into the SM scene feet first, and all these fantasies started to come out, fantasies of power and domination. We each like the other to be aggressive. It's a kind of battle of the submissives. The wonderful intimacy in being married is that I know every inch of his body and I'm comfortable caressing it.

You don't do SM every night. You don't have all your whips and chains out and do this massive scene with dungeon music. Sometimes we just get in bed and hump each other. He's hard, we fuck, I use the vibrator on my clit and go to sleep. That would be the basic pattern of our everyday sex—which is fine, because we both know it's going to happen, it's satisfying, it's comfortable sex on a nightly basis. On the weekends, or when one of us is really horny, he may come in, "I've been thinking about you all day," lift up my skirt and do it as soon as he walks in the door.

About a year ago, I started to have memories of incest. Midway through a fisting scene, I had a full memory of incest. I came and then just broke down and started to scream. Sobbing like a

164

Sexual Healing

kid, not an adult. The SM brought it out. What I remembered was my uncle playing with me from infancy. When I was ten, he did penetration, and that's when it became volatile and scary. Horrifying . . . . Once I started remembering, I'd break down and cry in every scene, but I didn't want to give up SM. About that time, Chris and I met a man who wanted to learn SM and play with us. He was a catalyst, a very dominant male, a daddy figure, who triggered and helped with the incest. In that six-month relationship, my master took a lot of the brunt of the trauma: he listened to me when I talked about it, he made me feel safe, he needed to take care of me. I needed the care-taking, and Chris needed the relief. I'll probably go into therapy at some point, but the feelings come and go.

Because of my molestation, I've used the power dynamic to get back at men. I knew all they wanted was sex. Now that it's dawned on me *why* I thought all men were shits, I've realized there are some genuinely decent men out there that you can have a relationship with—maybe not even sexual! *That* was an epiphany. It's had a lot to do with Chris: he's shown me the intimate side of a male. It's beyond physical pleasure; it's also emotional pleasure. I've matured in my attitude toward building a relationship, and I see that relationships and sex are more intertwined.

With Chris, I like being fucked, having him in me, that warm, good feeling. I've discovered that I can ask for what I like, that there's nothing wrong with wanting your nipples pulled till they're taut. I've learned that keeping a vibrator by the bed is not a crime. I've learned that Chris can come, and then I can come, and we can both enjoy watching each other come—as opposed to having this simultaneous orgasm that's supposed to move the world. If we have intercourse that's fine, if we don't that's fine. Sometimes we come home weary from work and it's: what do you want? Do you want to masturbate? Do you think you can focus enough for intercourse? It's negotiation, which I never thought it would be. I always thought it would be this mystic experience, but it's become a verbal experience. At times, we make concessions: he doesn't come when I give him head—too stimulating—and I've had to learn to deal with that. And I like oral sex okay, but he *really* likes doing it, so I let him do it maybe more than I would ask for it.

I love multiple orgasms. What's great about them is that moment when you start to grab, when you've got someone's fingers up inside you to contract against—or a dildo with finger or vibrator stimulation on the clit. You build, and if you can just hold it a little longer, the waves start to come. A full thirty second orgasm. A rolling effect. It's the sensation of water running through you, an ethereal moment where your body's just in pleasure. Waves and waves of water. Sparks of electricity.

Good sex is when you both come out feeling better than when you came in, to really touch the spirit of another person and feel their pleasure flowing through you. Satisfaction. Communion. You can have good raw sex, just passionate and physical, but it's so much better when you feel you've touched that person's inner being and you share that for a time. Anything else is only halfway there.

I started using safe sex at twenty-four, demanding that my boyfriend use a condom, and I never got any flack. Chris and I have made the choice to be fluid-bonded. We're a closed fluid system, and no one else is allowed in. If we have sex outside the relationship, there must be a latex barrier—even to touch us, a latex glove. Together, he and I have oral sex without barriers. For birth control, he pulls out and finishes in his hand. I haven't had to use chemicals or anything. It's a bizarre method of birth control for an enlightened feminist to use—the "oops method"— but it works for us. Sometime in the near future, we're planning to have children. Of course, we'll have to child-proof the apartment—put the whips and chains away.

Darrell

A square man whose face reveals his mixed American Indian and European immigrant heritage, Darrell grew up in rough industrial towns near the San Francisco Bay. Married three times, he is a forty-six-year-old construction worker serving a one-year jail sentence for molesting his oldest son, now eighteen. Five months before incarceration, Darrell began to receive therapeutic counseling at Parents United, a guided self-help group in San Jose.

My father was physically brutal. If he ever put a hand on you, it wasn't for a hug. My mother left him, and I was put in a foster home at age eleven. There was no love there, no one to put an arm around me and say, "You're really special." At eleven, I turned to heroin because I couldn't face the situation I was in and the pain of desertion. My foster-father was an alcoholic, owned a bar, never counted his money. I stole a lot of money and found things to do with it. One of those things made me forget where I was and why I was there. But soon I couldn't steal enough to support it. A guy who was buying heroin at the same place I was said, "I know where you can make lots of money." He was older, had a car. I started going to San Francisco with him, started selling myself to men at a house there. I was working for tips, and there was a lot of nights I made a hundred and fifty dollars—a week's wages in 1956. When I'd walk out of there, I'd feel sick to my stomach. I'd cuss them and call them "no-good dirty faggots." And yet, for the first time, I was having somebody hold me, tell me that I mattered, that they loved me and cared about me. And whether it was for a minute or whether it was for real didn't seem to matter. There was a reason I kept going back, and the reason was a lot stronger than the heroin.

At sixteen, I met the first girl I ever really cared about. I don't know why they call it puppy love, because I don't think I've felt an emotion as strong. At that time, there were a couple girls I was having sex with quite regularly, but I never had any sex with the girl I was so in love with. She was a strict Catholic. We dated and things, but she wasn't playing any games.

167

I joined the Navy. When I got out, I thought a lot about the homosexual part of my background and decided I was going to prove I was a man. So I proceeded to see how many women I could talk into going to bed with me. Sex was proving something to myself and the world: I was a man, I could bring women to a climax. Those years were probably the most frightening years of my life. At that time, I don't think I even knew what pleasure in sex was about. I'm not saying the sexual act wasn't pleasurable, but it was *proving* something. Without knowing someone. Conquest. Ego. Being a man meant you never let anybody see that you hurt. When I went to work in construction, I had to do it faster than anybody, lift more than anybody, drive a bigger truck with nicer mags. "Look at me. I'm somebody." Because of what I can do, not who I am. I never let anybody know what I was feeling.

I met my second wife in Las Vegas. I don't know what the attraction was, 'cause all we ever did was fight. Her love was PCP. She had these two little boys. I couldn't handle Las Vegas and decided I was going to get my life together in California. For fourteen months, these two little boys saw me come into their life and leave, come into their life and leave. I came back one more time, she and I fought, and I started to leave the house. Jeff grabbed me by the arm and said, "Dad, I don't want you to leave me. I want you to be my father always and to always be there." *No one* had ever said that to me.

She eventually filed for divorce, and because of her police record, I got custody. I don't know how long after they came to live with me that I started molesting Jeff, but it wasn't long. Improper kissing, fondling, oral sex. Both ways. That went on for eleven years. My feelings with Jeff were like I couldn't get *enough* of him. I couldn't be close enough *to* him. I stopped doing anything except for being with the kids. There were two incidents where I approached my youngest, and he rebuked me viciously, "Get away from me, faggot!" The molesting wasn't pleasurable. I felt bad every time. I felt almost the same things when I was having sex with my son that I'd felt with those men in my youth. But there was also something driving me to do it, and I suppose it was mixed-up feelings about love and sex: I didn't know that you could love somebody without having sex with them, or that sex had anything to do with love.

Sexual Healing

I don't think I've experienced good sex. As close as I ever came to it was with that first girlfriend, just lying there in each other's arms. Not copulation, not sexual touches, but talking and putting my fingers through her hair. I'd feel ten feet tall, like I was floating. Sexually aroused, but it didn't matter that I didn't have sex with her. It didn't lessen those feelings.

Sex is really scary to me. Still scary. I've never had an appropriate sexual relationship—even being married, it never felt like a spontaneous, "I really love you, and this is what we need to do together." I'd like to know what it's like, but I'm still afraid of it. I would like to have a relationship where I could be open and feel that my lover could be open with me. Where I could tell them what I had done to Jeff without them thinking less of me. Where they could really know me and be willing to be vulnerable enough for me to know them. I wouldn't be in there to prove something. I'd be there because that was where we each wanted to be. Not a service to them or me. Where the feelings would all be there. Where we'd do all of the foreplay and *feel* like doing all of the foreplay. And being able to talk to them afterwards, and sometimes just be able to lie there and hold each other, not even completing the sex act, but just to be there, touch and feel good about being with them. Sex has taken a lot of my life away from me. But there's still a part of me that says, "Yeah, I'd like to find someone to make the stars go off." I can believe that it's possible. I have to learn as I go.

Maya

At six, she found sex games with other children safe and fun. At seven, Maya hated the family friend who molested her on the school playground. Even after the man's arrest, it was a matter her parents did not discuss with her. A Latina from Denver, Maya is now a radiant twenty-one-year-old college student in California.

The year I was eight, I was walking to school, and this guy comes up and starts talking to me about my pussy, and he asked me if he could see it. He was a huge, fat black man, and he told me if I tried to run, he would kill me. He took me to a dark place under a building, and I lifted up my dress: "*Okay?* I'm gonna go now." He raped me. I went to school, crying and crying. I had on my mom's rabbit foot around my neck, and I took it off: "Here! It's *not* good luck." They took me off to the school nurse, and I said I had a headache. I cried about it forever and ever.

I matured later than most girls, didn't have breasts all the way up till ninth grade, so nobody paid attention to me. All my friends lost their virginity early. It was a big joke, "Maya's the virgin." In my senior year of high school, I ended up having sex with a good friend, and it was a good experience: we made love three times that day, and I came the second time. After the first guy, I had another boyfriend, who was really nice, and we had good sex. He had this huge penis. We tried a lot of new positions, and it was more fun with him, because he was more interactive with me and cared that I was there. In college, I met a really nice guy, sensitive and tender. He was a football player, black, lean, handsome. We'd touch, and we had lots of oral sex. Later, I had a boyfriend for two years, and we had sex all the time. He was the best lover I'd ever had, because I loved him. I could completely trust him, and it gave me freedom in being naked and just being me. One negative thing that came out of the early rape experience, though, is when I'd make love, and my boyfriend's penis touched a place in me, I'd just break out crying, get in this little fetal

170

position and couldn't look at him, touch him, or believe he was near me. Because it reminds me, it reminds my whole body. Not good sex. I'd cry and he'd hold me, but it was an uncontrollable reaction.

I went away to Russia for a year as part of my college program. When I got there, I realized it was a very different society, sexwise. I was living with a family, and I was unsure of my responsibility towards them, so I was celibate for six months. I found myself having wet dreams and waking up every morning coming, so it was *fun* to be celibate. There was this guy who lived in the same apartment building, and he spoke English really well. We played tennis and were friends. Then my mother came to visit me in Russia, and she really liked Sergei, and the more I saw him interact with her, the more I liked him. We drove to a villa near the Black Sea—Sergei, his mother, my mother and me. I was finding him sexier and sexier. I didn't know what to do about it. I was being all coy, but I wanted to jump his bones.

At night, after dinner, it started to rain. Buckets of rain. I walked out on the porch to look, it was so neat and sexy. Our mothers went to bed. He came over and kissed me. He laid me down on the couch, and we were kissing and kissing and kissing, and he kissed my breasts, and we were wanting each other. The water was coming down, and the moon was shining. It was like a fantasy. He was very attentive and really wanted to please me. He took my hand, licked it and rubbed my body with my own hand. I was kind of letting him do all the work and just appreciating the way he was treating me. But as soon as I took my hand and put it in his pants, I felt *the most beautiful penis* I've ever felt in my whole, entire life. Smooth, perfect, straight. I just had to have it. I took his hand and led him downstairs into a room which was almost filled up by a pool table. There was a couch, and he started taking off my clothes, and I was still resisting and feeling cautious. But then I made up my mind. We made love for a while, and I came, with him on top, kissing me all over. Then he lifted me up and put me on the pool table, and I was kissing him. We made love till we came at the same time. Very hard. All wet, just like the outdoors.

I really like being that close to someone, touching bodies, having a penis inside me. It's the ultimate hug. I've always known what I enjoy, how to make myself feel good, how to move. Good sex is when two people know their bodies and care about their partners emotionally. It's tender but also steamy and excited and happy. It's a solid, beautiful expression of connection. Being with Sergei helped me, and it helped being in a culture that doesn't sell sexuality, like ours does. Here, you have to watch everywhere you step just to make sure someone's not coming on to you. I don't come on to guys, but people have always told me, "You're sexy." I never wanted to be that. In Russia, a man could touch me and be sincerely touching me like a person, a young girl, not an object. It was a relief.

I don't want to tell you how many people I've had sex with. I get very sexual automatically. Because I was naïve, I've had sex with people who hurt me. The orgasm wasn't worth it. With them, sex wasn't empowering: something was taken away from me. One of the problems I have with being promiscuous is that I consider my pussy to be the flower of my body, where my babies are going to come from, and I've dumped the trash there. A lot of American men, even the ones who cared about me, they were really after getting a nut off. Come and go. Sergei could come any time he wanted to, but he got pleasure from pleasing me. Coming wasn't his priority. Now I want to be with someone I love. I can't do sex for fun anymore, because it's just not *fun*. I haven't done any dating since I got back, because I feel Sergei and I have something special. But he's so far away. He's so far away.

Jim

Dark-eyed and pale, Jim is a handsome twenty-year-old who grew up on a small horse farm in upstate New York. As a teen, he began showing horses on the Eastern circuit and making sexual contact with the mostly closeted gay men who worked the horse shows. Back home, Jim found little support for his emerging gay identity from his violent stepfather or from his classmates, some of whom responded by trashing his parents' property. Today, Jim lives in San Francisco with a close friend and sometimes lover. He works a clerical job and plans to be a teacher.

Sex is a huge part of me. It's part of my identity, and I'm not scared of my sexuality. I need sex, that physical act in order to make myself whole. And I make time for it. There's energy that builds up inside me until I have this release with another person. It can be filling up a void, if I'm lonely or depressed. For me, sex is physical, whereas making *love* is intimate and emotional. I've only done that twice in my life. One of those times, I was visiting somebody's barn. I was seventeen. There was a guy I thought was so hot, and we both knew that we were gay. We ended up renting a hotel room that night, and it was the first real good queer sex I'd had. It was beautiful. My favorite thing to do is deep kiss, and we did that for hours and hours. We had unprotected oral sex, mutual masturbation. There wasn't any anal. It was a huge release for me, because it was the first time I was able to do something with a man I liked. I liked him a lot; he's a good guy. The orgasm was the most incredible I'd ever had, it was so intense. I still think of it as the hottest experience of my life. It was making love, intimate and hot.

When I'm with partners, I set my limits, and then they can do what they want. I really like the submissive role, where they're making all the advances, taking the initiative and getting their pleasure. Once at a horse show in Louisville, there were two guys I didn't know—a couple. We went back to their hotel. It became a dynamic where they were using me for their pleasure.

They took their turns fucking me and getting me off. The key power aspect was me being on my back with my legs up, powerless. Them seeking me, them driving me to their hotel, two against one. I know being used is not a good thing. It stems from the battering and verbal abuse I suffered when I was little. It's destructive, but I really get off on it. I have fantasies of being abused during sex—slapping, bondage, golden showers, scat scenes—but I make sure those things don't happen.

I didn't hear the word AIDS till 1989 when I moved to Manhattan. I wasn't worried at first. But in the last year or so, I've made the commitment not to have oral or anal sex until I'm with somebody I really care about. I have really, really good sex without penetration—with friends or at sex clubs. There, I'm looking for something more group-oriented. Normally, it's just a mouth-to-mouth thing, nipple play and mutual masturbation. Nipples. I can almost come if somebody plays with my nipples. Roughly, with teeth. Also, the tendon in the groin area is really sensitive, and the underarms. Biting my sides and tonguing the body. Usually, I don't get off with somebody else jerking me off, because most people concentrate on the shaft, and I like more stimulation on the head of my cock, with not too much lube. I like friction to get me off, a little on the rough side. I don't like to take off my clothes in a sex club, because I'm scared somebody's going to come up and ram me.

I was sexually assaulted in January. Somebody I picked up, really cute. We decided to go back to his place. He knew I didn't want penetration, but he ended up forcibly fucking me without a condom. It was awful. He kept saying, "It's okay. I'm clean." That assault really affected me—at first I couldn't tell anyone. There's all these issues: "You deserved it. It was your fault." It's hard enough for a woman to come out as being raped, but man to man, there's the assumption that you're equals. For a while, I really denied what happened. One night when I was with a friend at a sex club, I saw the guy who raped me. I was so angry, I didn't know what to do. I wanted to attack him. He came up to me, "How are you doing?" Like nothing ever happened and we'd had a great experience. I shoved him as hard as I could. I didn't know what to do. I decided it was important to me not to leave the club, that I didn't have to leave just because he was there:

Sexual Healing

"He's not going to win over me." I still wonder about pressing charges, but I don't want to go through the legal system.

Since that assault, I've cut back a lot, and that's why I'm looking for a monogamous relationship. I've been dating somebody for three months. We're not having any sex. We have such intimate contact, it's very satisfying to me. We're just sleeping nights together, kissing and holding each other. He's twenty-three and still a virgin. In San Francisco! I want to make love with him. He's so hot, but I don't want to push him. I go off on the side, but it's not as gratifying. In one instance, I had a threesome with a friend and a friend of his, somebody I didn't know. There was the safety net of being with my friend while still having anonymous sex.

Good sex is playful and long, with somebody I'm comfortable with, exploring what's within my boundaries. I'd like to get somebody to finger-fuck me with a latex glove. Latex is hot, just stretching it, pushing stuff through it—although it's not biodegradable, and it tastes *awful*. But it can be so slippery with oil. I separate intimacy and sex so much that I don't plan on having *sex* for the rest of my life, because I'm really looking for somebody to have a beautiful, monogamous relationship with. Making love to somebody is less of a physical act than an emotional act. It's more of a holding, and you don't even have to have an erection. It's touching and exchanging spiritual energy.

Rachel

As a young teen, Rachel spent weekends cruising the tree-lined streets of a wealthy New York suburb in a green Ford driven by a boy who tried unsuccessfully to kiss her. She came out as a lesbian a few years later. In her thirties, Rachel moved to a six-story walk-up on Manhattan's Lower East Side and began teaching adult education in schools and prisons. Her affairs with women followed a pattern. "In longer relationships, I maintained dominance and distance," she says. "In short relationships, I opened myself up and got scorched." A small, ardent woman with wire-rim glasses and a schoolmarm manner, Rachel has spent the last ten years recovering from sexual assault—years of near-celibacy and abundant romantic fantasy. At forty-eight, she has begun dating again.

I tend to like butch women who are going to take me. Somebody who's around my own age, in my peer group, a friend, with equal power—butch *or* femme, and usually white. My past loves, I could be in love with them right now. I can sleep with just one person, but as Jimmy Carter said, "I'll lust in my heart."

When I came out at seventeen, I was a fuck being. It was mindless, born out of hysteria. I was compelled by an insatiable appetite that I couldn't possibly meet. Couldn't possibly. It was hard for me to have an orgasm. It was an insatiable appetite that freaked people right the fuck out. I think they were shocked. It was kind of like the librarian who took her glasses off.

Sex was a vehicle for love, for *something*. Some attention. My first lover seduced me, and the kind of attention that she poured on me was beautiful. She was twenty-two, four years older than I, gorgeous. And she was looking at me, coming after me, and I couldn't get enough. I became aware that I was a lesbian, because she fell on me once in a room full of people, and my body went on fire. So I knew. I got it. But she abandoned me. After she got married, I continued to see her for four years and didn't sleep with anyone else. During that time, it was all secrecy and burning.

176

Sexual Healing

I remember she took me into her bedroom, pushed me against the door and kissed me. I've never had another kiss like that. There was so much need from both of us.

I think that set the tone for my sexuality, and it was very destructive. This young woman—a kid, really, that I thought was a woman—was terrified of her sexuality, much more terrified than I was. Because I went on to want to be a lesbian, where she went on to get married. There was no place for appreciation, no way to rest and make love. It was all secret, fear, hysteria. And that hysteria was always my romantic image. I was looking for that—not the play, the fun, the sensuality.

I went from hysteria to hysteria—little affairs, one seven-year relationship that was heavy-duty. That relationship had a lot of passion. It often came out in beating, battering, as well as sex. There were lots of times I felt sexual but didn't want to acknowledge it, and so we went to war. That relationship had sparks, but we were not meant to be sexual partners, we couldn't have what I'd call good sex.

Good sex is where you're comfortable with somebody, where there's enjoyment, passion, fun. You can be serious—nothing wrong with that. But afterwards you feel good. You can do anything, as long as you're two adults in agreement. You feel fuller, richer, you don't feel jealous or ripped off. Good sex deepens communication—or it is a form of it. I had good sex with my girlfriend Christina, years ago. She was a working-class tough. Cute and hot, Italian and raring to go. She loved sex. With her, I had a fabulous orgasm: I came in colors. I loved her to eat me, and she would go for hours, loving me.

I love being taken from the front or the back. Gentle, but strong. With somebody I want. I don't mind taking somebody either, if I know it's going to be all right. Once in Provincetown, I was with a friend, and I just took her, grabbed her, in a bar and kissed her. Later, I was eating her, and she had this incredibly deep orgasm, and the resonant feeling in my body was spectacular. I love to begin body to body, to feel that eroticism. Kisses. Mouths. Tongues. Shirt off. Skin. Hands. Mouths on breasts. Into bed, naked. Lots of exploring, hands and mouths all over, breast to breast. I want hands in my hair, hands on my face, fingers in my mouth. Cunts pushing, riding thighs. Sweat and body juices, tasting them and going everywhere. Finger-play and fingers inside. I have incredibly deep orgasms, radiating up into my gut, my thighs, my ass, my breasts. Pleasurable and moving.

Twelve years ago, when I was living in New York, I had a traumatic rape, at night in my own home. That's the highest terror I've ever known. He could have killed me with one hand. And yet that rape involved one of the tenderest moments I've ever experienced. At some point, I told him I was a lesbian. He stood up, backed off and apologized. But a few moments later, he knelt at my side, pulled up my shirt and put his mouth on my breast. It was the most incredibly gentle experience. The two of us were utterly vulnerable. That's the moment of this rape that disturbs me the most. I did want to kill him. If I'd had a gun, he'd have been a dead man.

I think I withdrew from sex, and it's only recently—since coming to California—that I've felt a need to come into a new sense of sexuality. I've never really had one, never really felt myself as a woman. I've begun to experience more pleasure in my body. I'm much more comfortable now with my clothes off than I was when I was young. That feels new. I imagine that sex now would feel fabulous. And extremely frightening, because I haven't done it for a long time, because I don't have an easy time coming till I really trust somebody, and because I don't know about myself in that way. It cuts into such tenderness, such fragility. I think positive sexuality has to do with staying connected to your physical being and the earth, with getting real. It's feeling yourself as clear as possible in the world, with its eucalyptus leaves, its flowers, and coffee in the morning. The world is experiential!

VI. ECSTATIC OUTLAWS

Pleasure is a little subversive in a culture that upholds the Protestant ethic of delayed gratification. But rebels are everywhere. In the eleven interviews making up this chapter, men and women lay claim to shameless sexuality as part of an exhilarating largeness of life. "You have to throw off other people's expectations—the results of their own actions and pain," asserted Ginger, a New Orleans-born writer. "We live in a time when it's *scandalous* to talk about the beauty of the body. AIDS has made people even more closed in. I want to celebrate the body, sensuality and sexual magic."

For some people, just breaking away from the missionary position can be a surprisingly daring act. As Phil recalled, "Early conditioning about sex went, 'As a man, you are the commander-in-chief. Do it well. Be a soldier.' I was afraid of doing something perverted, like cunnilingus or being on the bottom. In time, I was pleasantly surprised to find that some women thought I was not a pervert—and sometimes even asked for what they wanted." Numerous interviewees made similar blasts against formulas for proper coupling and the limits of traditional sex roles. In one account, Angela, a young college student, described her uphill battle against good girl/bad girl stereotypes. "You get shit from all kinds of people. I met a guy who said, 'You enjoy sex, don't you?' As though he was really *surprised*," she marveled.

Rules change with the territory. Queer culture is perceived by the mainstream as free, fringe and permissive. Yet sexual minority communities also impose their own restrictions on behavior, and they have their own renegades. In one interview included here,

179

Toni described the lesbian butch/femme bed rules of the 1950's. "You were confined to roles: butches made love, femmes got it. I like to do everything, and I always worried, 'Am I too kinky?'" she explained. "To me, sex is not 'politically correct.' It's individual. Nowadays, everything is fair game." Another upstart, Mike, discovered that the thrill he found in anonymous sex in public parks was not universally lauded by other gay men. "You could blast through convention and all kinds of order to get to a sexual *core* that was radiant and powerful," he said, almost ablaze with passion. "I was always amazed by people who viewed it as the most tainted, the most degraded, out of control, people who can't have 'normal' sex."

Lust, of course, has a bad reputation. Even the most socially valued sexual partnership—durable monogamy, especially within marriage—is whacked with the scourge of negativity. Marital twosomes are dismissed as dull, if not altogether sexless after the first year's honeymoon. Martin, a disabled man wed six years, objected to the bad press. "I'm always looking for new ways to expand our sexual relationship," he told me. "It's important and constantly has to be updated, refreshed, given new life. We get creative."

Wild or tame, real-life erotics expand the range of sexual images far beyond Hollywood hunks and Miss February. Indeed, although corporate advertising suggests that the "vavoom factor" peaks at twenty, the sex histories collected here provide evidence that sex improves with age. By all accounts, selectivity informed by experience helps enhance choices in sex-partners and pleasures. "If you're twenty-two, you don't know how to be passionately connected to another life," said Lena, reflecting on her own fifty years. "The more life you bring to the sexual sharing with somebody, the better the sex. If you've walked in the world with appetites and generosity, love and lust, then that's who you bring to your sexual life." For these eleven outlaws, sex creates opportunities to take risks—first and foremost, the risk of being oneself, without reservation. As one man summed it up, "Here I am, giving myself away."

Mike

"I was always a fairy from age nine or ten, but I didn't know it—even though I had crushes on boys, sex with boys and at sixteen was buying physique magazines on Hollywood Boulevard," Mike says grinning. Mike came out in high school. Now a handsome forty-four, he teaches college in San Francisco and dubs his sexual proclivities "Jewish affectionate sex: kissing, hugging, polymorphous perverse sex where the entire body is a site of arousal."

Before AIDS, which has changed everything in the gay community, there was a kind of hierarchy of sexual expression. The highest was to meet somebody in a bar, which had the sanction of being a social place as much as a sexual place. The next step down were the baths, where you would meet people in mini-rooms that weren't exactly your *home*, but there was a little cot and so on. The lowest form of sex was anonymous sex in the bushes or the tea rooms.

I always felt it worked the other way around. For me, it felt great and absolutely spirited to meet people out in the open air, in the sunlight, among the trees, unformulated by rank and class, just spontaneously as men loving men. It's funny—it really is wrapped up with social ideology for me. I felt that the bars were pretentious, stupid, alcoholic and smokey. At the baths, presentation, beauty and privilege were evident. But in the bushes, there was a much more egalitarian sense. Frolicking in the bushes seemed the least tainted, and I was always amazed by people who viewed it as the most tainted, the most degraded, out of control, people who can't have "normal" sex. To somebody who didn't experience it, it would be hard to get across the nature of the abandon and the wildness of those times: wild, spontaneous fucking and sucking in the middle of cities or on the beaches—and totally, essentially kind. In some way, it was the most naked of all possible encounters, and I have been thrilled by that. I call it vertical sex.

In today's world, the free expression of sexuality has taken a rap and suffered. Now, anonymous sex is necessarily curtailed by AIDS, because the range of acts is proscribed. But anonymous sex is also *un*necessarily curtailed, because it's been maligned by association with AIDS, when in fact it has nothing to do with AIDS. *Unsafe* sex has something to do with AIDS, anonymous or not.

Nowadays, you negotiate with the official design of safe sex, at least I do. Everybody has their own guidelines, and I don't hold up my behavior as a model for anybody else. You establish your own guidelines for behavior, and you try to stick close to them under all possible circumstances, so that you protect yourself and other people. Frankly, those lines are hard to enforce. I think everybody is lured over their lines. There may be people who don't deep kiss, but I still do. Oral sex is my most transgressed rule. I don't use condoms for oral sex, but since 1981, I haven't come in anybody's mouth and haven't let anybody come in my mouth—even though it's a grievous loss, both ways. I completely eliminated anal sex from my repertoire, because of the danger of unprotected anal sex and then my questions about condoms breaking.

I miss various acts. I miss the lack of inhibition. In the past, you could blast through convention and all kinds of order to get to a sexual *core* that was radiant and powerful, without following any of the conventional routes to get there. You were ecstatic outlaws. Today, maybe that's a little more difficult to achieve. The loss makes me feel angry, scared, lousy—and I'm still able to have a decent sex life. It isn't as cool as it was before AIDS, but it's still pretty cool. I call it vertical sex. With vertical sex, good sex is a good blow job. No, it's not. A good blow job is a good blow job. But good vertical sex means that you perform some kind of dance with somebody with ease and grace and lots of unspoken, natural consanguinity. You know how to respond to each other, how to give and take, how to have a natural sense of mutual boundaries. It could be a completely silent dance, and it could be really deep. God, I've had some very deep exchanges with people whose names I don't know—just by doing that mutual dance. And I would say that's different than what I would describe as good sex in bed with somebody. The range of acts is different in the park, where you may or may not kiss somebody. The territory in which you touch each other might be circumscribed, the number of acts might be circumscribed. I'm more tempted to say that it's more loaded in bed, but gee . . . . Penetration and licking somebody's dick, or fucking, whatever— and again, I want to emphasize in the era pre-AIDS—how can you say that isn't intimate? It's *shockingly* intimate. Indeed, one of the best turn-ons is how shockingly intimate it is. To meet somebody in an almost public situation, which is supposed to preclude intimacy and instantly get down towards intimacy . . . . The vulnerability is so charged and so sudden and so true.

I've been seeing somebody for about four months, somebody with whom I'm having a wonderful sexual relationship. It's much more satisfying than vertical sex, because it's more thorough and complex, lasts a whole lot longer, and infuses sex with emotion and more complex kinds of responsibility. The eroticism is greater and much more subtle. For me, kissing this man makes me swoon in special ways. Kissing a lover is a much more supercharged act than kissing somebody you don't know—and that's just the *beginning*! Making love to somebody you know while you look in their eyes is such a frank enlargement of sexual vulnerability. To me, that's completely exciting. And coming to know each other's body, being able to talk about your body, to describe to each other acts that turn you on, to refine them, search them out, awakening somebody's entire body, having your own entire body awakened. That's what I would call good sex. It's different—and rare. For me, it seems to be rarer and rarer. I thank the Goddess that I'm having it.

Ginger

As one of nine children in a warm extended family on the outskirts of New Orleans, Ginger got mixed signals about sexuality. "I was trying to preserve what the Church told me to," she says, "but the social scene said, 'Cut loose, cut loose!' and everybody's daddy wanted you." A writer whose varied day jobs have included a stint at an anti-pornography organization, Ginger lives with her husband in a gilded Victorian house.

The female form is such an exquisite piece of symmetry in nature, such an outrageous source of power, the cauldron of life and sustenance. And as far as I know, human woman is the only creature in existence with a bodily organ designed sheerly for pleasure. I find that incredibly interesting. Yet so much time is spent teaching us to be critical of our bodies; entire industries are built on how we should decorate ourselves. When I fantasize, I dream of a time when women were free, and sexuality was not associated with pain and violence and sin.

It is very difficult to have a relationship if you don't know who you are or if you're pretending to be what someone wants you to be. When I was coming up—the sixties—first there was a notion about femininity that came down to being the bracelet, looking good on his arm. For a lot of black women, this meant that they had arrived at luxury, at respect, but it was boring there and pretentious. And it wasn't real: we got that old Queen of the Nile bullshit, but you never got *treated* like a queen. You got treated like something that looked like a queen when the presence of a queen was necessary. Then in the late sixties, in the height of the black revolution, there came the business of being Amazon Queen. You had to look good in the daytime, but at night, when the police was vamping on the community, you had to be able to pick up a gun, rustle down, handle a demonstration, do time. All this while maintaining a queenly notion of femininity and walking three steps behind. If you tried to be a woman of your people,

Ecstatic Outlaws

who you were could change from one year to the next, depending on the perceived need at the time.

Then there was that time in the early seventies, when all the conversation about what a black woman ought to be dropped away. And we were left to ask *ourselves* the question, "Who should we be?" The answer has come up, "A bowl of roses. Different colors, different shapes, sizes and scents." I think the person who recognizes that she has the right to define herself is in a better position to have quality short-term and long-term relationships.

My first sexual experience was awful, one step away from rape. I wondered, "Is this it? Why do people do this?" Then the first time I ran up on somebody who really made *love* to me, I became what we call dick-drunk: "Let me after *this*." In my twenties, the long-range thing was no way on my mind. I wasn't interested at all. Of course, the rhetoric was that you were supposed to get married. The older women would say, "Every man is a dog except one. It's up to you to find him." In my way, I kept looking for Mister No-Dog, and then it started to occur to me that this wasn't happening. So I slipped into what I call my "little-black-book stage." A book full of friends that you can also sleep with. No expectations. I found that to be a very good way to operate—but then, that element of interdependence was missing. I can remember being so lonely, I used to send for junk mail so there would be something in the mailbox when I got home.

I remained in the little-black-book stage for a long time. I was receiving spiritual counseling from a Puerto Rican sister down in L.A., and she told me, "The Goddess wants you to get married." I said, "Tell the Goddess she's out of her mind. I'm not interested in nobody bossing me around!" Then I had a poetry reading and read a poem, "I found him last night in a dream." At the end of the reading, a man came up to me and said, "You know your poem laying out what your man has to be like? I'm him." That was my husband. We've been married eleven years.

Eleven years is a long time. When I was younger I could take, and maybe even favor, a "wham, bam, thank you ma'am." But now I find it more interesting to insinuate and to tease for days before actually going into the artistry of sex. I need to move slow and really engage the senses. One of my favorite things is playing with foods. Food is very interesting. I like textures. Jewelry, especially gemstones. Incense. A bath—water with crystals, flowers, color. Big pillows, brightly colored fabric, and the tension involved in not rushing . . . where you tease all weekend and actually build up sensuality: bathe, massage, drink a little, sing, bite into a piece of fruit together, entice and entice and entice.

I like lots of foreplay. Days of it. A combination of vigor and tenderness. *Vigor* indicating strength and power, not getting close to violence, but vibrant, alive. The texture of the thing needs to change in order to keep my interest. I am fortunate in that my husband is a jazz musician who does improvisation, and in sex, we can move into something that will not be the same twice. There's a sense of fluidity, constant touch and motion, moving muscles like wet clay. There's a feeling of power sharing and an ability to read what's happening from one moment to the next, with enough of a second sense that I don't always have to say, "Touch me here, touch me there." Penetration is special. I love it. That's the sense of being fed.

Sounds. My goodness, the *music*. The music of it all. There are sounds that we as humans utter in sexual interaction that there's no other opportunity to utter. There have been times I needed to say something to somebody, and the only way to say it was to be erotic with them. In the past, I was so rebellious against the idea of a woman being "the other half," that notion of, "We two make one," that today I say, "This is the three of us: me and you—two *whole* people—and the interaction, a third entity where we come together." So that there's a sense of intermingling and being boundless, but not a sense of loss of self. I have notions about ecstasy, feeling deeply connected, ancient and something akin to innocent. I get excited about eating, colors, scents, but good sex is all of those senses put together plus something else that's difficult to articulate. There's a passage in the poems coming out of West Africa in which the goddess of love and the lord of destiny lie down to forget the world together . . . . To forget the world together . . . . But it's not about forgetting yourself.

Peter

Peter's first impressions of sex came from talks with his mother, who equated sex and love, and from sometimes gruesome pictures in medical magazines. The oldest of four boys, he grew up on Long Island in a well-to-do Italian American family. Now forty-five and self-employed as a wood-worker, Peter lives adjacent to his Marin studio. Iron John sits on the bookshelf. Masks adorn the walls. Drums lie on the inlaid floor. Adamantly monogamous, Peter has just begun a new relationship.

I was a virgin till I was twenty-two, posing, acting the role of a sexually-wise person, but women could tell that I didn't know the first thing about it. I was a jet pilot in Vietnam. I had my Corvette Stingray, and I'd put on my love beads and drive away from the ship, stalking women. I was really bad at it. I couldn't be cold and calculating. My first sexual experience was horrible: I date-raped some woman who was drunk. My Navy buddies had set me up with her because she was "an easy lay." Classic. I felt totally horrible afterwards and thought, "If this is sexuality, I don't want to have anything to do with it!" Two months later, I met an opera singer from North Carolina. We walked off a diving board fully dressed, wound up in her apartment, stripped off our wet clothes. I had a relationship with her for six months that was wonderful. It felt like coming home.

My second marriage was with a woman I chased for four years and left about six times. She became a follower of Bhagwan, the guru up in Oregon, and she moved into the ashram. The only way I could get to her was to go into the ashram. So I did. I joined up, put on my red robes and went to the encounter groups. The ashram was a corrupt organization, all about sex and control. In the midst of it, Bhagwan was this wonderful, enlightened being who'd drop pearls of wisdom, and everybody'd be transfixed, but then he was unavailable. He was cloistered, became celibate and went into silence. You were left with the so-called teachers, who were systematically fucking all of the most beautiful people in the ashram. I wanted to be monogamous. My lover would bring me women to fuck, and I had to show her how open and spiritual I was by being with these other women. Then she'd say, "You *could* have been with me, but you chose to be with her." Double messages. Not malicious, just confused. We were both desperately trying to put meaning in our lives in a profane culture. Eventually, she escaped from the ashram and came to me, saying, "I want to be with you." We took off our red clothes, gave up the spiritual thing, got married, moved to the Bay Area. Mostly what I got from the ashram was crabs.

Till I was about thirty-five, the way I was sexually was about pleasing the other person, being accepted, performing in order to get affection. I believed when I was really young that women had the secret to life and that men had to learn it from them. But a good lover is coming from a place of solid self-love, and men cannot love themselves if they feel there's a big chunk of themselves that has to be provided by somebody else. I've learned that once a man has experienced—in the company of other men—his *own* strength to provide for himself, to nurture and love himself, he can become vulnerable and bare his soul to a woman, because he knows if she doesn't love him, he won't die.

The other person is a universe over which I have no control, a total mystery I can let go into and learn from. Some of the most intensely pleasurable parts of being sexual have nothing to do with orgasm or even penetration. The sensations I get through my hands. Touching her and seeing her with my fingertips. Running my hands all over her body, over the different contours, especially the really female contours: the pelvis, the ass, the breasts. The *feminine* part is what gets me off. I really like what women look like from the back. When you can see their ass and vagina at the same time, it's a feast. I don't like anal sex at all, but I love women's asses. It's not about penetrating them, it's about *adoring* them! I love to eat pussy. For long periods of time. It tastes good, it smells good, it feels good. I love to get girl-juice all over me . . . . I like lots of tactile stimulation everywhere. I love oral sex, and one of the biggest parts of it for me is visual. There's something about a woman's face, the epitome of the feminine. To feel and see the contact of the most male part of myself with that feminine face is incredibly exciting. A lot of the pleasure comes from watching, not just from nerve endings.

I've been multi-orgasmic for the past two or three years. For me, it was about separating orgasm from ejaculation, and the vehicle for that is to opt for not ejaculating and still allow yourself the orgasm. I learned it through masturbation. Opting to *not* ejaculate allows you to make love all night, if that's what you want to do. And opting to have *orgasms* allows you to let energy surge up your spine and . . . for me, it blows out the top of my head and out my hands. It's a fountain of energy and bliss, a connecting force with my partner. When I'm making the decision about ejaculation, there's a little place inside me like a hungry ghost that's never quite wanting to draw boundaries and take responsibility, urging me, "Come on! This is what we want." There's another part of me that says, "No. I know *exactly* what I want." Once I push through that wall and make the decision, then I don't ejaculate. There is a grace that falls on you that has nothing to do with ability, with a technique that you have devised. It's all about getting the small personality out of the way and having more ecstasy.

Good sex is connection with the deep self. It includes poetry, being able to laugh in the middle of sex, being able to talk about how you're feeling, being uninhibited. It includes owning your gender, being a complete person. When I make love, I want to be with somebody who's in touch with raw animal power, with emotion and spirituality, though you can have an experience that's pleasurable physically that doesn't have to include all those things every time. Sex is circular, non-linear, timeless, a state of having arrived. I feel there is ecstasy and infinite possibilities.

Patricia

Young Patricia learned self-reliance early. She was the only child on a rough Saskatchewan homestead, a tract of wilderness broken into a farm by her resolute Scottish parents. Patricia won a science scholarship to college, where she met the men who have been her life partners. A slim, sparkling woman, she married, raised three children and worked in genetics research. Today, the white-haired seventy-one-year-old says she's looking at her life in a fairly positive way: "Considering everything, my relationship record is not too bad. It's rather good, you see."

I grew up in the country. I think that my parents were fairly open. My mother had big bundles of prejudices, but it was her intent to be honest. Sometimes too honest. Still, being open-minded about a wide range of behaviors doesn't mean that *you're* permitted to have a wide range of behaviors: "Our kind of people don't do that sort of thing." There were stories with sexual elements, stories I overheard from my parents. For example, we had neighbors, Amos Wheatley and his wife. One night while washing dishes, Mrs. Wheatley told my mother that she let Amos "use the other hole." Then they had a baby girl, and I heard my father comment that Amos must have got it right at least once! Sometime later, Amos, who was uneasy about the expense of having a new baby, told my father he'd rather have had a team of horses. My father said, "Isn't that expecting rather a lot of Mrs. Wheatley?"

One of the real negativities sexually—which was both a driving force and a terrific handicap—was something that happened to me at age eight or nine or so. It was something that I never dealt with, although I remembered it, until I was actually in therapy after my divorce. We lived out on a farm. We had an outhouse, and the dog was always following along, interested in smells. I remember pushing the dog away, but finally something just overcame me and I thought, "I wonder what it would be like." And actually I found it was quite nice. One day my mother caught me sitting on the couch with my legs spread and the dog licking my

190

vulva. She was terribly upset. She was crying, and I was crying. I remember saying, "Mama, please spank me. *Please* spank me." And she said, "I can't bear to touch you." My father came in and asked what was going on. She said, "I can't tell you. It's too awful." He put his arms around me and comforted me, but nothing was ever said about it. I always felt that there was something very bad about me, that nobody would be able to bear to touch me, if they knew this terrible secret. Through therapy, in my forties I realized that this was not so terrible. Still, I've always felt that I wasn't as daring as I would like to be, and I think that this is part of the reason.

Jack, my first husband, took better care of me than I ever took care of him, orgasmically. To some extent, through fooling around with him before our marriage, I got addicted to manual stimulation as release—with a partner and by myself. Four years later, I had an affair with one of Jack's friends, when I was living with him and his wife. I was working at a pulp and paper mill, and my husband was spending a year in Montreal to finish his degree. One New Year's Eve, I came in from a local party quite looped. John invited me into bed at five o'clock in the morning, and I was sufficiently unconcerned that I thought, "Well, so what? Once won't hurt." But once having started, it continued. I would get wakened up every morning with a cup of coffee—because he always got up early. Sexually, he never failed. He just wouldn't come until I came. This was a glorious experience. We weren't in love with each other, we just liked each other. I didn't worry about telling him my dark secrets. His had been such a strange life that he gave everybody freedom.

Probably the most perfect experience I ever had was after Jack and I were separated, and I was involved with this Swedish fellow. He was going through a divorce, I was going through a divorce, and eventually we crashed. But at that particular moment, we met up at Mount Diablo for a picnic . . . . It was absolutely the most perfect togetherness that I have ever felt in my entire life. He was a fairly competent lover, although I don't remember anything unusual about it—it was just tremendous feelings. It was truly as if time stopped still. I remember thinking, "I'm in eternity. There is no past, there is no future." It was like that all day long.

Nearly twenty years later, there was Howard. I knew Howard

from college days, and I always felt that he was the brother I'd never had. He was in some ways—whatever these vibrations are—the most powerful man that I had ever encountered. I remember feeling this power just emanating from him, and I thought, "We can't go on like this much longer." We were sitting on the couch, embracing, and I sort of grinned at him and said, "Why not?" He said mournfully, "It's too soon." But he was fairly easy to push over, and I did. Afterwards—and I treasure this comment so much—he sat up and said, "Now that we've got *that* over with, maybe we can settle down to enjoying each other." Such an honest remark. I had never had anybody say that to me, my whole life before. It was a long road to get to sixty to find that.

I felt that this was somebody I could so completely trust. To have him look at me and say, "I wonder if you know how much I love you." I was sixty, but I remember thinking, "This is the first time in my life I have been truly content." It was this feeling that here was someone that I could trust. Even if our actual sex life was not fantastic—it was good, not fantastic—I didn't care. The thing that was so good was that I could lean up against his back, look at the back of his head and feel so safe and comfortable. I felt in the electricity between us that I had never experienced that kind of total, physical rightness. That was a real unexpected bonus out of life.

I used to think that if you could have a really good orgasm, that was good sex. That seemed a fairly simple definition. But in looking back on various incidents in my life, I find that there was something else. The specialness. I think good sex is comforting. I'd like to have both aspects, but I keep coming back to this sense of emotional completion that is hardest to do without. Now that Howard is gone, I don't fantasize about sex. I just think it would be nice to have his arms around me, holding me close.

Buzz

A blond string bean from Minnesota, Buzz found boyhood thrills in an eye-opening dirty magazine—"an abomination and a treasure"—and in the Boy Scouts, where he learned to swear and masturbate. Today Buzz is forty-two, a graphic designer who lives with his long-time love. HIV-positive and on AZT, he has responded to the AIDS epidemic by encouraging safe sex jubilees, events that allow and teach people to have sex without risking infection.

When I was with my mother shopping in downtown St. Paul, I was propositioned by an older gentleman, and we made a date. We met later, he drove to a deserted place, I pulled down my pants, and he played with me. I was fifteen and absolutely a willing participant. However, a patrolling police car came by and checked us out with his flashlight and hauled us both off. I was charged with sodomy, a word I didn't know and had to look up in the dictionary. I was put on probation for six months, and once a month, the probation officer came to my junior high school and my name would be announced over the school loudspeaker. I was an honor student, an officeholder with the student council, and my classmates thought I was being called to the principal's office for student government, but I knew it was my probation officer. That was a very formative situation around my sexuality—my community seeing me as an exemplary junior achiever and me considering myself something else, which was a sexual criminal, a deviant, homosexual low-life. I worried that people would find out what I really was and I would be abandoned.

It wasn't till I was out of university that I began the early stages of coming out. 1972. That was my summer of love. Later, I moved to San Francisco for the winter, and I've been here ever since. I was overwhelmed by the San Francisco men: they all knew something I didn't, and it started with how they wore their jeans.

I met Wes. We began our affair very sexually, and that's been a crucial part of our relationship, which has gone on for eight years. One of his gifts to me is that he has never been judgmental about any of the things I've done in the sexual arena. He's a little bit kinkier than I am by experience and disposition, and he gives me room to experiment. The year we met, AIDS reared its ugly head, and I also became involved in the Radical Fairies. That's sort of a loosely organized social conspiracy, more vegetarian-organic oriented, more prone to be in touch with alternative healing and feminist spirituality. There, sexuality is acknowledged as a gift of spirit, a manifestation of the divine in us, not the shame in us. I was shocked and delighted to observe in my first meeting that while business was being conducted, guys would start making out, then cool down and rejoin the circle, and none of this was inappropriate. "Yes, this is the way it was meant to be. We are all naturally sexual creatures, and why should we not allow each other to see ourselves expressing that part?"

Around that time, a friend invited me to the San Francisco Jacks, a jack-off club. That's where I learned to be a voyeur and found that consensually watching people have sex together could be beautiful. In a group setting of guys masturbating together, there are clusters of energy that get drawn together, like pockets of gravity pulling people in. A particularly attractive guy could start it, or a particularly hot pairing. A circle forms, and sometimes a circle around *that* circle. The sexual energy flows through all the people who are watching or beating off or pulling on a nipple or standing behind the guy and touching his back. I might not be the center of the vortex, but I'm still part of the tornado. There we all are, being sexual beings together. I find that profound. And I find it profound to watch men regard each other in that situation, how they are touched and respected, the courtesy that is shown, the tender heat. All roles drop to the floor, like the clothes you take off when you enter, and you become only men.

When the bathhouses closed, and there wasn't going to be anything else like that, I signed a five-year lease on a building with offices for my business and party space for the San Francisco Jacks. In the course of time, other community sex organizations heard about it, and I started to rent out the space, up to eight times a month. It was like a VFW hall for kinky people. We had a Kinky Spring Festival, women's parties, the first Carnal Carnival, SM parties, piss parties. Quite a range. Mostly for gay men, but not exclusively. The parties had to be safe sex. It was *very*,

very important to me. I could not take money and allow people to become infected. In order to clarify that, I created house rules, and they were in the written contract for every party that I rented to.

We had the world's first Jack- and Jill-Off party. We didn't know what was going to happen. It could have been like the junior high dances, where the boys stand on one side and the girls stand on the other, but it wasn't. It took a while for the ice to break, but once it did, my goodness . . . my goodness . . . . There were gay men that touched their first pussy. There were straight men much surprised to find the hand around their dick was another man's. I remember one gal on a couch with a guy sitting on each side working a breast, and two guys at her feet, one man massaging her pussy. She was absolutely transported and started to have multiple orgasms. After the whole thing was over, a gay guy said, "Wow! They really *can* do that, can't they?" People had their first bisexual, trisexual, group-sexual experience, and all within an atmosphere of playfulness and without oppressive pressure. It's a sexual world. Heterosexual, bisexual, gay: it's really pretty arbitrary, and the divisions are limiting.

I've been in the presence of thousands of people having sex with each other. Outside that context, I like to have sex with someone that I know. I have this relationship with Wes that's very dear to me, but I also like to have another boyfriend. Wes likes one-nighters, but I've had outside relationships that have gone on for a couple of years. I like going away, the excitement of being with someone else, and also the trust and intimacy that can develop between two people who know each other. In a sexual situation, I am very passionate. Not restrained. I like switching, playing with the arbitrariness of top and bottom. Overwhelmer and overwhelmed, the daddy and the boy. Hard energy. I like to talk. I like to talk *filth* about unsafe sex. In practice, safe sex for me means using condoms for intercourse, latex gloves for ass-play, not swallowing come. "On me, not in me" is a succinct phrase for it. I insist on feeling connected to the other person, and I like a partner that is sexually expressive, uninhibited. I hate shame being brought into the mix.

Good sex connects you with yourself and with your partner. Orgasm brings a sense of union. It's losing your mind and coming to your senses. I worked for well over a decade to become an integrated person, and sex comes right out of the center of my being. I have no shame about who I am these days. I have a really good relationship with my family, and I don't hide my gayness. I try not to hide my life. Good sex takes you away from the ho-hum, humdrum life as we usually know it. Sometimes merely to a hilltop and sometimes hurtling into the stratosphere.

Angela

Brought up in Berkeley during the sexual revolution, Angela learned early that sex was a positive part of her parents' lives. Her father urged her to postpone sex till her college years, but just before turning sixteen, Angela began making love with her high school boyfriend. From the first, sex was orgasmic and involved birth control. Now a sparkling twenty-three, Angela is a young African American finishing up her senior year at UC Berkeley.

Guys will sleep with you at the drop of a hat, but they won't view it the same way. When I was seventeen and in college in Los Angeles, I was involved with a guy from Southern California, and he was the first man to ever ask me how many guys I'd had sex with. Of course I didn't tell him. I tested him out, "What if I said three?" He thought that was okay. "What if I said twenty?" He said, "Then I'd think you were a slut." But he could tell me about all kinds of wild sex *he'd* had: he was in a fraternity and had had group sex with women. Men will tell you openly that they're sleeping with a woman and consider her a slut, and you're supposed to accept that. I wonder, "What do you think of yourself, if you're sleeping with someone you're calling a slut? I revere *my* body." So I began running into the contradictory, hypocritical attitudes that some men have about sex.

For instance, I told my boyfriend that I'd had an abortion, and he was really negative—which was such a trip, because he'd had three girlfriends who'd gotten pregnant by him and had abortions. After that experience, I stopped being open about it. I know women who pretend they're virgins: "Guys think it's better if they're the first." Men get attitudes. They ask you, "Am I the best?" I've realized that you have to lie to guys. It's too bad. Hopefully, I'll meet someone as expressive as I am. The ideal person would be someone who I could tell everything to, and I don't think I've met a man like that.

I decided, "I'm just going to be who I am and take the risk, because it's worth it." But after going through those different experiences, I found that it wasn't fun to just try someone out, to just have sex, and I didn't have to do that. I also realized I had to get serious about birth control. Not, "The full moon is out, we're on the beach, who needs condoms?" I had to get more realistic.

My father died of leukemia six months ago. This has been the most difficult time of my life. I went back to seeing an old boyfriend from high school. It was comforting. During the whole last year, the only thing I looked forward to was sex. Going through a tragedy makes you feel things more deeply. When I first had sex shortly after my father died, it was the most incredible experience, because I was feeling all these things. The guy I was with felt it too, the energy was so overwhelming. It was almost scary. Since my father's death, I treat every sexual experience as the last. I consume it more and try to feel every little part. That's why orgasms are that much more intense. I feel I'm absorbing the other person more and care more about them. When sex is over now, I want to talk about what I'm going through—but I don't want to pour out everything, because I'm afraid my partner will close off.

I don't think I could have sex the same way I used to. Now I have to have some kind of emotional attachment to the person. Kissing, touching and affection are important, but I also have to feel close with my partner. I think sex is a way of expressing yourself, seeing someone's deeper side. Someone can seem straight and conservative and not be that way in bed. When two people climax together, that's a spiritual event. I don't know if it's nirvana itself, but it's great, lasts a day or two, then you come back down and want to do it again. I don't always allow myself to have multiple orgasms. If I'm with a man I expect to be a permanent partner, or if I've known my partner a long time, I enjoy sex more and allow myself more orgasms.

With great sex, you feel totally open, free and able to express yourself with someone. You're in the ultimate state of freedom from inhibition, and the other person is as well. The defenses are totally down. It's not just the orgasm: it's every look, every touch, every word. The whole experience has meaning, has depth. It's not what you're trying to get towards; it happens as a natural consequence of everything else. Orgasm is like an explosion. You're in this kinetic world where everything is in motion. You're going up and you can't stop, you couldn't stop if you wanted to. It's almost frightening, because you lose control. Something else takes over. In that experience, I feel wiser. You feel you are going somewhere. Everyone's trying to find the answer, "Why are we here?" You feel closer to that.

Phil

Growing up in a black middle-class family in Cleveland, Phil began his sex education with parental information "as clinical as calculus." Sex at sixteen induced his first orgasm. "I had never done that before, never masturbated," he explains. "It was kind of a weird feeling: "Oh goodness, am I going to pee in her?" Now forty-nine, Phil works as a consultant in organizational management.

One thing that to some degree shaped my sexuality was that I got this part-time job by accident in a porno store. I was a college student in Washington, D.C. Somehow I got into a conversation with the guy who ran the store. I guess he didn't have very many black customers. He asked, "Do kids up at the college look at dirty movies? I'll give you some stuff on consignment, and if you sell it, I'll give you a percentage." For a while, I became Mr. Porno. We had stag movies, pictures, magazines. It began to expand my awareness, made me more interested in unusual things. But one of the more negative effects was the good girl/bad girl thing, because the women who *do* all these things are the bad women.

For example, oral sex. No self-respecting man ever would go down on a woman. It was at best smelly and nasty, and at worst dirty, disgusting and humiliating. You want her to suck *you* off, because it makes you feel good and proud, powerful and strong, macho, masculine. But on the other hand, that's all she's good for: "I don't want to kiss somebody like this." It made it very hard to feel passionate love or warmth towards a woman I was having sex with. Some of the women I was most interested in sexually were not people I was interested in having relationships with. And with the "nice girls," sex was dull and *pro forma*. That was a problem for a long time.

It had a racial aspect to it. Ninety percent of the women I went out with in my senior year of college were white. Some of that was economic: all the black women I knew in D.C. lived in the

200

Ecstatic Outlaws

dorms or at home, so you couldn't do much there. All the women I knew who had their own places were white. Economics. But the other part was sexual: a higher proportion of white women were into the sexual openness of the late sixties. A lot of the black women were into the Church. They were less prone to political radicalism and cultural radicalism, which would include sexuality. A lot of the white women were being radicalized by women's liberation, SDS, and the pill. I didn't ever think about having any long-term relationships with white women. I always assumed there was this ideal black woman out there whom I could take home to mama. It never happened.

Most black women I had sex with, you always did the missionary position first. You might get into other positions, but it took much longer. Sex was a performance, never a conversation. But if I spent a weekend with a white woman, I could have sex in all different positions, experiment, stop and start and even discuss parts of it. The first woman I ever went down on was a white woman. It would never have crossed my mind to go down on a black woman. I would have been scared that she would have thought I was a sexual degenerate. With white women, I felt that I was not a pervert. The women were less passive, and I didn't have to be in control.

I remember one night, going over to one woman's house, having to please her sexually for the whole night. First she had me kiss her all over, lick her, caress her, starting with her feet. She led me over to the bed, tied me to the bed, straddled me, wanted me to kiss her nipples, her breasts, the back of her neck. She massaged herself, up and down, while I was lying there. She fucked me. Then she said, "You bad little boy, you came! You weren't supposed to do that," and lightly slapped me on the face. "I'm going to make you eat your own come. Suck me out until I come." Then she stroked my penis for a while with a feather, and I'm just, "Please do something, please do something." She let me come, started clenching my balls to the point where it was getting painful but not awful. She got in bed next to me, turned off the light, went to sleep, woke up and got on top of me again.

I like the possibility of getting caught. I remember one night out in the sand dunes by the Cliff House in San Francisco. It was getting dusky. She put the blanket around her shoulders and sat down facing me, pulled down my zipper and started massaging me. I was rubbing her breasts. People were walking by, and cars were close by. The turn-on was that we might get caught. Once a long time ago, riding Amtrak across the country, I went down on a woman I was traveling with. Late at night, when they turn off the lights. There were other people sitting around. I was on my knees on the floor of the coach, and she threw a coat over my head. I was sucking her off, and she was moaning, sliding down to get a better angle. The conductor came by and asked for the tickets. He didn't see me.

Sex helps me feel like I'm a full person. Complete. Exercising and discovering new parts of myself. At this stage of my life, I think about it more than I act. I'm much more careful than in the past. I use condoms now. I don't like them. AIDS has made me think about getting more serious, trying to find a Miss Perfect who I can *have* sex with, do all the things I might want to do. If I'm not in a relationship, I wonder if I'll be able to find a partner I can discuss sex with, or if I'll have to keep hiding these things. That old problem has not gone away . . . . Good sex is where both partners feel comfortable enough with each other that they can experiment and play around. Being able to feel free. Safe and free. You can fail, try something new or experience something old in a new way. And talk about it.

Toni

In mid-fifties Philadelphia, coffeehouses and jazz clubs gave Toni an introduction to culture beyond the constraints of her working-class Jewish neighborhood, where her parents encouraged dates with sensible boys who were going to be pharmacists. She came out as a lesbian in her late teens and moved to San Francisco ten years later. Strong-spoken and funny, single and forty-eight, Toni is a painter who has kept her day job as a secretary.

I'm a womanizer: I love women as a species. Their bodies, their smells, their feel, their sensitivity. I could sit on the bus and look at someone and think about sucking up her thighs.

I was a mother's helper the summer before my senior year in high school. I worked for these jazz musicians. I was looking in their bookcase one day and found this book, *I am a Woman in Love with a Woman*. By the time I finished the book, I knew I was a lesbian. It was like bells went off. I ran over to my school chum, who I was crazy about. I remember telling her on her step—everyone in Philadelphia sits on their steps in the summertime and talks. I don't know how it began, but she and I started having long make-out sessions. Long kisses. When you're a teenager, you can kiss for twenty, thirty minutes and never feel the need to go below the neck. Then when I started wanting to go below the neck, I got smacked away, until finally I was allowed to. We never, in all the years we were girlfriends, had true, true sex. I was in love with her. She had me twisted around her finger, and I would do anything she wanted. But she wouldn't let me do what *I* wanted. So I went to others.

One of the others was this prostitute, actually a famous and well-known prostitute in Philadelphia. But I had no knowledge of this, I just picked her up because I thought she was hot. I'll never forget sitting in a bar and telling her, "I don't know how to do certain things"—in other words, how to go down on someone. Oh, she didn't mind. She just took me in hand and taught me everything. I took right to it. That was one of the milestones in my life.

In that era, if you came out in the bar culture, you had to be butch or femme. No flip-flopping. I didn't have to decide to be butch. They told me. If you were butch, you made love. If you were femme, you got it. I went along with the program for a while, but then I realized this was not exactly fair; I had desires, too, and I wanted to be made love to, too. A few years later, I got involved with a butch. Handsome. She used to race sports cars. We went together, and that was when I finally started getting some myself.

The one and only time I slept with a male, it was not someone I was involved with or cared about. He manipulated me. He told me a far-fetched tale—which if I had not been eighteen and naïve, I would not have believed. He said that if I didn't let him do this, something awful would happen to my best friend. It wasn't something I wanted to do. Took ten minutes, maybe. If I had realized what was going on and said no, I would be happier. But on the other hand, I have a daughter. So I figure it was karma.

At twenty-eight, I drove cross-country with two acid-dropping, dope-smoking religious fanatics. I got to California and felt at home. The women are more gorgeous out here. I thought I had been let loose in a candy shop. I've had a lot of sex partners, a lot of relationships, lived with people. Generally, in bed, I make love to them first, and then they do me. I get very excited by making love to them, and the more excited they are, the more they open up. I've had a number of lovers who are really vocal. A lot of screaming and yelling. I find it exciting, but my conservative side is worried what the neighbors are thinking. It doesn't make me stop. I'm vocal, but not to that point. I'm pretty free, sexually. I like doing everything, just about. Cunnilingus, penetration and anal sex. With fingers. I think that everybody does ass-play. The first time that ever happened to me, I said, "No no no no no!" After a while, I decided that I liked it, and so it became part of my repertoire. Nobody else has said no.

I have plateaus of building up. This may go over the course of forty minutes or an hour. Then I have multiple orgasms. It's pretty intense. You're out of control, and your body takes over. I get extremely wet and ejaculate almost. Sometimes I see colors. In a way, it's paradoxical, because you're in your body but you're out of your body. You could almost say it's a spiritual experience.

Some religious people say you can maintain that state through meditation. Fine, I say. You want to get there through meditation, that's great. I'll get there through sex.

I've been with partners recently who've gotten me to do things I've never done before. Dildoes. When friends used to tell me they had sex toys, I didn't know what they were talking about. I vaguely remember going to adult bookstores long ago and seeing dildoes, and they were *huge*! Two feet *long*! You could beat someone to death with them! They looked more like weapons or billy clubs than sex items. The new ones out are different. Some can look like penises, but some are amorphous shapes or look like vegetables. Last year, at the behest of a girlfriend, I timidly went down to the sex shop and picked out a dildo. I discovered that I liked it, liked using it, strapping it on. It brought something out in me, definitely did something that I found erotic or forbidden. It's not about men. It's attached to a woman, and women smell different, they feel different, their bodies are different. And you can go *forever*. I also like holding the woman—because when you're going down, you're separated. There's something about having two bodies next to each other and having all that heat and sweat. I could be on the top or the bottom. At this point, I haven't had anyone do it to me.

In good sex, both people are present. They both want to be there. And there's a sensitivity to each person. An awareness of that other person, what they want, the non-verbal messages that they're sending, how they want to be treated, touched, held, felt or fucked. Technique matters. I like women who are femme, because I like that they like to wear slinky underwear and skirts, high heels, stockings and all those accoutrements. But once you're in bed, you can be anything. Butch/femme is not so much what you do in bed anymore, but how you are in the outside world. One time, one of my previous lovers used wrist restraints with lamb's wool inside, so as not to cut off the circulation. She tied me down, all four limbs spread-eagled on the bed, and sucked my nipples, bit up and down the body, licking, putting a whole hand inside, fisting me. I was totally out of control. I couldn't stop, I couldn't stop it.

Martin

Martin came of age in a poor refinery town across the bay from San Francisco. He was one of five brothers from a mixed-race family—Chicano, American Indian and white. Boyhood sexual rites included masturbating with his best buddy and cruising San Francisco with his brothers to gawk at prostitutes and transvestites. Today thirty-eight and sporting a long brown ponytail, Martin teaches independent living skills to the disabled.

B eing a sexual person has always been part of my identity. Not just me: my whole father's side of the family has been what I might dubiously call real ladies' men. I enjoyed girls at a young age, dated and was sexually active at a young age. Losing my virginity was classic. It was in the backseat of a red '57 Chevy in a church parking lot. The devil's car. I was fifteen. I didn't care about the person; I was just into losing my virginity. Not long after, I met a woman I did care about, and we were sexually active within a month or two of dating. We mapped out our whole life: marriage, kids. Then I had my accident. I was diving into a swimming hole off a little bridge and landed in too-shallow water. I broke my neck and became paralyzed from the shoulders down.

She was pregnant. We got married when I was in rehab in the hospital. The whole aspect of sexuality was real difficult: doctors didn't know what to tell you. My wife and I were used to missionary position intercourse. Really, we hadn't spent enough time together to experiment. We were young and knew how to do it one way. There were no groups to talk about sex, no counseling. Other patients were the best resource. One really experienced paraplegic said, "Well, you still have a tongue, don't you?" That was a profound revelation, that you could be sexually active in different ways. Growing up, I'd gotten the impression that oral sex was dirty, unpleasant and not quite right, although it was unclear what was actually wrong with it.

Our marriage broke up, just from too much pressure. I got

206

accepted at UC Berkeley in 1973 and that changed my life in terms of opening up my sexuality. Leaving where I grew up was important, moving away from that town and those friends who had a very narrow view of sexuality, were homophobic and limited in scope. Berkeley was a much looser environment—free love, free sex, openness, experimentation, women willing to be with disabled partners. I remember sleeping with two women at a time; I had experimental relationships with men. In the mid-seventies, I didn't see my disability keeping me from meeting people: women would come up to me and talk about my disability. It was an ice-breaker. Even though I was an assertive, sometimes aggressive male, I think there was something about the wheelchair that made it safe and easier for women to talk to me. Conversation didn't immediately lead into something physical. Sex had to be approached verbally, so I learned more skills on that level.

I met my wife through work. I had a rule I didn't date women from work, but I had to break that rule. We went to a star-gazing party in the Santa Cruz mountains, and that was the first time we made love. First times . . . . The adrenalin, the anxiety, leading up to the unknown: how's she going to feel, how are you going to feel, are you going to like each other, each other's bodies? And then the knowing, the finding out . . . . We've been together over seven years. She has cystic fibrosis, and she's not real strong, so she can't transfer me into bed or onto the sofa. If we want to have spontaneous sex, we have to be more creative. I have a bed that raises up, so she can lie down, and I can lean over and go down on her. We used to work together in an old Victorian, and the kitchen counter was just the right height. Occasionally after work or during lunch, we'd lock the door, close the blinds, unplug the phone and have sex. We've experimented with having sex in my chair. It's not that easy, but we've had quite a bit of success. Visual stimuli is arousing: videos, lingerie, even just a woman's body, a strip tease. Tactile things, like feathers. Sex that goes on for a couple of hours in the warm sun in the morning. Preferably outside. Numerous positions, with a lot of caressing and time for lying together afterwards.

I have tactile sensation above my shoulders, and I can feel pressure sensation and weight below. I like my partner to caress and lick my neck, suck and bite my ears, touch other parts of my body, as well as my genitals. Usually, if I have an orgasm, it's triggered by touching my neck. I'd say I'm orgasmic half the time, maybe forty percent of the time. I don't know if this is a male trait, but I think it is: I probably get as much or more pleasure out of satisfying my partner than being satisfied. As I've gotten older or more mature, I've wanted to be satisfied equally. But when I was younger, it was more important to satisfy my partner, and the issue then was whether I could perform. After I'd been with a half-dozen women, I think the *doing* part became the best. There's a lot of joy, satisfaction and real arousal from my partner coming, so I've gotten very adept at making my partner come to orgasm. I don't think that's uncommon for people with disabilities similar to mine. Once you get into oral sex, you really get into it, in terms of technique and enjoyment.

Orgasm's hard to describe, but it's similar to what I had before. Deeper, more emotional. It has the physiological aspects, though not as intense. With my disability, I have muscle spasms—not constant pain but discomfort—and when I have an orgasm, there's that endorphin release, and my body melts. I feel floaty, blissed out, sometimes my body goes limp. I feel grounded, powerful, satisfied. It restates who I am in a physical way, because I've always been a real physical person, even though I've had a pretty severe disability for twenty-one years. I drive a fast chair and fast cars. I like dare-devilish things and always have. Roller coasters. Gliding. There's something freeing about soaring, just up there in a plane with no engine. It's the same feeling after orgasm, a real high.

Don

Born and raised in Berkeley, Don works in a plant nursery. He runs rap groups for gay black men and works as a volunteer AIDS counselor for men and women. Now thirty-eight, he met his boyfriend Martin six years ago at a San Francisco gay bar. Martin left his native England, wife and daughter to live with Don. They would like to get married. "Domestic partnership is nothing but a crumb," says Don. "Marriage, period. Sink or swim, like everybody else."

Not everybody knows I'm gay. I know how to let it hide. I'm black, I'm big, and I've got a deep voice. I've worked in the most popular gay bar in San Francisco. I would have one boy on my right leg, one boy ȯn my left, and another boy stand in the middle, and then people swore I was straight. You don't say nothing good about a homosexual in the black community. If you talk about them in a hateful way, you can get away with it. I just love a man. *One man.* So I'm anything in the book.

I don't fit the stereotype for the gay community, either. I smoke cigars, and I wear hats. For a little while in the seventies, I had some long hair, and I had it curled up. Just nice. That special kind of *clean*: yeah, this boy's gay. I went, "I don't need this. You have to find out who you are and how to be more yourself."

I don't treat intercourse as the main event, especially with Martin. He told me he was a top. I told him I was a top. I said, "Well, we'll figure out something to do." We went to bed as both tops and sucked each other off, touched and kissed, looked into each other's eyes. It wasn't about no intercourse. It was about opening up, feeling him in me and me in him—not physically. I was giving to him, nurturing him, which I do good—better, for the most part, than the other way around. I'm going, "Don't waste your time with me. I don't need it. My hurt, my pain is mine, and I need it to be me." But I do need to nurture somebody and hold somebody. That's very important, that soft side, and *he* really needs to be cuddled and held.

In those days, when we had sex, he'd come and then *disappear* off the bed and go to the bathroom: "I want to clean this stuff off." I'd be, "What the hell's wrong with you?" So one time we were doing something and he came, and he went to go for the bathroom, and I grabbed him by his ankles: "You ain't going nowhere. Do not leave me." And now it's a hell of a lot better.

I like to kiss, hug, lick all over. I like to be sucked, I like to suck, I like to rim, and I like to fuck. Being a top means I like to fuck. I will penetrate my partner. When my lover gets nurtured and feels open and safe, it seems like he is *pulling* me into him. I use my tongue to penetrate him, and he has mental multi-orgasms. He told me a tongue was okay, but he couldn't take a man's penis. But one time I put it in him. I said, "You know I'm in you?" No. He thought it would hurt, and it didn't. He said, "I wouldn't with anyone else but you."

Now, 'cause we're monogamous—and people will disagree, and I *do* do HIV counseling—we do not have what they call safe sex. We have sex. No condoms. He ain't going to nobody else, and I ain't going to nobody else . . . . Anonymous sex where you just kind of go in there and go for ejaculation is still foreign to me. I never understood it. I can understand feeling like you want to be with somebody else. I've been trained to look. I looked so long and used my imagination so long, it became a friend. It's the way I survived. Now that I got what I was looking for, I just can't turn it off. I choose to accept it and overcome it. But I don't try to erase it. Everybody act like you have to be perfect, but no, you just hold yourself in check.

Good sex is oneness with your partner. Being in a room, alone and safe, for me to hug and know that there's no one else I want to hug or be with or lay with, and have him tell me he loves me. Holding him and feeling: "This is the way my father held my mother, my grandfather held my grandmother, and that all over the world, this is how people are loving each other. To feel his skin with my hands, and him next to me. To lay on top of him or have him be on top of me. To squeeze him sometimes so tightly, to see if I can squeeze him inside my chest. When he looks at me with that look in his eye, "How lucky I am to love you." You go, "God, this is life." And that's just the beginning. What I love to do is have him lose it, have him lose his control,

Ecstatic Outlaws

to where he is himself through sex. It's overwhelming him, whatever it is that comes up inside of us when we feel this safeness. I don't know. I just know when it happens, I go, "Gotcha." To have it build and then even after you climax, to hold each other: "That was good. Yes." And then stroke his hair, look into his eyes and kiss him, and reminding yourself he's very vulnerable. And you have to pull him a little bit closer, hold him more and not rush. Because once you get out of the bed, the world comes back in.

One time we made love on a bed of flowers, rose petals. The smell of roses . . . . Two years ago, when I went to England, he said, "I'll give you whatever you want for your birthday." I said, "Good. I want a banana split." I had a piece of plastic I laid across his whole living room floor, and we listened to Nat King Cole. I made my banana split *on* him. Bananas, whipped cream, blueberries, grapes and syrup. He wanted to put the whipped cream on me. I said, "No no no. It's *my* birthday."

Lena

*Lena's first sexual experience made her feel like Elizabeth Taylor.
She was nineteen and just married. Lena's childhood was marked
by the illness and early death of her father, a blond American
military officer. Her tiny Puerto Rican mother, a probation officer
in Watts, raised the family in a government housing project and
taught her daughters independence. "I always think it was great
I went to Catholic girls school, because I didn't have to act stupid
or dress for anybody," Lena says. "It's much more healthy for
women—sensually and sexually—not to form yourself in the opin-
ion of men." Today an attorney and the mother of a grown daughter, Lena has had four husbands—Latino, black and white.*

We were very poor, and I was working from the time I was
fifteen, any kind of job. I worked at Fredericks of Hollywood as a cashier. 1960. Most of the strippers got their clothes
there, as did the female impersonators. G-strings, pasties, crotch-
less panties, fetish clothes. There was no homophobia. Fredericks
was the first place I saw that was racially integrated—the sales
staff and the displays. I became aware of how closely racism is
tied with sexuality because of the number of bomb threats we
got for having black, gold and white mannequins.

My friends and I were in a fringe Hollywood scene. We got
to know these animal importers and learned that there was money
to be made in animal shows in Tijuana: tarantula shows, those
weird bars where women do their acts on stage, kind of a carnival
scene. Then we got this eleven-foot Peruvian boa. Somebody
suggested that I should dance with this snake. I got a manager,
and she placed me in truly horrible places. Suburban dives, one
notch above a truck stop. I'd wear a G-string and a leopard top,
big gold armbands. The thing about a snake is you have to move
similarly to how a snake moves. Nothing abrupt. It was prepared
to strike, so I couldn't move too fast. It would wrap around me.
My challenge was to keep it off my neck and to look sensual as
I was doing this. The audience thought it was erotic: they were

Ecstatic Outlaws

spellbound. It didn't feel sexy at all. I had a hard time understanding why other people felt it was sexy.

For me, the motive was cash. It was the quickest way to earn money. I was physics major at UCLA, just a wholesome, shapely person, trying to figure out how to graduate from college. I did taxi-dancing, too. The deal *there* was you were supposed to rub up against these guys, turn 'em on and meet them later. Or somehow jack 'em off while you were dancing, but the dances were so short that *that* was unlikely. It was twelve and a half cents a minute. Lonely, lonely guys. I remember one man sat at a table and talked to me for twenty dollars' worth.

I got involved with a jazz musician. Jazz clubs in the sixties were totally involved in prostitution. That's what kept these clubs alive. Not *music*. I was boring, because I was only interested in my boyfriend, but I was around an overtly sexual scene. I was always monogamous. For me, sex was about love. But my boyfriend became a strung-out junkie, and we separated. I married a blues musician when I was twenty-seven. We met and moved in together the same day. We were going to have nine kids, start our life. We sat out on the porch, and there we were. It was a wonderful life. There was music twenty-four hours a day. We grew all our own food. I can remember having a wonderful sexual experience after we were both down on our hands and knees picking bugs off the tomato plants. Or he'd go crab-trapping, come back at two in the morning, put the water on to boil and we'd make love. Opulent. It was an opulence of life. But then he became famous. I couldn't stand the drugs and the people. He and I were together for six years, and we dated for four years after our marriage. Sex with him was always good. Even when we had problems in our personal lives, we never had problems in our sex life.

Great sex is sharing and communication, passionate, loving, caring and fun. I feel a completeness of myself. I feel that this is who I most like to be. You don't get to be that person very often in life . . . . If I'm turned on, I have an orgasm. Or two or three. Sometimes slow, sometimes fast. It can seem like a journey, like flying over the city. Beautiful colors. Blossoming, like a flower opening. That certain time of day where it's not dusk and it's not day, where everything almost stands still, and it's slightly warm in color. For me that happens with a partner. I don't get anywhere like that by myself. Making love is more of an exploration with a person: how far can we go? Are we going to find the edges? There might not *be* edges. There might be no end to the getting together.

When you're fifty, you look around at men and you have to like what they're about. It's easier to be turned on when you're younger, because you don't know what anybody is yet. Now men have to turn me on by who they are—not necessarily their achievements. About two months ago, I met someone new. I think of him as having fallen from the sky. He's an exaggerated person, gentle with me, fierce with the world. Not fancy, not questioning his maleness, not fearful of my femaleness. In recent years, I met men who were consumed by their self-definition. Especially white men. It's not emotionally fulfilling to be with someone involved in his self-definition rather than in loving or having fun.

With this man I'm seeing now, we have a very sexualized relationship. I'm sleeping a whole lot less and actually stayed up seven nights in a row making love. A week unlike other weeks. My orgasms are much longer, and there's a floating sweetness about it . . . . There's a lusciousness to sexuality if you're willing to be totally, passionately emotional. The more life experience you bring to it, the greater the sex is. I have nothing to protect in myself anymore. There's no holds barred in the way of sharing. So sexuality and orgasms are much more vital and beautiful. I don't like boundaries, I'm committed to passionate expression, and I always hope that a relationship could be as big as the world. It's just a question of how far a person is willing to go.

NOTES FROM THE AUTHOR

The idea for this book struck me in the midst of a birthday party. I was talking with friends about sex, and though frank, we were in some ways inarticulate. We needed magnitudes of language, beyond Kinsey and *The Kama Sutra*. In fact, plain talk about positive sexuality is hard to find. Daytime TV and talk radio, handy sources for common conversation, invariably team sex with perversion, terminal illness or violence. Film and fiction—including pornography—occasionally supply sunnier images, but they often rely on stereotypes and generally give short shrift to real-life complexities, such as everyday mismatches in sexual timing and communication. Sex manuals favor clinical language and tend to reduce erotic interplay to a matter of technique. After spending a few fruitless weeks scanning bookshelves, I thought, "Okay, I'll write it." A long-time radio reporter, I hoisted my tape recorder on my shoulder and set forth to document plain speaking about sex.

I sought referrals from senior centers, disabled activists, therapists, writers, churches, Jewish community centers, universities, and advocacy groups for gays, bisexuals and transsexuals. I located sources through AIDS organizations, service agencies for prenatal care and counseling centers for incest and rape recovery. I interviewed women who sold sex toys or worked in the sex industry. Networking among the straight and married posed unforeseen challenges, because people more closely aligned with the dominant culture do not run support groups based on conscious sexual identity: "Hi. I'm openly heterosexual and do public education on what it's like to be a 'breeder.'"

Over time, I recorded eighty in-depth interviews with people aged seventeen to seventy-three. Sixty-two of those stories appear in these pages. All the participants reside in Northern California, although the majority grew up in other parts of the country, and regionalisms pepper the anecdotes. More than half are parents, and while a few have made public presentations on sex-linked issues, virtually all are private citizens—so private that my first phone contacts were sometimes mistaken for crank calls. As an elderly man told me, "I could not believe the message you left on my answering machine, saying you were writing a book about *sex*. I listened to it three times. I got my neighbor to listen to it. I got my *daughter* to listen to it." I found that describing my project to strangers in thirty seconds or less took practice, and I made a few false starts. In one conversation, I called *Good Sex* a kind of X-rated Studs Terkel. But the man I was talking to didn't know about the celebrated oral historian. "I thought you must have been talking about a porn star," he said, puzzled. "*Studs*, you know."

Many who sat down to talk with me were in effect thinking aloud, putting their perceptions of sex into words for the first time. Frequently, my questions to them about the very beginnings of carnal knowledge woke memories of vast, commanding silences. One man recalled the first time he pronounced obscenities: he was an adolescent, mouthing secrets at his reflection in the bathroom mirror. Others spoke of the overwhelming absence of sexuality and the lack of affectionate touch between parents. They remembered family euphemisms that obscured the "facts of life" but not parents' sense of shame. Men and women lacked terms for sexual sensation, bodily secretions and details of the genitalia: "I guess it's my G-spot, if that *exists*." One seventy-year-old man had never discussed sex with anyone—not his late wife, not the girlfriend he had known twenty years. "The reason I'm talking with *you*," he explained, "is because you've asked me to, and you're a stranger."

What drew people to share their stories was not always clear, though many voiced hopes for breaking out of isolation. Diane, married to a transvestite, told me, "I wanted to reach out, maybe find other kindred souls who are struggling to live the best way they know how in a less-than-perfect world, people who are going against the grain yet trying to feel fulfilled and *alive*." The ache for connection seemed strong among those under age twenty-five. Our one-on-one exchanges gave them an opportunity to ask their own shy questions: Do women really have orgasms? Is it possible to find a sex-partner you can talk to? Can relationships last? In a number of instances, people said they chose to kiss-and-tell

Notes from the Author

simply because they loved to talk about sex, and a few of those ardent conversations noticeably boosted the room temperature. Several men seemed intrigued by the idea of sitting with a young woman and talking dirty. One mistook the interview for a pretext to a date. Another sent me a thank you note for the "good therapy session."

In more than ten years of reporting, I have never investigated a subject so frightening to people. Interviews were regularly canceled or "forgotten." Slightly more than a third of those participating opted to use pseudonyms. Even so, men and women worried that they would be identified through their jobs: "If you say I'm a carpenter, everyone will know who it is." Several young women made panicked calls to me, saying they "just couldn't go through with it." Those individuals who braved the two-hour talk sessions were invariably vulnerable, no matter how practiced in deeds or words. Some women sought refuge from exposure by spinning out the details of relationships, not S-E-X. A few men tried to gain the upper hand through intimidation: one boasted of ten thousand sex partners, another rushed into an unexpected rhapsody on handguns, and a third snapped photos.

Among the raw details, the only shocking comments were those concerning safe sex. Worries about the AIDS virus were universal, but many of those interviewed seemed to regard anxiety as a talisman against infection. Measures to reduce risk of transmission were reported most consistently by three groups: gay men, bisexual men, and women affiliated with the sex industry. Many straight men and women voiced confusion about AIDS and safe sex. Jay, for example, told me he took precautions against AIDS by staying in long-term relationships, then noted he has been with his girlfriend for six months. HIV-negative, he bought condoms "just in case" but doesn't use them.

Even the sex educators I interviewed—a small number—were unlikely to use latex with their own bedmates. One reviled condoms as tokens of her lover's infidelities. Another, who said half her peer group had died from AIDS, admitted, "I tell my daughter all the time, 'Use condoms, use condoms,' but I'm as guilty as anybody. I'll think 'I trust this person,' when it has nothing to do with trust." Like all opinions in this volume, comments about AIDS, safe sex methods and the reliability of latex shrink-wrap provide clues to current attitudes and behavior, not guidelines for emulation. To reduce confusion, safer sex tips are provided in an appendix. The recommendations, like all pointers on prevention available today, are controversial and may quickly become out-dated as knowledge about the virus increases.

My interview subjects were not scientists, but they were experts on sexual chemistry—or what one woman innocently misiden-tified as "the Jung and Yang." In the course of each interview, I asked for a definition of good sex. Eighty people gave me eighty definitions. The responses were blunt, gentle, confident, tentative, passionate, cool. They were occasionally gussied up with meta-phors, but sex itself was not described as metaphysical. "I'm transported—I couldn't tell you where," mused a one-time peep show dancer. "But the transcendence is not an out-of-body experi-ence, it's an in-the-body experience." Presented in the context of a life story, the definitions of good sex invariably mirrored the storyteller's needs, secrets and strengths. Sex was described as a statement of self, a body language for the hidden faces of the soul, a freedom to communicate. By all accounts, sex is a person-ally encoded communiqué, continually reinvented.

The hours I spent sifting through other people's stories and impressions inspired cycles of self-reflection. As I thought through my own history and choices, I began to suspect that my dual interests in sexuality and investigative reporting originated in my family role, for I was the child encouraged to monitor and some-times translate the household's subliminal currents. My parents, an affectionate twosome, were fairly sex-positive but bashful and indirect. Much to their amusement, I named my first doll Lolita. When I moved into adolescence, I viewed sex as the ultimate doorway to adulthood, a powerful state I very much wanted to claim. So at fifteen, I tried a stab at intercourse with my best friend in a determined tumble we found funny, sweet and decidedly non-orgasmic.

College life featured earnest philosophies of sexual liberation and the urgent young men who concocted them. In that environ-ment, I rapidly began to understand the difference between sexual activity and sexual independence, which was less popular and harder won. I also found myself forced to relinquish the sexist and self-protective notion that boys would just *naturally* know

Notes from the Author

more about sex. Over the next few years, I engaged in a series of deep romances with men and tucked in a few quiet affairs with women, in which we all identified as heterosexual. Ten years ago, I took up with the woman with whom I happily share a bed and mortgage payments. She's a private detective, so of course I can't cheat.

As I carried out this investigation, the immense variety of perspectives on sexuality flung open the doors of possibility and torpedoed some old assumptions. I realized that prior to this project, I had in effect strapped sexuality to a continuum of risk. At one end perched the dowdy duo of monogamous heterosexuality. Beyond that sauntered increasingly daring partnerships, gender junctions, vassals and taloned masters. Farther still, an unimagined horizon. It was a tidy progression, commodified and competitive. But Libido-land makes neatnik anxieties about order quite irrelevant. It's a maverick realm. Interviews tangle up seemingly divergent sexual behaviors, and they advance unexpected opinions about personal risk. For example, a surprising tribute to fidelity came from an SM playboy, who noted with admiration that "long-term monogamy is the most *challenging* power relationship."

Good Sex is more like a fistful of polaroids than a clipboard survey poking towards a conclusion. As a group, the interviews suggest that sexual savvy depends less upon "how-to's" than on self-knowledge, which evolves slowly, awkwardly and through many different routes, including the silk road of sexuality. Vehicles for interaction—the SM four-on-the-floor, the standard wedding limo, the sporty convertible—may accelerate at different rates, but they do not determine the distance achieved.

I'd like to thank the people whose enthusiasm, generosity and assistance made it possible for me to explore this undulating trail: Tamara Thompson, Francie Koehler, Randy Ontiveros, Carol Queen, Lani Kaahumanu; my Cleis editors, Felice Newman and Frédérique Delacoste; and the courageous men and women who shared their stories.

Julia Hutton
February 1992

About the Author

Julia Hutton is a broadcast journalist whose documentation of cultural politics has included work on AIDS, police brutality, witches, education, aging and job safety. *Good Sex*, Hutton's first book, reflects her long-standing interest in sexuality and its representations from Hollywood to Queer Nation. Hutton's radio documentaries, produced with support from the Corporation for Public Broadcasting and California Public Radio, have included *You Can't Lead If You Can't Read*, which won the Ohio State Award in 1984, and *Almost Home: Violence Against Asian Americans*, which received Honorable Mention from the National Federation of Community Broadcasters in 1986. For the past decade, Hutton has been program director, promotions manager, producer and reporter for National Public Radio and Pacifica stations in the San Francisco Bay Area.

APPENDIX:
SAFER SEX GUIDELINES

The following recommendations are based on excerpts from the San Francisco AIDS Foundation's public education pamphlets and AIDS Hotline Training Manual *(August 1991). The guidelines are based on current knowledge about preventing the spread of the HIV virus. Though clear and useful, the guidelines do not address every concern or sexual practice. Supplementary information is available through the AIDS hotlines listed below; these services, which are completely anonymous, can provide the latest updates, as well as counseling and referrals.*

The Nature of AIDS

AIDS is caused by a virus called Human Immunodeficiency Virus (HIV). HIV can be spread through an infected person's blood, semen and vaginal fluid. Paths of infection include: unprotected sex; direct blood contact, via shared IV needles, blood transfusions, accidents in health care settings, or certain blood products; mother to baby, before or during birth, or through breast milk.

Evidence suggests that pre-ejaculate fluid (precum) may also be infectious, as it may contain small amounts of semen. Feces may be infectious, because they may contain small amounts of blood. Breast milk and urine contain enough HIV to be infectious if ingested in large quantities. Saliva, tears and sweat cannot spread HIV.

221

Before You Get Started

Talk to your partner: It is good to know your partner's feelings about safe sex as well as past sexual history and state of health. This information may not provide you with any direct clues as to your partner's current health or likelihood of carrying HIV, but it will give you a sense of your compatibility and how safe sex with this partner is likely to be.

Set limits before you start: When talking with your partner, you should establish which activities you will engage in and which you will avoid. It is not possible to overstate how important this can be. By explicitly stating your limits beforehand, it will be much easier to stay within them when the heat of passion tempts you to engage in a riskier activity. If you know where you want to stop, but have not made it clear to your partner, it is too easy to be carried away by the heat of the moment.

Number of partners: With any activity that might transmit HIV, the risk increases with the number of partners. This is simple arithmetic. The more times you have risky sex, the more chances you have to contract the virus.

Wash before and after sex: This activity has several purposes. It removes any traces of fecal material, urine or other fluids from the skin that might transmit the virus. Also, if you wash with your partner, it gives you a chance to examine each other's bodies and is an opportunity for "foreplay."

Safe Sex

These activities do not transmit the virus. Participants can engage in them without further precautions.

Solo masturbation: With solo masturbation there is no fear of self-infection. Anything done solo is okay as long as someone else's infectious fluids are not present; i.e. don't fuck yourself with a dildo that someone else has used.

Mutual masturbation: The skin is an effective barrier against all sorts of organisms, and will stop HIV. If you get a possibly infected fluid on your skin, simply wash it off. A scab that is older than one day is as effective as skin. Breaks in the skin might allow passage of the virus, but the breaks would have to be of a fair size for this to happen. If there is a break in the skin on a

Appendix: Safer Sex Guidelines   223

finger that is inserted into the vagina, it is more susceptible to infection and should be considered only possibly safe.

Dry kissing: This is also known as social kissing and is any kiss with the lips closed. No infected fluids can be passed during this activity, and even saliva (which we do not suspect) will not be passed.

Breasts: Touching your lover's breasts is safe. You can lick, suck, kiss and bite them, too—as long as there's no blood or breast milk.

Body massage, hugging: With only skin-to-skin contact, these activities are risk free. Of course, if both people have open sores, virus transmission could occur.

Body-to-body rubbing: also called *frottage*. This is basically the same as massage. Remember, though, that body rubbing can be unsafe if you rub yourself raw.

Unshared sex toys: This refers to dildoes, butt plugs, French ticklers or any other device that may come in contact with an infected fluid. If the toy is only used on one person, there is no worry because the person cannot infect him/herself. Condoms can be used on sex toys that are shared, but the activity is then only "possibly safe."

SM activities: This is safe only if there is no bleeding or bruising. It can include bondage, tit or nipple play, spanking, discipline or any of a number of other activities. If you shave each other, use different razors.

Fantasy, voyeurism, exhibitionism: These can be elements of many safe sex activities. It can include costumes or uniforms and can appeal to senses other than touch. Needless to say, these should be done only when legal. Being a Peeping Tom or removing your clothes in public may be safe for AIDS, but it may get you arrested.

Phone sex: This can be commercial or private (on the extension or from another house).

Possibly Safe Sex

This category contains activities with latex, low risk activities, and activities that are possibly unsafe.

French kissing: Saliva is not suspected as a route of transmission for HIV, but because there is not absolute proof, wet kissing remains in the "possibly safe" category. If one or both partners has bleeding gums or cuts in the mouth or on the lips (from toothbrushing, flossing, eating, etc.) blood could be passed along, and the activity would be considered "unsafe."

Vaginal intercourse with condom: Latex condoms can stop HIV, just as they stop viruses like herpes and hepatitis, but condoms are not always effective. When used properly, condoms almost never break. However, sometimes the condom is too old and therefore weak. More often, it is put on incorrectly and has an air bubble inside. Oil-based lubricants cause breakage. Sometimes not using enough water-based lubricant causes breakage. Contraceptive foams or jellies which contain spermicides increase protection.

Anal intercourse with condom: Because there is no 100 percent guarantee of preventing condom breakage, anal sex with condoms is "possibly safe." The lining of the rectum is thin and easily broken. HIV may infect the mucous membranes directly or enter through cuts and sores. Just as with vaginal intercourse, contraceptive foams or jellies which contain spermicides increase protection.

Putting your fingers inside a woman's vagina (finger fucking): This can be risky. To be safe, wear latex gloves. If you use a lubricant, make sure it is water-based, like K-Y Jelly. Oil-based lubricants, like Vaseline, damage the latex. Sores or cuts on the fingers, mouth or vagina increase the risk of infection. They can provide a way for the virus to get into the bloodstream. If you touch her vagina and then touch your own genitals, you could spread the virus. Be sure to change gloves in between.

Oral sex on a man with condom: Condoms are not foolproof; however, oral sex is much less risky than anal sex, so with a condom the risk should be almost non-existent.

Oral sex on a man/no condom/no ejaculation: It is assumed that pre-ejaculate fluid contains HIV. For this reason alone, this activity should be considered "possibly safe" at best. Additionally, though, this is an activity with a high degree of user error. Some men are not able to control their orgasm as well as others and may not withdraw in time.

Watersports/external: Urine on the skin should present no risk, but here again we have an activity that may have a high degree or error. If during this activity, urine gets into a cut or splashes into the eyes or other mucous membranes, it would be considered unsafe.

Appendix: Safer Sex Guidelines   225

Unsafe Sex

These activities are very risky and almost sure to pass the virus if one or both partners are contagious. These activities are probably responsible for the bulk, if not all, of the sexual HIV transmission that has occurred.

Vaginal intercourse/no condom: The lining of the vagina is stronger than that of the rectum, but tearing can still occur. Also, this stronger lining only extends as far as the cervix, where the tissue is thin. It has recently been shown that HIV can also infect certain vaginal cells directly and may also be absorbed through the mucous membranes.

Anal intercourse/no condom: This is the riskiest activity for transmission of HIV. The lining of the rectum is very thin and easily broken, even during defecation (shitting). During anal sex, the tears that result can provide a direct opening to the bloodstream for infected semen. The insertive partner may also be at risk from infected feces and blood entering the urethra, where the tissue is equally thin and also easily torn.

Fellatio to climax/no condom: Since we know that semen can contain the virus, taking semen into the body by any route is very risky. The biggest risk in this activity does not come from swallowing the semen, but rather from having it in the mouth. Since the virus can penetrate mucous membranes, the mouth can be a good entry point. Also, it is very common to have small abrasions in the mouth from eating, brushing teeth or flossing. Larger sores in the mouth increase the risk even more. The number of proven cases by fellation is small, but may be masked by other sexual activities. That is, an infected man who practices both fellatio and anal sex is presumed to be infected by the anal sex.

Oral sex on a woman/no barrier: The virus is found in the vaginal and cervical secretions of an HIV-infected woman. It is possible to transmit the virus during cunnilingus. Contact with menstrual blood is especially risky. A latex barrier (similar to ones used by dentists) can be used for to avoid contact with vaginal secretions. Or cover her vulva (genital area) with a double-thick piece of household plastic wrap. This will keep her fluids out of your mouth.

Sharing sex toys: Any sex toy that may have infected fluids on it should not be passed from one person to another without

226   GOOD SEX

thorough cleaning to kill the virus. A condom can be put on a dildo to reduce the risk, but the condom must be changed before use by each partner. Sex toys should be washed in hot, soapy water.

Rimming/oral-anal: Since we know that feces almost always contains minute amounts of blood, ingesting it is very risky. All the considerations that apply to ingesting semen hold here also.

Watersports/internal: Taking urine in the mouth, the rectum or the vagina is risky for all the same reasons that taking semen is risky. Again, even if you try to limit this activity to only external exposure, caution is warranted because mistakes can easily occur, especially splashing in the mucous membranes in the face.

Fisting: Fisting refers to inserting the hand into the rectum or vagina. It is included in the unsafe category for several reasons. First, early epidemiology of AIDS showed a correlation between fisting and AIDS. Now many people feel that it was a statistical illusion. People who like anal fisting like all sorts of ass-play and are very likely to be having anal intercourse also. Also, during fisting, cross-contamination from semen, or possibly pre-ejaculate, can occur when the hand comes out for a moment, the top masturbates briefly and the hand is reinserted. Second, fisting causes considerable trauma to the tissue in the rectum and colon (or vagina). If any infected fluid is present, it gets very easy access to the bloodstream. There may be additional risk to the top from the virus entering through cuts on the hand or the cuticles. For anyone who is going to continue fisting, precautions can be taken. Examination or surgical gloves should offer considerable protection, especially for the top. Wearing a condom on the penis to prevent cross-contamination is also a very good idea. No anal intercourse, even with a condom, should be done during the same session. Unshared sex toys can be used.

How to Use Condoms

Pinch the air out of the top half inch of the condom. This leaves space for the semen.

Put the condom on a fully erect penis. Hold the tip of the condom as you unroll it.

Unroll the condom completely, making sure there is not air inside. Air bubbles are the biggest reason why condoms break.

Use plenty of water-based lubricant, like K-Y Jelly. Birth control

Appendix: Safer Sex Guidelines

foam and jelly give extra protection: they contain the spermicide nonoxynol-9, which kills the AIDS virus.

After coming, hold on to the base of the condom and pull out. Don't spill it. Don't reuse the condom.

Never store condoms in your pocket, glove compartment or any place they will be exposed to heat.

Use condoms within one year of purchase.

AIDS Information Hotlines

San Francisco AIDS Foundation Hotline
9 A.M. to 9 P.M. weekdays;
11 A.M. to 5 P.M. weekends
1-(415) 863-2437 (English, Spanish, Tagalog)
1-(415) 864-6606 (TDD)

Centers for Disease Control National AIDS Hotline
1-(800) 342-AIDS (English - 24 hours)
1-(800) 344-7432 (Spanish - 8 A.M. to 2 P.M. daily)
1-(800) 243-7889 (TDD - 10 A.M. to 10 P.M., Monday - Friday)

SELECTED BOOKS FROM CLEIS PRESS

SEXUAL POLITICS

The Good Vibrations Guide to Sex: How to Have Safe, Fun Sex in the '90s by Cathy Winks and Anne Semans. ISBN: 0-939416-83-2 29.95; ISBN: 0-939416-84-0 14.95 paper.

Madonnarama: Essays on Sex and Popular Culture edited by Lisa Frank and Paul Smith. ISBN: 0-939416-72-7 24.95 cloth; ISBN: 0-939416-71-9 9.95 paper.

Public Sex: The Culture of Radical Sex by Pat Califia. ISBN: 0-939416-88-3 29.95 cloth; ISBN: 0-939416-89-1 12.95 paper.

Sex Work: Writings by Women in the Sex Industry edited by Frédérique Delacoste and Priscilla Alexander. ISBN: 0-939416-10-7 24.95 cloth; ISBN: 0-939416-11-5 16.95 paper.

Susie Bright's Sexual Reality: A Virtual Sex World Reader by Susie Bright. ISBN: 0-939416-58-1 24.95 cloth; ISBN: 0-939416-59-X 9.95 paper.

Susie Bright's Sexwise by Susie Bright. ISBN: 1-57344-003-5 24.95 cloth; ISBN: 1-57344-002-7 10.95 paper.

Susie Sexpert's Lesbian Sex World by Susie Bright. ISBN: 0-939416-34-4 24.95 cloth; ISBN: 0-939416-35-2 9.95 paper.

LESBIAN STUDIES

Dagger: On Butch Women edited by Roxxie, Lily Burana, Linnea Due. ISBN: 0-939416-81-6 29.95 cloth; ISBN: 0-939416-82-4 14.95 paper.

Daughters of Darkness: Lesbian Vampire Stories edited by Pam Keesey. ISBN: 0-939416-77-8 24.95 cloth; ISBN: 0-939416-78-6 9.95 paper.

Dyke Strippers: Lesbian Cartoonists A to Z edited by Roz Warren. ISBN: 1-57344-009-4 29.95 cloth; ISBN: 1-57344-008-6 16.95 paper.

Girlfriend Number One: Lesbian Life in the '90s edited by Robin Stevens. ISBN: 0-939416-79-4 29.95 cloth; ISBN: 0-939416-8 12.95 paper.

A Lesbian Love Advisor by Celeste West. ISBN: 0-939416-27-1 24.95 cloth; ISBN: 0-939416-26-3 9.95 paper.

More Serious Pleasure: Lesbian Erotic Stories and Poetry edited by the Sheba Collective. ISBN: 0-939416-48-4 24.95 cloth; ISBN: 0-939416-47-6 9.95 paper.

Serious Pleasure: Lesbian Erotic Stories and Poetry edited by the Sheba Collective. ISBN: 0-939416-46-8 24.95 cloth; ISBN: 0-939416-45-X 9.95 paper.

Since 1980, Cleis Press has published progressive books by women. We welcome your order and will ship your books as quickly as possible. Individual orders must be prepaid (U.S. dollars only). Please add 15% shipping. PA residents add 6% sales tax. Mail orders: Cleis Press, P.O. Box 8933, Pittsburgh PA 15221. MasterCard and Visa orders: include account number, exp. date, and signature. Fax your credit card order: (412) 937-1567. Or, phone us Mon–Fri, 9 am–5 pm EST: (412) 937-1555.